T0031163

Witch
of
Wild
Things

Witch
of
Wild
Things

Raquel
Vasquez Gilliland

BERKLEY ROMANCE

NEW YORK

BERKLEY ROMANCE
Published by Berkley
An imprint of Penguin Random House LLC
penguinrandomhouse.com

Library of Congress Cataloging-in-Publication Data

Names: Vasquez Gilliland, Raquel, author.
Title: Witch of wild things / Raquel Vasquez Gilliland.
Description: First edition. | New York: Berkley Romance, 2023.
Identifiers: LCCN 2022058280 (print) | LCCN 2022058281 (ebook) |
ISBN 9780593548578 (trade paperback) | ISBN 9780593548585 (ebook)
Subjects: LCGFT: Romance fiction. | Novels.
Classification: LCC PS3622.A834 W58 2023 (print) |
LCC PS3622.A834 (ebook) | DDC 813/.6—dc23/eng/20221213
LC record available at https://lccn.loc.gov/2022058280
LC ebook record available at https://lccn.loc.gov/2022058281

First Edition: September 2023

Printed in the United States of America
2nd Printing

Book design by Daniel Brount

For Jagel, my best friend

Everything we need to survive and all that
nourishes us comes from the Earth, its soil,
the atmosphere, the sun and the stars beyond.
We are simply walking pieces of earth.

—MARY REYNOLDS

They say I'm a bitch.
Or witch. I've claimed
the same and never winced.

—SANDRA CISNEROS, "LOOSE WOMAN"

M Y GREAT-AUNT NADIA SAYS IT'S A BAD IDEA TO REJECT
a gift from a ghost.

It's 'cause ghosts like to slide inside all kinds of worlds. They
don't just roam the land of the living or the dead. They can show
up in our dream worlds to meddle. They can touch the world of
shadows and eat the light from your own home, just sucking up
the long, thick gold of nightlights and fixtures like dead black
holes. "Just ask your prima Cleotilde," Nadia always says, her
wine-red acrylic nail in my face as she points. "She once offended
the ghost of her abuelo, and boom. Lamps didn't work around her
for *years*."

The scariest world that ghosts can touch is the world of gods.
The old gods. The ancient gods. The gods we've heard of and the
even more numerous gods we haven't. Nadia pours one cup of
espresso to these gods every single morning. This woman would
rather light St. Theresa's on fire than skip this daily offering.

And if you've got a ghost haunting you, there's no way to tell if one of *these* gods favors *that* ghost. So you offend a ghost? You reject her gift?

You might be offending a god.

Apparently, it's a *really* bad idea to offend gods. That's how you end up with the women in our family and our *gifts*.

This means that when I climb in my janky-ass minivan and see the cup of coffee in the console? Yes, *that* cup of coffee—the mug, a gift from one of my former students, hand thrown and glazed the color of lilacs against a lightning storm. The one steaming with notes of raspberry and a hint of chocolate. The one that I most certainly did *not* place there. The second I smell it—because yeah, I smell it first—I throw myself into my seat and press my face into the steering wheel. "Shit," I say in a long exhale.

I hate gifts from ghosts.

In order to distract myself from the sweet steam swirling around me, I grab my phone, hitting buttons as fast as my fingers can go.

Laurel picks up even before the first ring ends. "Hey! You on your way yet?"

I glance at the back of my van. Every seat is pushed down to make way for half a dozen boxes, triple that in plants, and an antique reading chair. Most of the boxes contain books—I can see a sliver of Joy Harjo's *She Had Some Horses* peeking through cardboard I hadn't bothered to tape shut. It's my favorite of her collections, because it reminds me of the stories Nadia used to tell us when Teal, Sky, and I were tiny enough to squeeze onto one twin bed. I can still hear Nadia's smoky voice filling our room. "In the beginning, there were only gods. Gods and this earth . . ."

Now Teal, Sky, and I will *never* be all together again. I take a shuddering breath as this reality sweeps over me for the millionth time in eight years, like the garnet-sharp winds of a tornado.

There and gone in a moment, but leaving behind painful, devastating destruction. That's how grief works.

"Sage Flores, are you ignoring me?"

I blink and jerk my face toward the console. The coffee is still there. Jerk. "No, of course not. I'm just about on my way. I'm in the van and everything."

"Okay, well, that's a good start. Next step, take your key, you know, the shiny silver thing in your hand right now, and push it through that teeny hole on the side of—"

"Literally giving you my middle finger right now," I say, but I'm laughing.

"Seriously, Sage. You've got this."

I glance up at my apartment—well, I guess it's not mine anymore. It's the third floor up, and the balcony still has dirt on the rails from when I watered my basil plants a little too violently. I take a deep breath, hoping the scent of that basil can calm me.

All I smell is ghost coffee.

"Want me to distract you?"

I put the phone on speaker and place it in the cup holder next to the mug. "Go for it."

"You'll never guess who I saw last night. At Piggly Wiggly of all places."

I sit back in my seat. I get the key in the ignition as I say, "Piggly Wiggly?" I think of who wouldn't be caught dead there. "Amá Sonya?"

Laurel draws out the response long and slow. "Tennessee. Reyes."

It may well be the absolute last name I'd expected her to utter. I think I would've been less shocked if she'd announced it *were* Amá Sonya at Piggly Wiggly, naked as birth, juggling plums in the middle of produce.

My breath's gone way too shallow, my hand gripping the key so tight it's cutting into my fingers. I turn the ignition, hard, but stay in park while clearing my throat. "Tennessee Reyes?" As though there were any other on the planet. "You're certain?"

"It was him, Sage. Trust me."

I close my eyes. "But . . . he moved to Denver and then got off social media and, like—"

"Disappeared off the face of the earth? Yeah. But I guess he's deigned to walk the earth's face once more, because he is in Piggly Wiggly, in Cranberry, Virginia. Or was, as of yesterday."

My heart's finally gone back to a normal rhythm and so I slowly begin reversing the van, angling my head back. "How does he look?" The question's out before I can stop it.

"Oh, gosh. Somehow *better*."

"Better?" It comes out like a squeak. *Better* doesn't seem possible.

"He's . . . I dunno. He's grown into those legs. And he's got this yummy almost-beard thing happening . . . hold on." Her voice gets distant. "No, hon, of course I'm talking about you! Well, I mean *if* you grew a beard thing!" Laurel sighs. "I think my husband just heard me verbally ogling another man."

Normally I'd laugh and keep up with their teasing each other, but my stomach keeps making stupid, roller-coaster-y loops somehow in my rib cage. Because Tennessee Reyes is back in Cranberry.

Tenn is back in Cranberry.

"Well, that's something." I've made it to the edge of the lot now without hitting any parked vehicles in my emotional state. That's also something.

"Guess that distracted you good, huh? You sound like you've morphed into some kind of zombie." When I give a flat chuckle in response, Laurel adds, "You okay, Sage?" in a soft voice. I hate that voice. It only comes out when I'm near tears. And to me? The consequences of crying are worse than those of offending gods.

I blink and blink and then respond. "Oh, yeah." I try to make my voice smooth, but it's as useless as ironing linen. "I'm just not looking forward to—you know. Moving back with Nadia." With Teal.

Laurel hears what I don't say. "Maybe she won't be as bad as you remember."

The last time I saw my sister, she cracked my lip open so wide, I needed four stitches. Later she said she didn't mean it—that she'd forgotten she'd worn such a sharp ring that day—but that just tells me that she did mean everything else. As in, the whole situation of her fist in my face.

"Oh, yeah." I finally make a right onto the main road as someone starts honking behind me. "It won't be that bad."

"I'll make you pollo a la plancha the second you get here."

I manage a smile. "Now you're talking."

"Nothing like Cuban comfort food to get settled in." There's a muffled noise in the background. "Ah, I gotta go."

"Tell Jorge I said hi."

"Drive safe and text me the second you get to Nadia's, yeah?"

"Of course. Love you."

"Love you more."

When I merge onto the highway, I do a double take at my reflection in the rearview mirror. My eyes are wide, the brown almost citrine in the sunlight, and my mascara is already smudged even though I applied it less than an hour ago. My hair—a mass of curls I'd braided and pinned up—looks like it's trying to break the hair tie keeping it from reaching down and steering this car without any of my help. I look like a twenty-nine-year-old who is freaking the fuck out.

I *am* a twenty-nine-year-old who is freaking the fuck out.

Why on earth is Tenn back in Cranberry?

I take a deep breath as I veer toward my first exit. It doesn't matter. What happened between us, it was over a decade ago, which feels like a dozen lifetimes by now. And that's exactly where anything between Tenn and me will stay—buried in the memories of seventeen-year-old me, back when I thought heartbreak was the worst thing that could happen to a person.

I have better things to worry about now. I take a long sip of my now lukewarm coffee.

Like ghosts.

silvergurl0917: what haven't you noticed today?

RainOnATennRoof: Wow

RainOnATennRoof: What didn't you say?

silvergurl0917: what didn't you laugh at

RainOnATennRoof: What didn't you do?

silvergurl0917: what didn't you think about

silvergurl0917: . . . you there?

RainOnATennRoof: You

RainOnATennRoof: I didn't think about you. Until now. :)

RainOnATennRoof: Who is this?

silvergurl0917 has logged off Messenger.

PRESENT

It takes exactly four hours and seventeen minutes to reach Catalina Street in Cranberry. Without even thinking about it, I slow the car down well before Nadia's house, eventually pulling over in front of Old Man Noemi's in-street parking. From here I can see enough. There's the emerald ivy curling over Nadia's place like a clawed, leafy hand. When I crane my neck a little, I make out the glow from her kitchen, through the daisy-patterned curtains she sewed herself when we were little kids.

From here I can look at my new life and think about all the senseless mistakes that led me to this moment.

Sleeping with the department head.

Deciding to never again sleep with the department head.

All that stupidity leading to a very convenient firing under the evergreen excuse of budget cuts.

In my mind's eye, I'm back in Gregory's office, tucked in the basement of the art department at Temple University. It is one big square with no windows, and there are piles of random objects everywhere. I had found the mess charming once, but this day, all I see is trash. A constellation of Skittles peeks out from under his desk. At the very bottom of a pile of abstract expressionists' biographies is a first edition of *For Whom the Bell Tolls*, covered in a thin layer of mold after a coffee spill.

My classroom is right above us—the jewelry studio. It's my favorite place on campus, maybe even in the whole city. It's got a dozen jewelry benches, each one made of rustic, knobbed wood. A wall of windows faces northwest, which means my classes get the most luscious gold afternoon light—the perfect setting for photographing finished pieces. A raw turquoise, blue as photos of the deep sea, bezel set in brass. A silver locket that opens to a faceted Montana sapphire that glows like a lantern made of cornflowers.

Every day, my students amaze me, but my favorite part of teaching is witnessing the ways they amaze themselves. How they go from *I can't do this* to *Holy shit, I did that*.

And now Greg is taking it all away.

Greg's arms are crossed as he gives me a big, fake sigh. "I tried everything, Sage. It's just . . ." He waves his hands. "You know how it is."

And that's how he dismissed me from the life I'd pulled together from nothing. The one I'd slept in my van for. The one I'd sold basil starts at farmer's markets for. The one I'd stitched and scraped and carved up from the thinnest air, all to get away from the one place I never, ever wanted to live in again.

And now I'm looking right at it.

Cranberry.

My eyes well with tears before I can stop them. "No," I whisper. "No, no, *stop*—"

A single tear makes it to an eyelash, and I violently swipe it away.

But it's too late.

Next to me, in the passenger seat, a figure materializes like the pale curls of coffee steam. It's only one tear, so her edges stay as blurry as a dream. It's only one tear, so the ghost is gone before either of us can say a damn thing.

And what would I say, anyway? *Sorry for killing you? Thanks for the coffee? Leave me alone now, please?*

I take a breath, as deep and long as I can make it, and turn the car back on.

S HIT." I BREATHE INTO MY STEERING WHEEL FOR THE SEC-
ond time today because, fuck me, my sister's boyfriend is
over. His truck is wedged between the driveway and Nadia's
creeping thyme, large and matte black and with a bed so small it's
useless.

I back up onto the street and grab my purse. When I step out,
I'm overtaken not for the first time in my life by how epic Nadia's
house is. It's two stories with a giant attic, covered in pale indigo
siding, illustrations of stained glass etched around the windows,
mostly of bugs and flowers. When we were little, we'd track the
progress of the roses and butterflies across the hardwood floors,
pretending they were real. We'd leave them snacks of popcorn that
Vieja, Nadia's calico cat, would gobble up.

There's a huge front yard for the garden—because there's
nothing behind the house. It backs into a cliff, and when you're on
the attic balcony, you can look way down and see the endless emerald of trees, and look way out and see the endless lapis of sea,
and look up and see the endless sapphire of sky.

"It's us," I once told my sisters. We, put together, were the landscape. Teal and Sky and Sage.

Not anymore, though.

I trudge toward the door, open it, and am assaulted by the sunflower yellow of Nadia's kitchen. Has she repainted it recently? Or have I just forgotten how bright it is?

"¡Mija!" Nadia appears out of nowhere, throwing me into her arms. She covers my face in kisses, and just like that, I'm ten years old again, unable to keep my smile in. She smells like she always does, like old books and cinnamon, espresso and the garden all put together. I wish I could put it in a candle to light when I'm feeling all kinds of lonely, which is just about all the time these days.

"How was the drive?" Nadia asks, pulling a tote bag off my arm.

"Not bad."

Nadia nudges a clay pot from my hand. She assesses the leaves of basil in it—blue spice. It's the most fragrant of all the basils, and the vanilla and licorice of it surrounds us now. One of my favorites. "I thought you'd given it up," she says, eyeing me close.

"I—" *How can you give up something that you're made of?* I want to ask, but then my sister steps into the room. The moment she does, lightning flashes at the window, the following thunder making me and Nadia jump.

"Put that away," Nadia says, gesturing to the storm.

Teal rolls her eyes. Nadia well knows she can't do anything about it. I used to feel bad for her—at least my gift doesn't reveal my emotional state at any given time. Teal's upset right now—hence the lightning and thunder—and it's because I'm here. After she punched my face, though, I don't feel bad anymore. Instead, I say a prayer that she hasn't learned how to aim those bolts yet.

"Hermana," she says, carefully stepping around Nadia to kiss my cheek.

"Teal." She's in a trendy, tight, hot pink spandex getup. She works at the gym and looks the part, right down to the long, beautiful muscles cutting into her shoulders and arms.

Nadia lets out a long, deep exhale. Teal and I didn't throw fists within thirty seconds. Thank all the old gods. "I'll take this upstairs," she says to me.

"Wait, Nadia, I'm coming—"

"Woah! Is that Sage?" Johnny Miller, Teal's boyfriend, driver of the trucklike status symbol on my great-aunt's creeping thyme, bounces into the room. "They'll just let anyone in here, huh?" He bellows a laugh that makes my skin crawl and throws me into a hug, not noticing that I don't return it. He kisses my cheek and it's wet. I have to fight myself *hard* to not pull out my hand sanitizer and douse my whole body in it.

"How are you doing, Johnny?" I ask, though I don't really want to know. I glance at my sister, but she's at the stove, cooking something that smells amazing. She won't meet my eye and I know we're both thinking about the same thing. My last visit three years ago. Me, walking downstairs around midnight to grab cold water and almost knocking into her, crying on the stairs. "Oh my God, what's wrong, Teal?" I had asked. Now I wish I hadn't. Maybe then I wouldn't have this scar on my lip.

"Oh, you know!" Johnny's voice is just under the level of a shout, breaking my trip down memory lane. "Busy with the channel. You know. My follower count keeps jumping, baby."

Johnny makes YouTube reaction videos. Now, I've got nothing against that, in theory. But I swear to God, all this pasty man does is film himself yelling, "WHAT?" and "BRUH," over and over again, like he's the leader of a fuckboy cult. I literally cannot believe enough people watch so he can make a living from it. And that's not even the worst part.

No, the worst part is somehow this bustling YouTube career has made Johnny think that every single thought and revelation his brain conjures is precious. Look at him now. He's going over to stand next to Teal. Yup. Leaning against the wall, crossing his legs, watching her cook with a smile on his face. Now, I bet you anything—

"So guess what, everyone? I found a *female* mechanic. Hired her on the *spot*. Do you know how many lady mechanics there are? And the fact that there's one in Cranberry, Virginia?" He laughs and shakes his head. "Do you know how many men would *trust* a lady, a *female* mechanic?" He might as well pump his fists into his chest and grunt, *Me good man. Me trust lady with big truck.*

Yes. Johnny Miller, YouTube reaction star, discovered feminism several years ago. Ever since, his favorite hobby, besides annoying the shit out of anyone near him, is to lecture Teal, Nadia, and me, if I'm so unlucky, about what a groundbreaking feminist he is.

"That's great, babe," Teal says like a hypnotized Stepford wife. A little flash of lightning in the distance tells me what she's really thinking.

If Johnny had an iota of awareness beyond himself, by now he would've noticed that storms follow Teal the way bees follow single-bloom dahlias. Since he doesn't, I can only assume that he thinks Cranberry has randomly gotten gloomy—and often violent—weather since the start of their relationship.

Johnny looks at me expectantly next. Right. He wants me to clap and cheer because he hired a woman to work on his truck. And I can't do this anymore. I can't pat this manchild's shoulder because of his recent discovery that women are also people.

Especially because it's not even true. If he really believed that, I never would've found my sister sobbing on the stairs three years ago.

"I gotta help Nadia," I say fast, and rush out of the room and up the stairs.

LA CASA DE NADIA FLORES WAS BUILT SOMETIME IN THE 1920s. Everything about it croaks and creaks and I can't help imagining each sound is a story, sliding right out of the floorboards. I climb the stairs fast, trying to run away from the specific stories inside these walls—but they rush toward me anyway. There's Sky's boyfriend, Ramón, who helped put in these shelves. The way they both stacked these hundreds of books as I studied for some exam downstairs, listening to them laugh and flirt. How I recently learned from social media that Ramón and his wife are expecting a baby, and how that means my baby sister would be old enough to be a mama now, and how unfair it is that life continues on without her.

I rush past the second floor and keep going until I reach the attic door. I find Nadia in there, pulling a strawflower quilt out of the teeny hobbit closet. "Nights can get cold up here," she says with a smile when she sees me. "I'd forgotten the blankets."

"I know. I used to live here, remember?"

"Oh, humor me, Sage. Let an old lady take care of her niece."

A wave of anger rushes through with something rude to say. *Bit late for that*, maybe.

Instead of saying what's on my mind, I inhale slowly until the resentment isn't so close to the surface. I take a look around. "Nothing's changed." The walls still have their thick white paint, chipping, revealing the forest green underneath. She left my collection of vintage botanical illustrations on the wall over the bed, in mismatched frames ranging from shiny gold to matte turquoise. The bed sits low on a brass wire frame. Along the southwestern wall are tiny windows with shelving just under them. It's where I started seeds as a teenager. And across from the bed, there's the balcony. I don't have the guts to wander that way.

"I knew you'd come back," Nadia responds, shrugging.

I freeze, because who likes to hear any version of *I told you so?* And because it sounds like she thinks I'm gonna be staying. Which I'm not. I can't. The thunder rumbling around us reminds me of all the reasons why.

This time, Nadia saves me from saying what I'm thinking. "Come on, mija. Let's see if we can get our friendly neighborhood feminist to help move in your things."

My laugh echoes in the stairwell on our way down. I think only I notice how dull it is.

TEAL'S COOKED UP CHEESE-AND-SUN-DRIED-TOMATO-stuffed chicken breasts with a wine and mushroom sauce. On the side is a salad, strewn with nuts and cranberries. She slices her chicken into a series of squares, barely dipping forks of salad into her vinaigrette on the side. I think of popcorn parties we had as kids, dipping the warm extra-extra-super-buttery crunch into anything from hot sauce to chocolate syrup. We'd stuff our faces, trying to see who could eat the most without spraying kernels all over the kitchen table. Teal always won.

The storm's cleared up some, but that doesn't mean Teal isn't glowering at her plate, choking me with her animosity at my existence. Nadia's pretty reserved, too. Then again, not a single one of us can get a word in edgewise.

"So then I took a step back, and held my hands out, and I said, woah. No. That's *stealing*. You take that headset to the front where I can pay for it." Johnny shakes his head, closing his eyes briefly with a smile. "You should've seen her face. I mean, she was near tears, you guys. I don't think any influencer has turned down their free merchandise, like, ever. Even though it's stealing." He glances around the table to make sure we're nodding our heads, waving palm leaves, possibly on our knees worshipping such profound morality in a single human. He seems dismayed at how quiet we are. "I mean, it's *stealing*," he says again, stabbing his chicken in emphasis.

"But it's Best Buy," Teal finally says. "They can afford the loss."

"Babe." He barely lets her finish the sentence. "It's still stealing."

"So you're like, super against stealing, huh, Johnny?" I say.

"Yeah, of course. It's—"

"Stealing, right. One of the commandments and everything." My voice is sarcastic but Johnny doesn't notice. Nadia and Teal sure do, though. Nadia's giving me pleading eyes that say something like *Don't start some shit, Sage*, and Teal's eyes are glaring, like *Go ahead, see what happens*.

I clear my throat and glance down. The words I really want to say are as crisp and angled as ivy, but in an instant, they dry and wither and fall all around me. What comes out is a shadow of those leaves instead. "I—I was wondering what LandBack activism group you're a part of. You know. Returning the land that was, like, stolen from Indigenous people."

Johnny stares at me for a full five seconds, his mouth slightly open. "Ugh, well, you know that was a really long time—"

"You could look online at maps, and see, like, what tribal nation your property belongs to." I pop my last bite of chicken in my mouth.

"Well, I—I mean, I pay for my place. Like, it's *mine*." Johnny snorts. "What are we seriously going to consider next? That dudes get no say in abortio—"

Teal reaches for my plate so fast, she nearly knocks my glass of water over. "Okay, wow, look at the time. I've got a shift to get to."

Johnny glances at his watch. "Oh, shit, babe. I need to get home early to film, too."

Johnny shoves his plate in my hands before giving Teal a re-volting kiss on the mouth. It's more of a lick than a kiss. "Come over after?"

"Sure."

He leaves without thinking of offering to help clean up. "Peace out, babes," he calls to us before the door shuts.

My sister has been with this man for six years. Six *years*. Why does she hate herself that much? He's not even cute. Like, *nothing* redeems that mess of a personality.

The second he's gone, Teal turns to me. "What the hell was that about?"

"What?" I play dumb. "Making conversation?"

"No. Belittling him. Like you always do."

I snort, taking Johnny's plate to the sink. "No offense or any-thing, Teal, but Johnny belittles himself just fine without any of my help."

"Sage," Nadia says, a warning thick in her voice. Oh, now she wants to comment, and it's directed at me, of course. Not at Johnny or Teal. It's always me.

"I can't believe it. You've been here for an hour and a half and you're already back on your bullshit." Teal takes a step toward me. I take one back, fighting the urge to touch the scar on my lip. Lightning flashes across the sky, thick as a river, white yellow like daisies. In an instant, all the house lights go out. We're lit only by the orange sunset line on the horizon and weirdly every-thing is in shades of blue. Like we stepped into an early Picasso painting.

"Shit," Nadia says, flicking the light switch back and forth. "Power's out."

"See what you made me do?" Teal snaps. She tosses all the silverware into the sink, the clanks high-pitched and echoing, and pulls her apron off. For some reason, I haven't noticed it until now. It's pink with a little turtle print on it.

"Cute apron," I say.

"Fuck off, Sage." She grabs her keys and is out the door.

Nadia and I both wince when it slams. She sighs very, very deeply. "We could've avoided that." Her voice is gentle, but her words are as sharp as the cutlery Teal just slammed into the sink.

"I just can't stand him." And her with him. She could do so much better. I told her as much three years ago, in the middle of the night on the stairs, my fingers softly wiping away at her tears.

"She's been through a lot, mija. Losing Sky. It did her in."

Now Nadia's words are swords, sliding right into my gut. How many times had I heard nearly the same sentence growing up? *She's been through a lot, Sage. Especially after your mom took off.* When the hell is Nadia going to realize that I also lost my mother? That I also lost my sister? That these events *did me in* so thoroughly, I can't even remember who I was before?

"I'm sorry," I tell her. *I'm sorry you still see me as the fuckup* is the part I leave out. "I'll do the dishes. It's late. Why don't you go and draw a bath?"

"Ah, you shouldn't—"

"Go, Nadia. You rubbed your shoulder all through dinner. I know it hurts."

"But the power—"

"I'll call them. But we've got plenty of hot water." A while back, Nadia got tired of ice-cold water after living with teenage girls who all loved long showers and baths. She invested in a water heater the size of an Appalachian mountain, and I'm not sure if she's run out of hot water since.

Nadia nods and turns. The floorboards creak under her feet as she goes, releasing more stories. In an instant, it's eight years ago. Summertime, the woods thick with tart, sweet berries, the leaves on the trees firm in their green. Sky puts an arm around me and kisses my cheek. *You sure you don't want to come with us?*

I think about that question a lot. How my answer changed the path of our lives, how one single decision carved out deep, bloody chunks of each of our hearts, never to be seen again. No matter how many espressos Nadia pours to the old gods, we're not getting those pieces back.

If I'd said yes, Sky would still be here. She'd be alive.

But I didn't.

It only takes three breaths to will the tears back in, and then I push my hands into the soapy water. The moment I do, the lights flicker back on, like a dream. Like another whole story descends upon me, in this house on the cliffside overlooking the sea in Cranberry, Virginia. For the last eight years, I've kept the narrative of my life tight in my fists, my hands and arms and entire body decorated with bronze armor so I couldn't ever be hurt again.

And now, for the first time in a long time, I don't know what's next.

I GUESS TEAL SPENDS THE NIGHT AT HER BEST BUY–FANATIC boyfriend's house, because she's nowhere to be found when I come downstairs in the morning. Nadia's all dressed up for work—she's a greeter at the Cranberry Wood State Park Welcome Center. "Coffee's still hot," she says, gesturing to the mint green percolator on the stove.

"Thanks." I grab a mug from the cupboard, freezing when I see it's *my* mug. The ghost mug. The only things I unpacked last night were my toothbrush, toothpaste, and a T-shirt. So I don't know how the hell this got here.

"You okay?" Nadia's paused in the middle of pulling her blazer on. Her eyes are lined in bronze, her perfectly tweezed brows furrowed.

I shake my head, turning to fill the mug. "I'm fine." I've never gotten around to telling Nadia or Teal or anyone about my ghost. I know they'd believe me, so it's not that. I guess it's that I'm scared. I kind of know what Sky the Ghost might say, should I ever give her the chance. And I don't want to hear the ugly truth, and I don't want anyone else to hear it, either. Teal blames me enough as it is.

"Oh, Sage, I almost forgot." Nadia turns, her giant black pleather purse on her shoulder. "I let Dale Bowen know you're back in town. He'll probably call you soon."

As though on cue, my phone buzzes on the table. Of course the name on the screen reads *Dale Bowen*.

"Answer it. He wants to hire you. And I *know* you need money." Nadia gives me a long look before blowing a kiss. "Have a good day!" The door shuts behind her.

I sigh. Nadia's gift is *knowing* things. Not all the things, but enough to be meddlesome. If she says Dale wants to hire me, well. She's not gonna be wrong. I briefly wonder if she *knows* what I really need money for—getting the hell out of Cranberry as soon as possible.

I accept the call and put the phone to my ear. "Dale! How are you?"

"Sage Flores. Heard from a little birdie that you're back in town for a while." Dale's voice is exactly as I remember it. Booming and bursting with joy.

I smile despite myself. "Yeah, well, I wouldn't say a while. A bit, maybe."

"Well, can't say I'm sorry to hear it. We've been needing an extra set of hands at the farm."

"Yeah?" I put the phone on speaker as I pour cream into my mug. "But the festival isn't until July, right?" That was where I mainly worked, back in the day.

"Oh, yeah. But we still need help tending the veg beds . . . remember? You used to weed and fertilize with the best of us! Why don't you stop by and do some paperwork today, will you?"

I nearly choke on coffee. This—this seems so *fast*. I wonder how much of it is Nadia's doing. Her garden has been a backup for lots of the popular roses from the farm for years, in case, old gods forbid, some fungus or virus wipes out the rose fields. She must've called in a favor . . . or maybe twenty. It unsettles me. "Well, ah. Here's the thing, Dale. I—I was thinking about looking around for a job first, you know? I don't know what Nadia told you, but you don't need—"

"Nonsense! Look, we would love to have you. Stop by as soon as you can."

I sigh silently. "When's good for you?"

"Me!" Dale laughs. "Didn't Nadia tell you? I retired a good six months ago. Nate took over."

I'm a little too flustered to point out that he's still technically working by recruiting me. "Nathaniel, you mean?"

"Oh, yeah. He's excited to have you on board. I'll tell him to expect you anytime, okay? Gotta go! Take care, Sage!"

I sit in my chair slowly, taking a sip of the coffee. It's now cold but I barely notice.

Here's the thing.

I've kinda been into Nathaniel Bowen for a while.

As in, oh, about eleven years.

I worked the Heritage Rose Festival—hosted by the Cranberry Rose Company, which Dale and his brothers founded like a gazillion years ago—for three summers in a row, from the ages of seventeen to nineteen. That first summer, I helped set up tables and signs and lined up rows of roses and vegetable starts to convince people that yes, they needed a second English tea, and absolutely, that gourd was squash bug resistant. The second summer, I went in to do about the same, but then Joan, the festival coordinator, had a bit of a freak-out. She couldn't find the labels for the rose cuttings.

These rose cuttings were pretty young—as in, greenish-brown sticks piercing Virginia mud in plastic pots. Some of them didn't even have leaves yet. None were blooming. There was virtually no way to tell them apart.

If you weren't me, that is.

In an instant, I'm there, traveling back in time faster than light sucked up from scorned ghosts. I'm on the edge of the barn where the roses are about to be loaded onto the truck headed downtown. It's early morning, so the light is thick and pale, the way it gets after the sky swallows the pinks and oranges of sunrise. Joan's near tears. "We can't sell these," she says. "No one wants to buy mystery roses."

"Let me," I say. I pick up one of the pots in her arms, gliding the tips of my fingers over the stem. I pretend like I'm studying the leaves . . . when really, I'm *listening*. It's as though those sticks, those cuttings, become an extension of my own body—the cells that make up me swirl around them, and the cells of the plant spiral around me, until nothing separates us. Until identifying cultivars is as natural as wiggling my own toes or pointing my own fingers. "This one's the Ballerina rose," I say.

"It is?" Joan is skeptical but she can't hide the hope filling her sea holly eyes.

"Yeah. And that one—" I point to the one in her arms. "That's Queen Elizabeth. Behind you there are three, no, four wild American ones. Pale pink."

Soon, Joan's writing everything down on notecards, sticking them in the dirt. The moisture from the Virginia mud seeps into the paper, but she either doesn't notice or doesn't care.

Then Dale walks by, tall and silver haired in his dirt-stained overalls. "What's going on, y'all?" Joan fills him in and he chuckles. "Oh, didn't Susan tell you? We put the labels on the bottom this year. Remember? We ran out of both the plastic and wooden sticks . . ." He grunts as he lifts a few pots to show her.

It takes a few seconds for Dale to look and see how the note-cards and labels match. They're all accurate. "Say . . ." He looks at me. "How in the blazes could you tell what was what, Sage?"

I shrug, my cheeks warm. "I . . . I study plants."

"Huh." Dale looks at me, his eyes bright with ideas.

Next thing I know, I'm set up at my very own table in the festival. I've got a sign over my head that displays, in big green letters, *The Plant Whisperer*. People bring me unlabeled cuttings, vegetable starts, even seeds. I tell them what it is. If I'm wrong, they get a free rose cutting.

I'm never wrong.

It's actually kind of fun until a group of guys—all Johnny Miller types—try to trick me. They don't even hide the fact that they've switched the labels on the four-inch pots they've got. I glance at the planters they slide in my face. "That's a Black Beauty tomato. The other's a Sunrise Bumble Bee."

"Wrong!" The men are drunk and slurring their words—clearly they spent a little too much time at the local brewery's booth. They laugh and laugh. "Give us a freebie." One points to the sign above me. "You owe us."

"You switched the labels," I say, bored.

"Are you calling me a liar?" I'll never forget the growl of threat in his voice—the biggest one. I realize I could be in real trouble here, looking at the way he flexes his beefy fists.

"What's going on?"

Out of nowhere, there's another guy. I recognize him immediately from photos in the office. Ridiculously tall, like six-four, and lean. His hair auburn, his eyes green as tomato leaves, his smile beautiful enough to make my stomach turn inside out just by looking at it in a picture. It's Nathaniel Bowen, Dale's only grandson, home from college. And he's not smiling now.

The guys try to explain how I'm cheating them, but Nate examines the plants. "The Black Beauty tomato has leaves that turn blue at the tips," he says, "and the Sunrise Bumble Bee is a grape. It's a smaller tomato, so smaller leaves." He switches the labels back. "Nice try, fellas, but if I see you harassing anyone else tonight, I'll have security escort you out." He looks even taller as he glowers at them, and grumbling, they all disappear.

When he turns to me, though, he's gentle. That smile widens over his face. "Hey. You okay?"

I nod.

"Good. You let me or anyone else know if they come back, okay?"

I nod again. "Sure. Yeah. Okay."

He walks away and I watch him disappear into the plant-enthused crowd. I swear, I've been thinking about that man's smile at least once a month for the last decade.

I blink and I'm back here—Nadia's kitchen. The sunflower walls, smooth white appliances, the midmorning sun touching the cup of coffee in my hand as gently as the creation of Adam.

That summer, when I was eighteen—sadly that was the last time I saw Nathaniel Bowen.

Until today, I guess.

MARCH 9, 2001
14 YEARS AGO

RainOnATennRoof: Hey, Silvergurl

RainOnATennRoof: If that is your real name.

silvergurl0917: i could say the same to you.

RainOnATennRoof: Yeah? Well I think you know me.

silvergurl0917: . . . so what haven't you noticed today, tennessee reyes?

RainOnATennRoof: Ha! You do know me!

RainOnATennRoof: Is this Kayla?

silvergurl0917: :(

RainOnATennRoof: Swati?

silvergurl0917: :'(

RainOnATennRoof: Hmm.

silvergurl0917: answer the question and i'll give you a clue to my identity;)

RainOnATennRoof: Okay. Okay. What haven't I noticed. Well that's a hard one. Because all I've got in my memory is whatever I *have* noticed.

silvergurl0917: i think that's what this philosophy guy (who said the question- i read it in a book) was going for.? like. he wanted people to start being aware of what they were missing?

RainOnATennRoof: Sounds like I've got homework then.

PRESENT

The Cranberry Rose Company for Heritage Roses is on the side of a blue Appalachian-like hill, maybe one that's been worn down a billion years, from tens of thousands of feet tall to this—a leveled mound, surrounded by maple, ash, and white mulberry trees, overlooking smoky rolling hills and the white shard of highway cut right in the middle of them like broken milk glass.

I take a turn down a dirt road, appropriately named Rosy

Lane, and my van jumps and grumbles until I reach a small, gravel parking lot, full of low-blooming weeds. There's a little barn, restored and painted yellow ochre, and a tiny farmhouse, white with navy trim, which holds the offices, a kitchen, and a bathroom with a high glass window so old and thick, looking through it transforms the landscape into a proper Monet painting.

Surrounding these are enormous hoop houses: five total, each filled to the brim with mostly—surprise!—roses. Behind the farmhouse is a field with rows of—surprise!—more roses, a messy labyrinth of them, twirling and curling among allium, garlic, and nitrogen fixers like blue false indigo and wild lupine, both reaching up toward the marshmallow-cloud sky with their violet blooms.

Right next to where I've parked is an herb spiral, made from stones Dale and his brothers all dug out of the field when they first established it. It's nearly ten feet tall and has been abandoned since I last worked there. I'm surprised to see it full of weeds and dry, sad soil.

"Yikes," I say once I pop out of the van. I run my palm against the spiral's rough stone sides. This was my creation. My way to convince Dale to sell herbs in addition to vegetables—especially basil. How I'd nearly forgotten it, I don't know.

There's some deep chuckling from behind me and I turn, my stomach dropping a little when I see Nate there. He looks exactly the same except, well, older. There are faint lines around his mouth presumably from that sunrise smile of his. Glasses frame the eyes that exactly match the Virginia creeper all around us. He's dressed very casually—a thin T-shirt and jeans, hands in his pockets. "Gramps said he tried to keep it up after you left, but . . ." He lifts his arms and gestures to the weedy mess. "I wondered if you'd be up to making it beautiful again. Your first task once we get you on payroll."

"Yes," I say, trying to ignore how breathless I sound with Nate uttering the word *beautiful* my way, even if he was just referring to my old herb spiral. "I'd love that."

He points to the farmhouse. There's no wedding ring on his finger. "We've got plenty of seed in there if you want to get started."

"Sure. Right away."

He grins. "Yeah? I mean, if you're this enthused already, you could start today. I'll have Olivia log your hours." He takes a look at my outfit for the first time and frowns. "But maybe not . . . ?"

I admit that I'd definitely overdressed to make an appearance at a farm. The sundress is white linen with a pattern of blue roses. I thought he might get a kick out of it—blue roses are a rose collector's wet dream, long sought after and nonexistent on planet Earth—but he looks all worried now.

"Yes. I mean, what, yeah, I'm *fine* with this." I pull up my skirt half an inch, dropping it immediately. "I can work on the spiral today. Yeah, for sure." Well done, Sage. Props on the articulation.

He inclines his head. "Come on, let's set you up."

And maybe it's something about the way he looks, all handsome and happy in the gold sunlight, but all of a sudden, moving back to Cranberry no longer feels like my dumbest decision in recent memory.

The paperwork isn't a lot since I've worked here before. Unfortunately Olivia, the office manager, can't get the printer to work for the tax form I have to fill out. "Oh, this old piece of junk," she says, all but kicking the massive machine. "Tell you what. Stop by before you leave, okay? I should have it by then."

One hour later, I am absolutely cursing my past self for mindlessly agreeing to do this today. For one, it's hot—I'm talking *no more clouds in our Southern summer sky* hot—and for two, it's humid—I'm talking *hold a cup in the wind and it'll fill right up with warm, sticky water* humid.

I've pushed up four wheelbarrows full of compost from the barn, all dark and sweet-smelling. I'm trying to mix it into the dirt already in the spiral, but it's been neglected for so long, it's like cutting in pieces of dry pottery. I water the whole thing, trying to soften the soil, and only then can I take a shovel and begin the real dirty work.

By the time I'm done prepping the spiral's ground, I'm covered in sweat. The compost has left an abstract painting of black stains on my dress, the clay adding highlights with its orange red. My white Converse are also blackened beyond repair. I'm pretty sure there's dirt all over my face, and there's definitely dirt—and maybe a beetle or two—in my hair.

As uncomfortable as I am, though, my whole body also feels weirdly good. I've been gardening in containers—little ones—the last eight years, so taking a shovel to earth hits a spot where I didn't even know I was needing it.

I think lots of people look at dirt and think it's just this inert substance we happen to walk upon, but ever since my gift appeared, I've known in my bones that dirt is *alive*. One spoonful of dirt can contain yards and yards of microscopic strands of mushrooms and one billion bacteria. I swear, sometimes I can put my ear to it and hear how loud it is down there. Dirt sounds like a song, but a song made up of broken-down stems and acorns, bones and stones, and the skinny, sly migrations of spiky and smooth invertebrates.

It's always been easy for me to connect with the dirt with my gift, probably because that's where most plants grow, so I close my eyes and do just that. I hover my hand over the spiral and sense its new body, the compost slowly softening the clay with organic matter. I pause, though, when my hand "sees" weed seeds—violet and vetch. Both lovely, but they spread too fast to grow much else near them. "Get out of there," I mutter, scraping until the seeds are collected in the palm of my left hand. I blow them toward the trees like birthday candles.

I dip my hand in my water bucket and trace my name right into that dirt mix. *S-A-G-E.* One of my favorite landscape designers, Mary Reynolds, writes, "Our bodies are made of the Earth and return to it eventually, but the land will always remain alive." The fact that we come from dirt and eventually turn to dirt is spooky and incredible to think about at the same time. My sister is dirt by now, surely. All of our ancestors are, too. This must make dirt holy, holy enough for the old gods to walk upon it from time to time, holy enough that Nadia gives it a little cup of espresso to drink every single morning.

I'm looking through all the seed packets stored in big buckets in one of the offices when Olivia walks up. "Here you go, darlin'." She passes me the form, not even blinking at the mud caked on my hand as I accept it. "Nate told me he wants you to see him in his office when you get a chance."

"Sure." My stomach flip-flops at the idea of seeing Nate again. I try to calm it down with water from the fridge. *There's no way he's single,* I remind myself. *Ring or no ring, there's just no way.*

I knock on Dale's old office door, assuming that's where Nate's set up. "Come in," calls his friendly voice. I smile immediately, burst-

ing the door open to Nate's happy face behind his desk. Unfortunately, the door keeps opening, revealing the other person in the
room—the only person in the whole world who would make my
heart lurch and my knees weaken on sight.

Tennessee Reyes.

8

I FELL IN LOVE AT FIRST SIGHT WITH TENN WHEN I WAS FIF-teen years old.

He was waiting at the car pickup at school, headphones over his ears, staring into the distance like the beautiful, broody teenager he was. His hair was dark brown and overgrown and curly, his eyes dark and intense, his skin smooth and brown. His jaw—I mean, I know it's a cliché to say a guy's jaw could cut glass, but Tenn's jaw was like that. It could cut Montana sapphires. Gray and black and white diamonds. And unlike most of the guys in school, who were lanky and wobbly with awkward, adolescent bodies, he was thick and solid, his shoulders so wide that the second after I'd fallen for him, I imagined what it'd be like for him to hug me, to feel that wide warmth all around me like an absurdly sunlit mountain.

Say something, I told myself. I was waiting for Nadia to come get me and Lord knew I had time.

Love at first sight wasn't to be trifled with. I'd read all kinds of stories about people who didn't make their move and regretted it. Okay, fine, I'd read *one* story, one of Nadia's romances, and eventually, the couple reunited and had their happily-ever-after, but whatever. I *knew* this was some type of a once-in-a-lifetime moment, so I walked over, heart racing, and said the first thing that I could think of. "Nice backpack."

He pulled his headphones down around his neck. "Come again?"

"I like your backpack."

He furrowed his eyebrows and I noticed how unfairly thick his eyelashes were. He could model for mascara. For falsies. He glanced behind him at his fairly unremarkable black Jansport and said, "Oh. Thanks . . . ?"

"Sure." I kept walking, acting like I had somewhere to be. My cheeks burned. *Nice backpack? I like your backpack?*

My once-in-a-lifetime moment, and I ruined it with my conversational ineptitude.

I swore to myself that I would make it right. I'd find a way to make an impression on Tennessee Reyes.

Unfortunately, I wasn't the only one. Whenever I saw him at lunch, or after school, there was always some kind of flirting contest happening with him and at least two or three other girls. Girls who were in his year and thus older, thus infinitely cooler, girls who probably didn't spend every second of their free time watching their little sisters.

So my chance didn't come until the next year when I took Yearbook. See, we had access to students' contact information, including email addresses. And back then, way back in the stone age of the internet, most of us had dialup with America Online. One of the best features of AOL was instant messaging. IM screen names always matched the emails. So when I saw Tenn's (of course I looked for it the very first day of class)—RainOnATennRoof—I memorized it and went home and spent two months watching him log on and off, mostly on Friday nights.

Laurel took an art history class with him and vaguely knew of my crush. Meaning, she knew I thought he was the hottest thing since buttered tortillas, but not that I was head over heels, wondering what he smelled like, daydreaming about kissing his full mouth nightly, in love with the boy.

After class, because she knew it made me unspeakably happy, she'd share tidbits about Tenn, like "Today he made everyone laugh by imitating Ms. St. Clair," or "He snuck a peanut butter cup after the pop quiz." One day she said, "I think he's, like, really into philosophy."

"Philosophy?" We were in the lunchroom, squeezed at the very end of a long table. Laurel had packed extra to share with me. I always made Teal's and Sky's lunches in the morning and rarely had time to do my own, and Laurel's mom was the *best* cook.

"Yeah. He had all these books and was debating with another guy on, like, I don't know. The meaning of life? When class started."

Somehow I knew that was the key.

I went to the school library and checked out every intro to philosophy book I could find. They all, sadly, were deathly boring and I was quickly losing hope. But then randomly thumbing through one, I found a question.

What haven't you noticed today?

I don't think I even wrote down which old, stuffy white guy had asked it. I just knew it stuck with me. So one Friday night, after everyone was in bed, I saw RainOnATennRoof log on. I took a deep breath, opened up an IM box, and wrote that exact question out. *What haven't you noticed today?*

The result?

Everything I'd been hoping for. Tenn and I became friends. Confidants. We shared secrets and hopes and dreams and fears. And, eventually, he developed feelings for me, too. Toward the end, I was beginning to think my goal of making Tenn actually love me back was a real possibility.

Over one year later, though? When I was seventeen? He shattered my heart into one hundred thousand pieces. Sometimes I can still hear all those bits shattering against the ground like paper-thin rose quartz. Sometimes I wonder if there are still bits of my heart slit into the floor, the story of my heartbreak hidden in the hardwood.

The very last time I saw Tenn Reyes, I was nineteen and working, once again, as the Plant Whisperer at the Heritage Rose Festival. And he was a jerk to me. Not as bad as the Johnny Miller guys my first year, but close enough.

I made myself stop loving him, or, rather, who I wrongly imagined he was.

And I got over it. Honest. Or, at least I thought I did.

Till now. Seeing him in Nate's office. I'm sixteen years old again, all anxiety and insecurity, all frizzy hair I don't know how to style yet, all exhausted from taking care of my sisters all the time, all madly in love with a guy who only flirts with perfect girls who are literally the opposite of me. A guy who doesn't even know my real name.

And this is how Cranberry, Virginia, fucks me over once again.

LAUREL WAS RIGHT. THIS IS MY FIRST THOUGHT AFTER I HAVE TO grab the door handle to keep from falling over. Tenn does look better. Impossibly, impossibly better.

He's still solid and thick, though maybe an inch or two taller.

Maybe six feet or just under. His hair is still that exact shade of rained-on tree bark, warm brown with the slightest coppery highlights. His jaw is still sharp as a dagger, his eyes still dark as winter nights. His eyelashes, still thick and long enough to make Cover Girl executives weep. He's got that sexy stubble Laurel mentioned and my eyes drift down to where his long-sleeved shirt is unbuttoned once, revealing a peek of chest hair.

I don't remember that chest hair in high school.

I also don't remember him looking at me like *that* in high school. Which, okay, to be fair I'm not sure he ever actually looked at me after that *nice backpack* incident. But while Nate's chuckling and saying, "Sage! I'd like you to meet someone," Tennessee Reyes is letting his gaze go over me all honey-slow, taking in first, probably, the dirt and the mud and the clay on my stupidly white dress, before settling on my eyes. And when that eye contact occurs, I feel it all the way down my spine to the tips of my toes, as though Teal did learn how to aim lightning bolts, and she sent one over to me at that exact moment just for fun.

Tenn gives me a half smile and crosses his arms. "Well, if it isn't the Plant Whisperer."

MARCH 16, 2001
14 YEARS AGO

RainOnATennRoof: So I've been thinking . . . you know. My homework and all.

silvergurl0917: yeah?

RainOnATennRoof: Today I didn't notice how the rain looked on the windows at school. I was just watching it, here in my bedroom, right? The little droplets, how each one like, reflects the world. I didn't notice that earlier.

silvergurl0917: that's. wow. that's really beautiful.

RainOnATennRoof: so what about you?

RainOnATennRoof: What didn't you notice?

silvergurl0917: hmm

RainOnATennRoof: I'm waiting:)

silvergurl0917: i'm looking around! give me a minute will ya!

RainOnATennRoof: ;)

silvergurl0917: okay. . . . i didn't notice how that streetlamp in front of my house, how its orange light . . . there's like a big sliver of it peeking through the curtains.

RainOnATennRoof: Sounds pretty.

silvergurl0917: real pretty, yes.

RainOnATennRoof: Like you:)

silvergurl0917: lol. i am not that pretty

RainOnATennRoof: prove it to me. Let's have lunch together tomorrow.

silvergurl0917: sorry . . . i think my aunt's up. i gotta go.

silvergurl0917 has logged off Messenger.

PRESENT

Well, if it isn't the Plant Whisperer. At his words, I'm sucked into another story, another memory. There I am, nineteen years old, taking up a job at the festival as the Plant Whisperer for the second year in a row. My heart's only just stopped aching at the thought of him, even though it's been two whole years since he ripped it to pieces with his bare hands. He's moved away to Denver. That part of my life is done.

And then, out of nowhere, *he* saunters up, hands in his pockets, his dark brown eyes twinkling. "What's a plant whisperer?" Tennessee Reyes asks me, a hint of a smile curled on his lips.

My mouth's fallen open, but no sound can make its way out. He lifts his brows. "Oh. Ahh—" He runs a hand through his hair, making the curls even more tousled. "¿Qué es una encantadora de plantas?"

Anger shoots through me, veined and white-hot, poking at all the places in my heart that I thought had healed but was infinitely wrong about. "I heard you the first time. God." My voice is much sharper than I intended.

He blinks in surprise. My stomach drops. It's actually really thoughtful of him to try Spanish, what with me staring at him like I had no idea what he was saying. It's probably not fair for me to be this rude to him. He never knew who Silvergurl0917 was.

"Sorry. Bad day," I say, and wince. The fact that I'm apologizing to him, after what he did to me . . . it doesn't sit well.

He rewards me with a grin, one I don't want to notice as basically breathtakingly beautiful, but too bad, I guess. "No worries. So." He claps his hands together. "What's a plant whisperer?"

I close my eyes, briefly, and gesture to the sign. "I can identify any stick, start, weed, or seed. If I'm wrong, you get a free rose cutting."

When I look back at his face, he's delighted. "Okay, hold on." He points a finger my way and disappears into the festival.

It's fifteen excruciating minutes until he returns, an assortment of plant goods in his hands. He slaps a little planter on my table. "That's a White Rose of York." I barely even look at it.

"Yes," he says. He lines up more pots. I name them all—cabbage rose in yellow, a tea rose in hot pink, a climbing rose the color of blood.

He stares at me for a minute after the last one. "There's a trick, right?" He picks up a pot, looking all over. "They're marked. Notched. Or something."

This isn't the first time I've been accused of trickery. Thing is, *him* doing it, him accusing me of essentially lying, is so antithetical to the person I'd thought Tenn Reyes was that I can't help the anger rising up inside me once more. It's hot and gooey and way too sticky around the general broken-heart area.

Then he reaches in his pockets and pulls out seeds. They're all in Ziploc bags, and really wrinkled, like they've been squished against his warm leg for a week. "These ones. These aren't from the festival." He winks. "Go ahead. Try."

I swipe the bags out of his hand, glaring at him the whole while. Apparently, not only does he think I'm a liar; now *he's* trying to trick *me*. Well. Let's see about that.

Without breaking eye contact, I lift up bag number one. "This is a wild squash you found south, here in Cranberry, near the coast. It's bitter. Inedible, if you were thinking about it." I dangle bag number two. "These are pink poppies, collected roadside near the Appalachian trail." By bag number three, his eyes are big, those lashes fanned out and framing them like pine needles. But I can't stop now. "A melon. This one's a family heirloom. They don't grow very large but they're sweet. And finally . . ." I hold the last bag up. "A squash. It's a Seminole pumpkin, from one of those tourist shops along the Florida Panhandle. They're almost non-viable. I'd sow those soon." I thrust the bags into his chest and he stumbles backward. He lifts his hand and instead of taking the seeds, he wraps it around my hand and wrist. His fingers are warm. They're calloused. They're big.

"You didn't even look at them. And how did you know . . ." His voice is so low, it's almost a whisper. He looks at me, up and down. "What did you say your name was?"

"The Plant Whisperer," I snap. "And I was right about the seeds, because I'm always right, so no rose cutting for you." It's kind of a sad way to end my ego trip, *no rose cutting for you*. He's not a three-year-old.

"Very well, Plant Whisperer." He's gotten his senses back. He lets go of my hand and stuffs the seeds back in his pocket. He nods at me as a farewell and when he turns away, I want to tell him to stop. I want to say, *It was me. I'm Silvergurl0917. You loved me, once, or at least like-liked me a lot.*

But I hesitate instead. And then he's gone. Gone, gone, gone, for ten years, until, without rhyme or reason, he showed up at Cranberry's Piggly Wiggly two days ago; until now, he's here, staring at me with a look of wonder as Nate keeps chatting, not noticing the electric air crackling like burning cedar between us.

10

So you know each other! I figured you must've, if not from high school, then one way or another." Nate's pretty gleeful about this revelation.

"I wouldn't say we know each other," I say, at the same time Tenn says, "We didn't go to high school together."

"Uh. Yeah, we did." I scoff out a breath.

"Pretty sure I'd have remembered you." He finishes his sentence with a wink that makes my knees feel like they're made of molasses again.

And just like that, the anger I thought for the trillionth, zillionth time was over and done for . . . it returns. It just ascends in me, like a thousand blackbirds deciding to fly up at once, pecking at all the places vulnerable and scarred. *Pretty sure I'd have remembered you.*

It's not that I need him to remember something he never knew. It's more like a reminder that he never valued what we had. Back when what we had was *everything* to me.

After a moment of them waiting for me to respond, I turn to

Nate. "Olivia said you wanted to see me?" I hope that whatever it is, it's quick.

"Sure. Have a seat. The both of you."

The *both* of us? Tenn isn't the least bit bothered by Nate's command like I am. He saunters to one of the two chairs, manspreading immediately. I hate him for it—for this easy confidence so many men have to take up space. They get it just from existing, far as I can tell.

"I'll stand," I say. "I'm filthy."

"It's not a big deal. That's why these chairs are plastic," Nate laughs. "It's a farm, remember?"

With that, I plop down, angling my body away from Tenn's.

"So, I was just getting Tenn up to speed on your arrival, Sage."

"I'm sorry." I lift my hand like I'm in school. "Does he work here?"

"New hire, just like you. And I've got a proposition for the both of you, if you've got the time." Nate doesn't wait for our responses. He lifts a stack of folders. "So as y'all know, Cranberry Rose has been one of the leading providers of heritage roses in Virginia for the last forty-five years. However, ever since folks started buying plants online, our revenue has had a slow—don't get me wrong, it's a *very* slow—yet steady decline."

"Okay." I'm dismayed at how aloof I sound. But I can *feel* Tenn sneaking looks at me and it's *irritating*.

"I've been studying the sales of the last decade or so, and we get a little jump after one of two things—an article in a state or national paper telling the story of our company. And the addition of the wild American roses did us a lot of good, too."

I nod. I remember when the wild roses were added. Dale's brother Owen had found them growing on the side of an abandoned factory in West Virginia. The land was destined for development, so he got cutters and a shovel and filled his pickup truck with roots and cuttings. They'd given Nadia a handful for her garden, too—she grows them along her tall white picket fence, the pink and peach five-petaled blooms bobbing in the wind like scoops of sherbet. Henry, who's in charge of seeds, was the one who named them. The Wild Graces—graced because they were saved just in time.

"It got me thinking. I mean, what we sell, heritage roses? They're flowers with history. With stories. So it's no coincidence that our sales increase whenever we've got a new story floating out there—whether it's about us or about the plants."

I can follow this. It echoes what Dale always told us before we worked the retail tables at the festival—people like to buy stories. Sure, they love the gorgeous-smelling wild roses and the beautiful hundred-petaled teas. But they also like to hear about how in the middle of winter, wildlife is sustained by the big, fleshy rose hips of the American pink, or how Olivia's daughter held a bouquet of lavender cabbage roses for her wedding. These little personal anecdotes were what sealed the sale.

"We don't have a lot of new stories. Not consistent, anyway." Nate looks at us. "We hired a social media manager, and her findings are the same."

"Wow, you guys hired a social media manager?" I ask. I'd always seen Cranberry Rose as old-school, relying on word-of-mouth recommendations, free farm tours, and the festival to sell. I didn't even know they were on social media.

Nate laughs. "It's nothing fancy. I mean, yeah, the manager is amazing—her name is Fern Santos, and she works remote for now. Gramps wasn't entirely convinced, but . . ." Nate shrugs. "Now that I'm the boss, I'm trying to get Cranberry Rose with the times, you know? We've got a decent following on Instagram and Facebook, but we get more engagement when we can personalize the plants we profile. Whether it's about their botanical history, their Indigenous history, or something more. This goes for the catalog, too." He claps his hands together with a smile. "That's where y'all come in."

"Oh?" I glance at Tenn. Not an ounce of apprehension on his face. He glances at me with a smile and I jerk my face back toward Nate.

"Yeah, Tenn here, we hired him to plant hunt. He's been doing it here and there. You know the heirloom melon we sell, Sage? The Goosebear, small and sweet?"

I nod. It's a weak nod. Because I think I know that melon. Not from the Cranberry Rose catalog, but from the Ziploc bag of seeds stuffed in Tenn's pocket ten years ago at the Heritage Rose Festival.

"That's Tenn's, and a handful of others, too."

Nate's waiting for me to answer. I don't know if he wants me to start praising Tennessee Reyes's plant-hunting skills, but that's not going to happen. I say, "Well, where do I come in? I thought I was here to maintain the veg beds."

"Sage, you've got a gift," Nate says, looking me right in my eyes. My heart drops a little. What does he mean, my *gift*? Did Nadia tell? "You've got a good eye for ID'ing plants." He smiles. "You're a real-life plant identification app. Our own plant whisperer."

I breathe out a sigh as silently as I can. No. He doesn't know the whole gift. Thank goodness.

"And that's why we want you to partner up with Tenn. We want you to hunt for plants. All season long, and if all goes well, into the fall, too."

I'm speechless. I mean . . . Nate? Wants me to work alongside *Tenn*?

It's not like we'd be maintaining the herb spiral together. We'd be traveling. In the same car. Or plane. We'd be in the same hotel, if we went out of town. We'd share meals and coffee together.

We'd have to talk. In person. Face to face. For indeterminate periods of time.

"I don't know if I can do that," I say quickly. Off to the side, Tenn gives me a long look. I can feel him reading my every inner thought. My every dark secret. "I just got here and was hoping to spend time with my family."

"Well, if it helps, you won't be traveling very far. We'd like for you to stay in and near Cranberry for the first month or two, and then branch out."

I steal a glance at Tenn. He's not looking at me for once—no, his eyes are trained out the window, like he's a million miles away in his mind.

"Can I think about it?" I ask.

"Take the rest of the week." Nate stands, and so do I and Tenn. "For what it's worth, Sage, I hope you accept." He gives me his bright sunrise smile and it's so beautiful, but everything is confused now. Tennessee Reyes is *here*. Nate wants me to work in close quarters with Tenn. Tenn keeps winking at me like he's got sand in his eye. I'm covered in dirt and I'm exhausted and I think I can feel a beetle crawling against my scalp. When my phone dings, I reach for it with such desperation, it's like I'm on call to stop the apocalypse.

It's Laurel. You coming over? I'm cooking . . .

I respond immediately. On my way. right. the. fuck. now.

11

LAUREL AND JORGE LIVE IN A WHITE BRICK BUNGALOW HER grandfather, a man who was epically named Tiago Mer Martin de Lourdes the Second, bequeathed to her in his will. It's near Church Lake, so called because of the wide, clean body of water that sits at the feet of St. Theresa's Catholic Church for Wanderers and Pilgrims. If you're on Laurel's wraparound porch, you can see the glitter of aquamarine-blue water between the trees in the distance. If you close your eyes on a just-right windy day, you can hear the water's lapping waves.

The house isn't big but thanks to tall ceilings, it feels full of wide open space. Abuelo Tiago built it himself in the forties and then raised seven kids there with his wife (who was not-so-epically named Patricia). I can feel the stories of that history here sometimes—standing on the porch like I am now, where little dents on the floor mark dragged-out chairs for dozens of birthday parties, and on the corner over there, a stain of wine where Laurel's mom and uncle snuck sangria when they were teens.

Laurel opens the door with a big smile. "¡Hermana!" Unlike

when Teal said it, this greeting of *sister* is warm and genuine. She wraps her arms around me, into a famous Laurel hug—long and swaying like the tall pines around us.

She takes a step back. "What the hell happened to you? Did you and Nate Bowen roll around in mulch on your first day at the job?"

A laugh chokes its way out of my mouth. "Oh my God. How do you know about my job already?"

"Oh, you know. Small town. Ran into Dale at Cheddar's last night."

I snort. "Laurel, *I* didn't even know about my job last night."

She laughs. "Really, *really* small town, then. Come in. I hope you're hungry."

The house smells like a mix of amazing food and purple Fabuloso cleaner. Everything looks the same—the old maple dining table leading to the kitchen. Same glass French press on the counter, same sage-green curtains at all the windows. Laurel's the same, too—her long, thick black hair up in an Ariana Grande–esque ponytail, a dusting of mascara and strawberry-red lipstick her only makeup. She wears a thin cotton dress, a small gold medallion of St. Theresa clasped around her neck, bare feet—Laurel's staying-at-home-for-the-day outfit. I have a seat at her insistence, smiling at the familiarity all around me.

"So what made you bring up Nate Bowen and mulch rolling?" I ask as she makes me a plate full of pollo a la plancha—chicken cooked with a thousand sweet onions. On the side are black beans, rice, and salty tostones. While Laurel's dad is Mexican American, like my family, her mother is from Cuba—and dang, that lady can *cook*, and lucky me, she taught Laur everything she knows. I dig in the second she sets the food in front of me—I hadn't realized how hungry I was, what with being all occupied with the weirdest morning of my life.

"Girl," Laurel says, getting herself a plate now. "I had to hear about Nate's—what did you call it?—*sunrise smile* for like a year of my life after he saved you from those guys at the festival that one year." She points a tostón at me. "The first thing I thought when I heard the news was Jorge and I should double-date you and Nate."

Is it hot in here? My cheeks feel too warm. I swallow a giant bite and say, "I don't think that should—or even could—happen."

"And why not?"

I shake my head. "I'm sure he's not single—"

"He is. His mom's friends with my mom, remember? I get all the good Bowen gossip." Laurel smiles with a big tostón hanging out of her mouth.

"Oh my God, stop that." I lightly smack her arm. "Well, I mean, I doubt he'd even want to—"

"Have you seen you lately?" Laurel looks at me, up and down. "When you're not covered in filth, I mean."

"Laurel." I take a breath. We need to stop this conversation as soon as possible. 'Cause once she gets an idea in her head, there's no stopping this lady. Laurel's the definition of headstrong. She wasn't valedictorian and debate team captain *and* star soccer player in high school for nothing. Which means I've got to throw her off this Nate Bowen trail big-time, and lucky for me, I have just the thing. "He wants me to work as a plant hunter for the summer." I pause. "Partnering with Tennessee Reyes."

Laurel drops her fork. "*What?*" She throws her hands up. "Dale mentioned nothing about this!"

"I guess this town isn't *that* small, then," I say dryly.

"Tell me everything," Laurel says, and I do. As much as I can without sounding like I'm sixteen with a ridiculous crush again, which means I leave out his chest hair and the winks and the fact that when he looked at me I felt like I was surrounded by one thousand calliope hummingbirds, their shimmer-green wings vibrating all along my limbs and spine.

Instead, I focus on the important parts. Like he clearly flirted with me because that's simply what he does. He acts all sweet to get you to lower your defenses, all so he can stick an arrow in your heart so deeply, you spend two years trying to get said arrow out.

"So what are you going to do?"

Both of our plates are clean. The light has slowly made its way across the blue marble counter, touching the edge of her electric kettle with a glare. I shrug. "I don't know. I mean, the money's good. Nate even said we'd make a percentage of sales for our finds for, like, ever."

"It sounds like there's a *but* coming . . ."

"*But*, I don't know. I mean, you know what went down with Tenn junior year."

Laurel nods. She knows. She is the only human who knows, who held me as I wept, who made up the guest room in her parents' house so I wouldn't have to go home snot faced and heartbroken. She helped me photocopy his senior photo so we could puncture it with darts, and later, when I declared I was done with Tennessee Reyes forevermore, she helped me burn the photo in an epic, witchy bonfire.

"It was a long time ago, but I still felt mad at him. I was actually kind of rude to him in a way that should embarrass me, but it doesn't. I'm afraid I'm not going to be able to let it go." I bury my face in my hands. "Ahh. That sounds so dumb. It was over ten *years* ago . . ."

"What he did to you junior year was fucked up, Sage. It's okay to still feel mad at him." She shrugs. "I'd be indecisive, too."

I want to change the subject again, so I look around. "Won't Jorge be home for lunch soon?"

Laurel's face darkens. "No. He's been putting in long hours regularly for the last month."

"Big project or something?" Jorge's an architect at a fancy firm downtown by the beach. All their clients are wealthy folks who want to design their second homes in a little beach town away from Philadelphia and New York City and the like. It's good money, even if all Jorge does is complain about his job when he's not there.

"That's what he says, but—" Laurel shakes her head. "Never mind. I don't want to sound crazy."

"Well, now you *have* to tell me."

Laurel stands and picks up our plates, shooing me when I try to help. After dropping them in the sink, she pulls out her phone and pulls up a social media app profile. It has the name *Cynthia Peterson* and shows a pretty woman maybe in her thirties making a kiss face at the camera with her plump, mauve lips. "That's the firm's new assistant. And Jorge's been putting in long hours since the *second* they hired her."

My stomach drops. "You think . . . ?"

"He says it's just a coincidence, that it *is* a big project, a series of big projects, even." Laurel's eyes are glassy and I kind of want to drive downtown so I can throw a brick through the window of Jorge's ugly-ass Beamer. "But just earlier this year he was still skipping lunch so he could see me faster at the end of the day. And now . . ."

I don't know what to say. Laurel knows I never thought Jorge was good enough for her, and this is why. He cheated on her— twice that we knew of—when they were dating. But then he followed her all over town, begging her to give him a chance, that he was a changed man, blah blah. Thing is, he knew Laurel's weakness: she wanted to get married. She wanted kids. He bought a platinum two-carat solitaire and that was it for her.

Sometimes I pull up Laurel's wedding photos and just stare at that look in her eyes, wide in fright even though her smile is big. Like she knows she can't trust him. It's only been four years since, but I've always thought that expression has just gotten stronger whenever he's in the room, and here's all the proof as to why.

I shift in my chair when the silence gets awkward. "Laur, you're his wife. I'm sure that it *is* true that he's working hard. You're still saving money to try for kids, maybe he's thinking about that."

She sits next to me, sniffling. "Yeah, he mentioned that, too."

"And if you ever want to follow this bitch around for a day or a week"—I gesture to her phone—"I'm your girl. If you need that peace of mind."

Laurel laughs until she snorts. "Yeah. Maybe. I'll think about it." She shakes her head. "Anyway. When are you going to start jewelry designing again?"

I bury my face in my hands. "Lord. Too many heavy topics today."

"That one stone-cutting place you used to be obsessed with is still around. I'm just saying . . ."

"Okay, okay, I hear you. Maybe I'll pull out my supplies this weekend." I wonder if she can sense the lie in my voice. I used to go to Brian's Lapidary, "that one stone-cutting place," all the freaking time, bringing my sketchbook so I could set the sapphires and rose-cut rutile quartz with pencil and ink before I could afford to do it in real life. I used to be able to look at a hunk of raw aquamarine, or polished ruby, and instantly know exactly the metal I'd use to hold it. And then create designs onto those metals, too—green gold hammered with a hundred little dents that each catch the light, or maybe wild violets carved and cast in silver. And nothing in this world was as satisfying to me as putting the final polish on a piece I'd worked weeks or even months on.

Well, almost nothing. Because once I got good enough to sell my work—and then watching those pieces become someone else's treasures? Knowing that someone loved my jewelry enough to pay me actual money for a pendant or ring or bracelet for a promise, a proposal, or even an apology?

Freaking *amazing*.

And then I had to be a dumbass with my boss.

It's not that I'm not ready to get back on the bench. It's more that there are too many dumb Gregory-related memories in the way.

We small-talk some more—Laurel's dream is to purchase this abandoned lighthouse on the northside of Cranberry and turn it into a B&B. That's what she's been saving photography money for. So far she's been working weddings and reunions and art openings for years, events she hates with her whole heart, so she can convert that old lighthouse to something whimsical and beautiful like her.

As we talk, though, I can't help but think about the words I really want to say. It's more than *I told you so*. It's more like *You deserve so much more than that man. You deserve this entire universe.*

But I'm afraid she'll get mad at me. I can't have another person who I love hate me—I've already got three. And one of them is dead.

Between my ridiculous morning at Cranberry Rose and watching Laurel cry over her dumbass husband, I'm in a bad mood when I pull into Nadia's this evening. I can't even appreciate the late-spring sky with its twinkling early stars, or the bright lightning storm rolling in over the blue-green mountains. No, I can't even park on the driveway at the place I freaking live because—once again—Johnny Miller's Small Penis Compensatory Truck takes up two spaces' worth, its wheels predictably crushing Nadia's creeping thyme.

All I want to do is shower and finish unpacking. That's it. So when I walk into the kitchen and see my sister cooking, Nadia nowhere to be found, and Johnny hanging over his laptop, shouting at it, I increase my speed toward my room, to the point where I'm jogging.

"And *there* is my hot Mexican girlfriend's sister," Johnny bellows, stopping me in my tracks. He flips his laptop around—it's on a strange sort of pedestal that resembles a torture device. "You're on YouTube Live, Sage! Say hi to my followers!"

I glimpse some of the live comments floating on the screen under my wide-eyed, mud-stained visage. *Wow, she looks dirty*, someone types. *I can't tell which sister is hotter*, another one adds.

I lift my hand to wave and glance at Johnny over the screen. "Hi. Sorry, Johnny, I've had kind of a bad day and—"

"Sage, I'm so glad you're here. You can settle a debate with me and my fans, huh?"

I open my mouth but nothing comes out.

"Some of these guys"—he lets out a chuckle as he thumbs at the screen—"they think I do too much for my girl." He twists the laptop toward Teal. The lightning storm I mentioned? Well. It's pretty much right over our house now. "Smile, babe."

"I'm cooking," Teal says with a laugh as fake as Johnny's goodwill.

"Okay, yeah, my girl's hard at work. But some people have been telling me, you know, they say, *Johnny, what's this about you picking your girl up from work? Why can't she drive herself home? What's this about you packing her up a lunch? She can do it herself.*" I swallow a snort because I can guarantee *no one* actually cares about any of that—he's definitely made up every single word.

Johnny shrugs. "And the thing is, I insist. It's what I want to do. Sometimes, feminism is about what you can do for women, as a *man*."

Oh, sweet baby Jesus. "Listen, Johnny, I really, *really* have to—"

Johnny cuts me off with a laugh. "Anyway, Sage, am I right? Sometimes this is what the right thing looks like, you know? It's not all about getting your food made for *you*—"

And this is when the rage threatening to boil over for basically my entire life . . . it just spills. *Everything*—from Nadia blaming me for anything she feels like, to the last time I saw Teal and she cut my lip open, to my mother leaving when I was seven years old, to Jorge cheating, because yeah, I'd bet money he was fucking Cynthia

Peterson, to Johnny Miller, standing in front of me with that big ugly smile on his face, clearly wanting me to join the act and pretend like he invented feminism.

I should just leave. At the very least, I should keep my mouth shut. But instead I narrow my eyes and let it all out.

"Yeah?" I say. "When's the last time you cooked for Teal?"

Johnny freezes. "Uh—"

"When's the last time you at least *helped* her cook a meal?"

"Well—"

"No, no, when's the last time you did *anything* but explain feminism to her while *she cooked your dinner*?"

Johnny blinks. "Well, see, feminism—"

"Right, I remember!" I smack my head like I'm the dumbest person in the room. Which is never the case if Johnny's here. "You're a *feminist*. That's why you think it's okay to hit a girl, right, Johnny? I mean, maybe you can answer that, huh? When's the last time you shoved my sister around so hard she had bruises on her arms?"

"Jesus Christ, Sage," Teal whispers, frozen over the stove, gray smoke all around her. I think the fish is burning.

Johnny sputters, "That—that's a *lie*—"

"Is it a lie? Like you swear to God in heaven, and Jesus and Mary, too, that you've never left a bruise on my sister? Because shit, Johnny, I remember them. I remember the one the shape of your *whole fucking hand*."

"And you know what," Johnny says as he swirls the laptop around. "We're gonna go on a break because, of, technical—" And then he slams the screen down and turns to Teal. She's got a steaming spatula in her hand and while I know she's pissed as fuck at me, for some reason she looks *scared* of him. I hate that. I hate that my tough, angry little sister is scared of anyone. *Don't be afraid*, I want to tell her. *I will beat his ass before he touches you again.*

Johnny's hands are curled into fists. "I can't believe you told her—that you *lied*, I mean—"

Oh, no he did *not* . . . "She didn't tell me, Johnny!" I yell. "I saw the bruises and I guessed! Because you know what, a guy doesn't spend his every waking hour trying to convince everyone he's the greatest human to walk the earth unless he's actually a really bad fucking person."

He won't look at me. "Can you tell your sister to shut up now?"

"Tell me yourself, asshole. Look at me and tell me yourself and see what happens."

His phone dings and he picks it up—yes, in the middle of this fight, the asshole—and yelps. "I've lost five hundred followers in the last minute because of you fucking bitches."

I gesture to him. "Ladies and gentlemen and our nonbinary friends, I give you *feminism*."

"Oh, shut the fuck up, Sage." This is Teal now, but I don't care. She's been telling me that for eight years. I don't even blink.

"You know what," Johnny says, turning to me, and I get this foreboding, you know? The moment before a bad lightning strike, when the air grows heavy in seconds, and everything gets way too quiet. The moment before someone goes for the lowest blow. And I'm not disappointed. "You're telling me *I'm* the bad person? Teal is always saying *you* could've stopped Sky from dying. And you know what?" He turns to Teal. "You were with her when she fell. You were there. How the fuck do we know that *you* didn't—"

I shove the table, startling him enough that he stops. "Johnny, I swear to the old gods, if you finish that sentence, you'll regret it."

His cheeks are red. His breath heavy. "Just like your sister regretted it, right?"

Finally, *finally* Teal directs the anger where it ought to go. She's blinking back tears as she shoves the smoking pan off the burner. "Get the fuck out, Johnny. And don't come back."

He stuffs his bag with his electronic equipment as he starts making threats. "You're going to regret this, Teal. You know what I have"—he lifts his phone and wiggles it with a sneer—"and exactly what I'll do with it."

I swear, it's like the breath has been knocked out of me. Because I know what he has, too. Teal told me three years before, through sobs on the staircase, about ten minutes before she punched my face.

"I don't even care," Teal says, though she's a shade paler than before. "Just *go*."

I'm right on his heels as he's out the door. "Get the fuck away," he yells.

We march through the little porch to the stone path that leads to the driveway. "I'm not done with you yet," I say.

"I said, get the fuck away from me!"

I sigh, because I didn't really want it to come to this. I glance around fast. No one is out. And even if they were, it's dark enough that they could convince themselves that they didn't see what they're about to see.

A vine from a moonflower reaches out and swirls around his ankle. As he trips, another one comes—this time it's a thick, old Virginia creeper—and the gnarly brown stem slithers around his chest, dragging him until his back slams against Nadia's dogwood. Petals fall between the both of us, pale and pink like pretty rain. The vines wrap around harder, holding him in place.

The dogwood curls one of its branches until it leans against his neck. It tightens until he makes a strangled sound. I make sure he's still breathing, and then I say in a low, deep voice, "After you beat up Teal, she told me she was afraid to leave you because you like to remind her about some private pictures you have of her."

His eyes are wide as he chokes on an inhale.

"That's what you have on her, right? That's what your little threat with your phone was about."

"What the fuck is happening—" The dogwood wraps its little twig branches around his mouth like a sharp claw before he can finish.

"What's happening is this, Johnny. You're going to get in your tiny-penis truck. And you're going to leave me alone, you're going to leave Nadia alone, and most of all, you're going to leave Teal alone. And if I find out any private photos of Teal made their way public—and I don't care if it's just *email*, Johnny, I *will* find out—you will find yourself *smothered* by plants." The claw of dogwood lightly strokes at his chin. "You see what I can do? I want you to imagine how much worse it would be." The tree limb around his neck tightens and he squeals. "*Do you understand?*"

"Yes," he squeaks out.

When the plants release, he clutches his neck and between coughs he calls me a fucking witch.

"Exactly," I say. "And don't you forget it."

Only then do I go back inside, not sparing Johnny Miller another glance.

13

EVERY FLORES WOMAN, FOR AS LONG AS ANYONE CAN RE-member, has been born with a gift. I mentioned before that Nadia knows things. My other great-aunt, Anya, who lives in Memphis, can talk to water. My mother can hide—if she doesn't want to be seen, you won't see her, not even if she's sitting right in front of you.

Mama named Teal and Sky all wrong. Teal's the one who messes with the sky. But it's not like Mom could know what our gifts were—they don't come alive until puberty, and even then they can stay dormant for a long while until there is a need. Until I was four-teen, apple picking, trying to reach the most perfect blush-pink fruit I'd ever seen in my life—and then the tree lowered its branch for me. It placed the apple right in my hand, and when I twisted it off, the tree pulled back, slow, like a dancer in that crisp fall light.

Teal's was easy to figure out, moody child that she was. When she was angry, lightning and rain loomed. When she was happy, the sun was brighter and more vivid over Nadia's house on the cliff overlooking the sea than anywhere else in the world. After Sky died, it rained here for twelve weeks straight. Teal nearly drowned Nadia's entire garden.

Sky gave us all heart attacks when she discovered her gift. Nadia looked out the window and screamed, and then *I* looked out the window and screamed, and then *Teal* looked out the window and screamed—because there Sky was, laughing against the wind as she scratched the belly of a *full-grown black bear*. Sky wasn't even scared. As tough as Teal seems, I'd guess she's about as scared as me, which is to say, we are terrified of nearly everything in the universe. But not Sky. Once Sky figured out her gift, it wasn't odd to see a bear or wolf or fox hanging out in the yard with her (Nadia had a strict no-animals-in-the-house policy after a wild hog incident).

Nadia says these gifts are a punishment. Someone in our lineage offended an old god—the worst sort to do that to—and, boom. Weirdly magical daughters, forevermore. I guess in a lot of ways, it does feel like a punishment. Nadia and Amá Sonya have basically sworn us to secrecy ever since we learned about what the Flores women can do. "Bad things happen when white people discover the gifts of brown women," they like to remind us. And those two can't agree about anything, so on this, you know they're serious.

There is only one person in the world who knows our gifts, and Nadia only okayed it because Laurel's own mother practices brujería. "Laurel and no one else," she said.

Thus, we can't really tell people about our gifts, so we only have each other. And if we lose each other the way I've lost Sky and Teal? Well, it's easy to feel like I've got no real family in the world besides Laur—no one who can stand the sight of me, anyway.

This is how Teal greets me when I make it back inside after almost killing Johnny Miller with a dogwood tree. "What have you *done*, Sage?" She can't even look at me.

"Don't worry about . . . what you were worried about before."

What she told me when I found her crying on the stairs, bruises inked on her arms.

Then Teal looks at me. Her eyes are so pointed and dark, it's like she stabs me with her gaze. "Don't you get it? Even if Johnny never posts . . ." She can't say it. Revenge porn. Ugh, I want to threaten him all over again. ". . . you've just *outed* me as a victim of domestic abuse. To *everyone*. I've gotten forty texts in the last ten minutes alone. Half of them are asking if I'm okay and do I need to call the police, and the other half are asking why did my sister lie like that?"

My stomach drops and I swallow. "Holy shit. I'm so sorry, Teal. I wasn't thinking about—"

"No, you weren't thinking at all. You weren't thinking about anything but ruining everything around you. That's what you do. That's *all* you do."

My heart drops. *This* is why I don't ever say what I'm thinking. Teal's right. I just ruin things.

Before I can try to apologize again, Teal runs up the stairs, leaving me alone in the kitchen, the smell of burnt fish all around. In the windows, the lightning crackles through the sky in sharp ribbons of light. Right now it feels like I am that sky, the white-hot electricity singeing me.

I DECIDE TO TRY TO GET MY MIND OFF THINGS BY FINISHING unpacking. But it's kind of like attempting to ignore a tornado as it whisks you up and into the sky toward the outer edges of the Milky Way. With every move I make, all I see is Teal. Everything I touch, all I feel are lightning burns.

I pull out book after book, setting them in great, tall stacks in front of the balcony doors. I turn boxes of my clothing on the bed into a pile resembling any one of the little blue mountains in and surrounding Cranberry. All that unpacking goes to hell, though, when on my way back to the boxes, I trip on a book stack and it knocks over a small shoebox, scattering dozens and dozens of photos across the creaky wood floor.

I sigh and sit, gathering them up, but of course since they're photos, I have to look at them, and next thing you know, I'm biting my lips to the point of tasting blood so tears don't make their way to my eyes.

We didn't get a proper digital camera until I was out of high school, so almost all the pictures we have of Sky are physical, like these. I sift through the images and pull one up of us in the kitchen, each holding up a platter containing a whole flan. I was sixteen, Teal was fourteen, and Sky was eleven. Our smiles are huge— we'd spent the whole day baking with Nadia, and those were the *best* days back then.

People always said we Flores sisters looked like triplets, but I never agreed. Each of us had a different father, and to me this skewed our looks in really different directions. I mean, sure, we all had gold-brown skin. But I'm the shortest at five-four, Teal is now five-six, and before she passed, Sky was already five-nine at sixteen. My hair's brown like leather, curly and thick, Teal's got black waves, and Sky's hair couldn't hold a hot curl and it turned deep honey every single summer. Teal's got narrow hazel eyes and a turned-up nose. I have a wide nose, defined cheekbones and big, brown owl eyes. Sky's face was long, covered in light freckles, and her eyes were black and crinkly, like she was always holding back a smile.

I never thought we looked alike until Sky died. And then every time I looked into Teal's face, I saw her. Every time I glanced in the mirror, Sky was looking back at me. I couldn't escape that hurt, and eventually it all pushed me away, in my shitty red van, where I'd rather live than see my baby sister's face in Teal's, telling me she was dead because of me.

I do not have the gift of ghosts.

I do not have the gift of ghosts, so when I look up with tears falling over my cheeks and see Sky there, sitting right in front of me, her legs curled over the hardwood attic floor, pictures of the past dropped between us like autumn leaves, I want to tear open the floorboards. I want to rip apart this house, I want to destroy every connection I have to whatever it is that has punished me with this particular trait: tears that pay for the sight of my dead sister.

Her ghost gets stronger the more I cry. Her edges are defined. She reaches for me, but of course her hand goes through my knee.

I just take her in, her blackberry eyes, her hair reaching her waist, her skinny legs curled up in front of mine. I look at this ghost and think, *Jesus, she doesn't look sixteen anymore.*

She opens her mouth to speak, and that's when I wince. This is it. This is when Sky herself says what Teal's loved to remind me of for years: that everything's my fault.

"Sage," she says. "I've figured it out."

I blink in surprise, and for a couple of beats, I can't talk. My voice comes out hoarse when I finally do. "Figured what out?"

The lightning outside has been traded for water. It hits the windows in hard, sharp slaps. Sky bites her lip as she gazes at it, the gray cold rain, and then her black eyes meet mine.

"I know what you need to do for me now."

14

RainOnATennRoof: Howdy, partner. Long time no talk

silvergurl0917: howdy???? you're named tennessee, not texas.

RainOnATennRoof: ;)

silvergurl0917: how'd you get that name anyhow

RainOnATennRoof: It's kind of a gross story.

silvergurl0917: yeah? how so?

RainOnATennRoof: My parents . . . conceived me . . . in Nashville. ***shudders***

RainOnATennRoof: What about your name?

silvergurl0917: don't think i don't see what you're doing here

RainOnATennRoof: And what's that??

silvergurl0917: your trying to figure out who i am

RainOnATennRoof: No offense or anything, but I seem to remember you promising me a hint as to who you are if I did my homework. Which I did, two whole weeks ago.

silvergurl0917: okay. . . . . . . good point.

silvergurl0917: i'll give you two hints. . . . okay? one is on theme with tonight's conversation. my mother named me something that is kind of witchy and natural.

RainOnATennRoof: Wow. Okay. That could be a lot of things.

RainOnATennRoof: :) what's the other hint?

silvergurl0917: i'm a sophomore.

RainOnATennRoof: You know what this means, right.

silvergurl0917: what??

RainOnATennRoof: I'm going to spend the rest of this fine evening with my yearbook, trying to find you in last year's freshmen.

silvergurl0917: there's a lot of us. good luck:)

PRESENT

While yesterday's rain didn't last, it's brought in its place thick clouds that have blessed Cranberry with cooler weather. Even with the crispness in the air, the last average frost date was nearly a month ago. It's perfect for me to sow seeds in the herb spiral.

I've dragged out a small folding table from the barn. On it are paint markers, little wooden stakes, and two boxes of seed packets. There are two chairs, one on either side of the table. One for me, and one for—

"This is boring," Sky says, looking around with a grimace. I guess I'd cried enough last night for her to stick around for another day. When I'd asked why she could only be seen by me when I wept, she said she didn't know, either. I guess I'll just have to file it under one of the mysteries of life as a Flores woman.

I put my hands on my hips and stare at her for a few moments. Last night and this morning, I'd braced myself for her to say something, anything about her death being my fault. But all she's done is annoy the hell out of me, whether it's been a critique of my outfit (*Uh, your boobs are, like, popping out of that thing. Aren't you going to a farm? Shouldn't you be wearing, like, overalls?*) to insisting I put on the Backstreet Boys on the way here (*I don't care what you say, "Everybody (Backstreet's Back)" is a classic and I will literally sing it as loud as I can until you find that CD*) . . . it's like no time has passed at all. It's like she's still alive, even. It's easy enough to pretend she is, as she whines once more, "This is so *boring*, Sage."

"So go," I say, waving my arm. "Go fly or something."

She narrows her eyes at me. "If I could fly, you think I'd be here watching you do everything the hard way?"

"What's that supposed to mean?"

"It means, use your gift, Sage. Make those seeds sprout and grow in seconds. This is taking way too long."

"Even if I did that, they'd still have to be placed in the dirt, genius. Besides, I'm almost done." And I am. I've planted calendula, salvia, parsley, annual bee balm, chives, dill, borage, and, my specialty, basil. Ten different types, even. I grab the last of the seeds—cardinal basil—for the very top of the spiral. It's been bred to make wide, red-violet flower heads, and it will become a beautiful bouquet up there, with bees and butterflies feasting on it.

"Hey! Looking good!" When I turn, I can't stop the smile on my face when Nate approaches, which is saying a lot, considering how the last couple of days have gone.

"Thanks. I've just finished up."

"Great. Gramps is gonna be thrilled to see this all pretty again." Nate leans against the stone of the spiral, surveying my work. He's wearing a plain green T-shirt, which makes his hair look positively red. Also his muscles under said shirt—a very nice distraction from the ghost scowling just behind him. "So, Sage, did you think about the position yet?"

I bite my lips and then release them. Right. He wants me to work alongside Tennessee Reyes, a man I was certain I'd marry before he did the emotional equivalent of cutting open my chest and tasing my heart. I certainly haven't had any time to think about that, what with *ruining everything* and all. "Um. Not exactly.

I know I have till the end of the week, but—" I scrunch up my face. "What day of the week is it, again?"

Nate laughs. "It's Friday." When he sees me panic, he holds up a hand. "Tell you what. Why don't you meet us at the Lounge tomorrow night. Everyone should be there—it's kind of our thing, if you'll remember."

I nod. I was too young back then to join them at the town's only cool bar after the workweek, but now . . . now I could. "Oh, sure. I remember."

"Yeah? Why don't you let me know your decision then?"

I let out a breath. "Yes. I'll do that."

Nate smiles even wider, making my breath feel funny and shallow. "It'll be good to see you there. I'll buy you a drink." He nods before making his way back to the farmhouse.

When I turn back, Sky is rolling her eyes. "He's . . . ugh. You *like* him?"

I close my eyes briefly. When I say I've been scared to cry for eight years because I'd see the ghost of my sister? It was because I thought she'd be upset. I thought she'd blame me. I even thought it might be like a horror film, where she'd appear more and more decomposed until a dry, smiling skeleton was following me with every tear. I didn't think about *this*—Sky, acting like a sullen, annoyed teenager, bothering the hell out of her big sister for no good reason.

This might be worse than what I'd feared, to be honest.

"You should invite Teal."

"What?" I mutter, packing up the seeds.

"What?" a gruff voice echoes behind me.

I shriek, dropping several packets. Tiny black basil seeds bounce all over the folding table. "Shit." I curl my hand to push them away from the edge and lift my head to glare at . . . Tenn

Reyes, a smug look on his face. I had no idea he could sneak around soundlessly, like a freaking Avenger or something.

He holds his hands up. "Didn't mean to scare you. I just came over to see if you needed help."

I want to tell him to scram, but I bite my tongue. He doesn't know, I remind myself. Which means what he *does* know is I'm mean to him for no reason at all. I take a breath. "No. I'm done now. Thanks, though."

"Here." He walks up, bending toward the packets that made it to the ground. "Let me."

"No. Seriously, I've—"

"Sage." His voice deepens as his gaze drops to my shirt, then back to my eyes. "Let me." He bends further, gathering up the crisp white packs. The way he's always checking me out is getting ridiculous.

"Are you always this bossy?" I ask with my hands on my hips, and get even more irritated when all he does is chuckle in return. I stand back and watch as he rises, using his hand to sweep the basil seeds into the packet.

"Well, he's *way* hotter than the other one," Sky helpfully observes from her chair. "My vote's for him."

I grit my teeth in response.

"What? It's the truth." She leans forward a little. "He smells good, too. Like tea leaves."

I forget the situation for a moment and begin asking, "Wait, you can smell? When—" Tenn startles a little, lifting his head, his brows raised. "Basil," I yelp. "Sometimes basil seeds smell like basil leaves." I have no idea if that's true and pray he doesn't know any better.

"Yeah?" He smiles and lifts a palmful of seeds to his nose.

"Oh, you don't have to—"

"I don't smell it." He shrugs. "Then again, I'm not a plant whisperer." He winks and tilts his palm toward the open seed packet.

"Oh my *God*," Sky moans. "This is the worst flirting I've ever *seen*."

I bite my lips to keep from sassing her right back, and then Tenn hands me the packets. *Be* nice, I remind myself. "Thanks," I say, popping them into the big plastic container.

He looks like he wants to say something, or ask something— it's like words are etched right on his mouth—but then he shakes his head. "Guess I'll see you."

He nods once, but before he turns, I shout, "Wait!"

I walk up, ignoring Sky as she mutters, "Oh, here we go," and I point toward his chin. "You have a couple basil seeds in your whiskers there."

"My whiskers, huh?" He laughs and runs a hand over his jaw. "Did I get it?"

I shake my head, taking another step closer. "I can . . ." I lift my hand. This is being nice, right?

He folds his hands behind him and bends down at the waist so I can reach better. I regret offering the second my fingers make contact with his chin. He's so warm. The scruff over his face is rough in a way that makes me want to shiver. I gently flick the seeds off and his eyes flutter, the thick lashes reminding me of the leaves of hummingbird vines.

"Got it?" His voice is raspy, and he stares at my lips.

"Stop that," I say, taking a step back.

"Stop what?" He laughs, raising himself to full height, putting his hands in his pockets.

"You know exactly what."

"I most certainly do not."

I wave a hand. "Flirting."

He takes a step closer to me, his eyes dipping to my mouth faster than a butterfly flutter. "You think that was flirting?"

"You're a flirt. It's what you do." With that, a memory surfaces in me. Me, sixteen, him, seventeen. My heart, one hundred thousand pieces, scattered between us and steaming like the second after asteroids made of porcelain slam into the earth.

That's just one of a million reasons why I can't let Tenn's mindless flirtations affect me.

"Flirting's not *all* I do," he responds with a wry smile.

Oh, *God*. He's *flirting about flirting*. "You can go away now." The seeds are gone. I turn back toward Sky and the seed table.

"Finally." She rolls her eyes as I walk up. "As I was *saying*, you should invite Teal."

"Invite her where?" I whisper, in case Tenn's still within hearing distance. My hands tremble as I slide the lid over the seed container.

"Invite Teal to the Lounge."

I take a breath. "I don't think Teal's gonna speak to me ever again, but sure."

"Remember what I asked you?"

"Of course I remember," I snap, but when I look up, she's gone. I guess the ghost-tear-power dried up.

My heart hurts. I don't like losing her like that. I didn't like having her, either, not quite alive and not quite gone, but this is much less preferable. I sigh. It won't be long before I cry again, with the way things are going. But Sky had explained that she *is* still around when I can't see her—just "fuzzier." So before I start for the farmhouse, I say, "Fine. I'll try. Okay, Sky? I'll try."

I turn back in the direction where Tenn was, but there's no sign of him. And I exhale a sigh of relief.

Being mean to Tenn is way, *way* less dangerous than being nice. Lesson learned. Lesson freaking learned.

That exact moment, my phone buzzes. Maneuvering the seed boxes onto one arm, I reach for my pocket. Don't forget, Nadia's texted. Dinner at Sonya's tonight.

Shit, man. I don't even remember Nadia telling me about this the first time. *Can't a girl get a break?* I want to scream at the sky.

I already know the answer is a firm no, so I don't even bother with it.

"WHERE'S TEAL?" I ASK NADIA AS SHE AND I CLIMB INTO HER Honda CR-V.

"She had a bad day at work." Nadia gives me a knowing look that says something like *Somehow I know that's all your fault.*

I look out the window quickly. This time, it's true. I only have myself to blame. I can only imagine how Teal's day might've gone after I revealed, live, that her hopefully-still-ex beat her. Stupid. Stupid, stupid Sage.

Though I find it odd that Nadia doesn't seem to know the details. Oh, well. She'll know soon enough. And then I really won't hear the end of it—not that I don't deserve that.

Amá Sonya lives in a gated community just inland of downtown, the type of neighborhood Jorge's always designing homes for. I don't know how the work could be as bad and hard as he says, because each residence looks like it was popped right out of a cookie cutter labeled *Devoid of Any Personality Whatsoever.*

Whereas Nadia's home is full of stories—from the chipped green-glass Tiffany lamp bolted on the living room ceiling, to the stairwell walls full of books, to the curtains, handsewn from a daisy print—Sonya's house looks like someone grabbed a giant, cosmic vacuum and not only sucked out all the stories but also all the color, all the laughter, and anything that might even resemble imagination.

I'm *so* not looking forward to dinner.

But as I'm looking out the window, something hits me. Something I haven't thought about in a long, long time.

My gift isn't ghosts . . . but *Sonya's* is. That's exactly her gift, isn't it? I close my eyes and try to remember what Nadia told us about it all those years ago. But that just gets me thinking about times when Sky was alive and that hurts too much right now.

Sonya is our maternal grandmother. The first thing anyone should know about her is that she is a *bitch*. When my mother got pregnant with me, Sonya tossed all her belongings on her giant, white porch, probably stacked symmetrically between the colonial pillars, and kicked her only daughter to the streets. That's why Nadia's house is the only house of our childhood. There's a reason that when my mom left, she made sure that Sonya wouldn't have a single hand in raising us.

Sonya also likes to pretend we don't have gifts at all. After her first husband, Mom's dad, passed away, she married a wealthy crop farmer (the kind of dude who takes pictures of himself on farm machinery and then hops off so his underpaid farmhands can do the toil of actual labor) and so now she basically lives her life as a privileged Southern belle. And Southern belles do not have *gifts*. That's why I keep second-guessing myself. It's been so long since I've heard anyone acknowledge Sonya's magic. *Was* her gift talking to ghosts? I guess I could ask her, and risk a big, dramatic, pearl-clutched *Bless your heart* (Southern belle for *Fuck you*).

Sonya bursts the door open before we can even knock. There is no greeting, unless you count her glaring at Nadia with a peck on the cheek as one, and then her turning toward me and saying,

"You don't look the least bit thinner, Sage. And what did Nadia tell me? You got yourself fired from your adjunct position?"

"It was because of budget cuts."

"Turn around. Let me see you better. Hmm. Four years at that college and you couldn't prove yourself against budget cuts, eh? Well. I guess that means you're here now, though." She definitely doesn't make that sound like a good thing for her. She stops me from twirling around like a marionette and looks slightly to my left, just above my shoulder. Her eyes narrow. "Is that . . . ?" I glance over my shoulder and turn back, brows knitted. She shakes her head. "Never mind. Come inside, the two of you."

Sonya's wearing a long-sleeved, crewneck white dress that flares just below her knees. The material's pretty, with the slightest bit of shimmer, but the fit is too loose. Nude three-inch stilettos adorn her feet, and everything else on her is jewelry: one-carat diamonds on each ear, a tennis bracelet, and her wedding set, which makes Laurel's look teeny by comparison, with a three-carat center diamond flanked by one and a half carats on either side. She's got the same complexion as us, but she dyes her hair what she calls a "strawberry blond" but to me is more like cherry ice cream. Her lips are painted shimmery, pale peach. And she's *always* scowling— like she just smelled a combination of dung and burnt fish.

The inside of her place contains only beiges and whites layered on top of one another, from the sofa to the throw pillows to the cabinets to the floors. It's cold in here, and the (white, of course) marble floors make our footfalls sound ominous. All around us are messages painted in neutrals onto canvases in stiff, feminine font. *Live Laugh Love. Bless This Mess. In This House We Believe That Freedom Isn't Free.*

Her husband, Kason, isn't here, so dinner has slightly more flavor than usual. There's garlic roast chicken alongside soft, buttery yeast rolls, asparagus, and roasted potatoes. You'd think, looking at this place, that she'd only serve lobsters and foie gras, but Kason likes things traditional, I guess. I keep glancing up at the all-capital-letters printed on the canvas hung over the dining table, yelling at us to *EAT*.

Dinner conversation is fascinating, because both Sonya and Nadia just insult the *fuck* out of each other with stuff that on the surface sounds like compliments. I wonder if they've always been those kinds of sisters, if they just popped out of the womb already well versed in passive aggression.

"Nadia, that dress is positively adorable. You must tell me which Goodwill you set foot in to . . . dig . . . for it." Sonya puts the smallest piece of potato in her mouth as she blinks rapidly. I know that's gotta annoy Nadia because I'm pretty sure she got that dress at a yard sale. It's really cute, though—bright orange like the cosmos that bloom at the end of summer in her flower garden.

"Thank you, Sonya. Your outfit, as always, is so immaculate. *Clinical*. It matches your beautiful home *and* your personality." Nadia picks up a chicken leg and takes a bite right out of it, causing Sonya to swallow a gasp.

After we're done eating, Sonya makes a big production over her fancy, expensive coffee, to have with pastries, and she somehow manages to insult both me and Nadia in a single sentence. "Ladies, you'll have to let me know if you'd rather I leave the sweets on the counter . . . so you won't be *as* tempted to overindulge." I inherited the same figure as Nadia—thick and curvy. Sonya thus, as far as I can remember, acts like her skinny frame makes her a better person.

"Leave it up there, Amá," I say. "As you said, less temptation." But when I walk up, I place three giant chocolate croissants on my plate, stacked so high they wobble. It makes Nadia grin and Sonya square her jaw, tapping her foot against the floor like an old movie-style bomb ticker.

After I demolish dessert, I excuse myself to the bathroom. I just can't take much more of this. Inside, I stare at myself in the mirror. I look angry. I think about all the things I wish I could tell both Sonya and Nadia. Instead, I settle for a pep talk. "Your life is a mess," I tell myself. "This is true. But it can't get worse, right? Not much worse, anyway." I exit quickly after that. But just as quickly, a bony, cold hand snaps over my forearm and pulls me down the hall, opposite of where the dining room is.

"What the—" I say, stopping when I see it's just Sonya who's got me, and she's pulled me into what looks like her bedroom. Everything is still white and beige, but I guess she decided to live life on the wild side in here because one of the throw pillows on her bed is pale *pink*.

"You brought a ghost into this house?" Sonya says, pointing one blunt, French-tipped acrylic nail at my heart. "In *my* house?"

"I—"

"I can *feel* it! It's floating all around, like noisy tissue paper!" Sonya's voice has gotten a lot more hissy than usual.

I frown. "Nadia said that *you* said you didn't have a gift."

"I don't." We stare at each other for a moment before she folds her arms against her chest. I guess I'm going to have to go with this old Southern tradition of saying one thing and meaning something else. Sonya scowls. "Well? Who is it?"

I shrug.

"Sage Esmerade Flores . . ."

"Fine! It's Sky, all right? You happy now?"

Sonya wrinkles her nose. "What's she still doing here? Did she say?"

I think about what Sky told me last night. *I know how you can help me now.* "She said . . . she said she thinks she needs me to do something, so she can . . . you know. Move on. To heaven."

"Do what?"

I look down. "She wants me to repair my relationship with Teal."

Sonya gives the most ladylike snort I've ever heard in my life. "Fat chance."

"Thanks for the vote of confidence."

Sonya closes her eyes, angling her head, like she's listening. I wonder if her connecting with ghosts feels like me with plants. If it feels like ghosts, for a few moments, become a part of her. I shudder and Sonya scowls before asking, "She didn't say anything else?"

I shrug. "I asked her if she knew where . . . you know. Where her body ended up. She said all she can sense there is . . . like, a light high—"

"Sense? What does she mean, *sense*?"

"I don't know, Amá Sonya. She said it's like a dream or something."

Sonya gives me a look of disgust. "Ghosts don't dream."

"Well, *like* a dream, she said."

"No. That doesn't sound right. This is one of the three laws of ghosthood. Ghosts do not dream. Ghosts cannot affect the physical world. And ghosts do not age."

I swallow. "Oh. Okay." Then I shake my head. They can't affect the physical world? "Wait a minute. You're saying ghosts can't give you a gift? Nadia always says to never reject a gift from a ghost, though—"

"A gift like a favor from one of the old ones. Not a gift like a diamond." Sonya laughs. "Or a cup of coffee." She slaps her knee and cackles.

A very specific cup of coffee comes to mind. One in my favorite mug, cupped in a lavender storm, smelling like sweet raspberries.

There have been dozens of cups of coffee like that. Gifts. Ones that I could hold, feel, drink, for goodness' sake.

"What happens if a ghost could do something like that?" I say. "Break a rule?"

Sonya stops laughing so abruptly, it's creepy. "Then they're not a ghost. End of story."

She means end of conversation, too, because she turns to the door and pulls it open. Before we walk out, though, I touch her arm. "You—you've never felt Mama? She's not a ghost, is she?"

It's been twenty-two years since any of us has heard from her. I don't wonder about her as much as I did when I was little, but when I do, often the worst comes to mind.

Sonya's eyes soften for half a second. Then they look me over, cold once more. "Never. I have never sensed her."

I breathe a sigh of relief and follow her out the door.

15

I SPEND THE NEXT DAY HELPING HENRY AND DeANGELO FER-
tilize the tender vegetable seedlings—tomatoes, peppers, greens,
and onions—and unpack as much as I can when I get home. My
books fill the old china cabinet Nadia had rescued from the Salva-
tion Army, giving it a gorgeous rustic look with mauve chalk paint.
I hang my clothes in the little hobbit closet. My basils line the shelf
in front of the short windows: holy, lime, lemon, chocolate, blue
spice, to name about half. There's only one box left, one of the large
ones, labeled *SCHOOL/WORK*. Even though I'd packed it as fast
as I could, I know all it contains: a set of pliers, a box of unset gemstones. Scraps of brass and silver sheet metal, a five-inch saw with
several packs of blades. A jar of paste flux, brushes, a butane soldering torch. Tweezers and tongs and blue jeweler's wax and shiny
carving instruments.

I barely open it when memories, when stories, waft over me—
my students, whom I loved; the work, which I adored to the point
of getting to the studio early and often leaving late. The look on
their faces when they successfully soldered for the first time. How

when I announced I was leaving for good, they brought cupcakes for my last class, right on theme: each one had a fondant gemstone ring pressed into the white buttercream. How hard I wanted to cry after they left.

I sigh, check my watch, and push the box to the wall. It can wait another day.

After I shower, my phone buzzes.

Laurel: Sorry, J and I can't make it tonight.

I'd invited her to the Lounge so I wouldn't stand there looking like the world's biggest loser among all the chummy Cranberry Rose folks. Jorge wasn't invited but I guess when you're married it's hard to see attending these things as anything but part of a unit. I guess I'd rather be alone than watch her and Jorge pretend like everything's hunky-dory, though.

Awww, that's too bad, I lie.

Laurel: Can you do something for me, though?

Me: Anything.

Laurel: Ask Nate out tonight. Double date, remember?

Me: Did I just write 'anything'? Bc what I meant was, anything but ask out my boss. Who hired me only 2!! days ago

Laurel: Come on

Me: No <3

Laurel: Just think about it, okay? Promise you'll THINK about it.

I sigh. Fine. JUST thinking, though.

I know what Laurel's up to. For the last decade or so, she's always telling me how sad I seem. She thinks if I find love, it's going to magically fix things. I don't have the heart to tell her that there's no way a man's love is big enough for that, not even sunrise smile Nate Bowen's.

I stand in front of the mirror in the bathroom. I'd put on a green dress—cinched at the waist with a deep sweetheart neckline. Moonstones gleam from my ears and labradorites shimmer on my fingers, everything bezel-set in silver. I'd braided my hair over one shoulder and put on mascara and lipstick—a deep red that's almost purple. After a spray of Pacifica's Dream Moon—a blend of patchouli, sandalwood, and, yes, pink rose—I'm almost done.

Now comes the hard part.

I trudge downstairs, my feet dragging along the wood. I stop at the second floor, right in front of Teal's room. I brace myself, lift my arm, and knock. After about ten seconds of no response, I knock again.

The door whips open and there's Teal. She wears yoga pants and a slim-fitting activewear hoodie in a mix of pink and turquoise. Her hair's thrown up and she's glaring at me. "What do you want?"

"I was wondering if you'd like to come to the Lounge tonight."

"No." She shuts the door.

Normally, this would be the point when I'd give up. But I told Sky that I'd try. So, here I am. Trying.

I knock on the door again. "Please?" I shout through it.

"No!"

"You're not working, are you?"

"What does it matter? I don't want to come!"

I sigh and rest my forehead against the door. "It's for Cranberry Rose. Nate Bowen's offered me a job and I have to tell him my final decision tonight. I don't want to go alone."

She's quiet for a beat. "Who's Nate Bowen?"

I lift my head up. She's not yelling now, so this is progress, right? "Dale's grandson. He runs the place now."

There's silence. I swallow. "I'll be the designated driver. And . . ." I wince, thinking of my bank account. "I'll buy you three—no, two drinks."

The door flies open. "Fine. I'll be ready in twenty minutes." She shuts the door again, then shouts through it, "But we're taking my car, not that grandma-ass shit you drive!"

"Fine!" I say grumpily, but I can't help but smile. What if this isn't going to be hard at all? What if I can get my sister back while helping my other sister move on and it's easy as pie?

I guess I forgot that pie's really tricky to make. All that butter that you've got to keep cold while you're folding the dough . . . ugh. My pie crust always ended up a weird mess.

And that's a good word to describe our car ride. Mess. It's all me saying things like "How's work?" and "Did you see you got some mail today?" and Teal not responding at all. I glance at her again—her hair is down with wild waves and she's got on shiny pink lip gloss and a one-strapped, skintight black dress that makes me feel like I look like a nun. I try once more: "I like your outfit." Nothing. Eventually I take a deep breath and look out the window, at the trees that get thicker and then more spread out, at the little ponds here and there full of Czech glass algae and amethyst lilies and smoky quartz water birds.

We Flores women weren't always surrounded by the maple tree woods and salt-worn cliffs of coastal Virginia. Nadia says our family, dozens of generations ago, lived in Texas. I guess things were happy and peaceful as could be, with a lineage of women with our kinds of gifts . . . and then the missionaries arrived. I mean, missionaries have been meddling in this continent, in specifically what we call Texas now, for centuries. But these missionaries took one look at my family, at the way they talked about the old gods, at the way they said things like *There are things older than God* (one of Nadia's favorite sayings), and they got really pissed off. Legend has it that they stole one of our daughters and tried to pray her gift away. When that didn't work, they tried to beat it out of her.

The girl somehow got free and ran home, and *whew*, were her mother and tías and grandmothers pissed. Nadia never goes into detail about what they did to those child-beaters, but I can only imagine what women who talked to water, women who aimed lightning bolts, women who communed with animals like venomous serpents might've done. And after that, I guess the family decided to get a fresh start and move here, to Cranberry.

Because Cranberry's in a seaside valley, a lot of its history is broken up. Historians aren't exactly sure when it was taken over by settlers, and they can only guess that it was named for the wild cranberry bushes that line the forests. But Nadia says *we* came here because these mountains felt like the stomping grounds of the old gods. She says that back when my mother was little, she'd take her hiking in the woods and if they were lucky, they would find a not-quite-human footprint lined in gold dust. "Look," Nadia would say, and they'd stare and stare at it, until finally Nadia took out a flask of espresso and poured it onto the dirt.

I don't know about all that. I've heard about the old ones my whole life, but Nadia never once took us to find some bedazzled Sasquatch print in the woods. I guess between us kids and her work and all her obligations at St. Theresa's, she never found the time.

Teal pulls into a parking space in front of a one-story building made out of slabs of stone and red brick all mixed together. Over its front door is a hand-painted sign in a font that looks like it's from a ren faire, reading *Lost Souls Lounge*.

I know, I know. With that kind of name, it sounds like they're trying way too hard. And maybe they are. But it's the only legit bar in town so everyone gives them a lot of leeway. Even when the inside's dark with low-level gold lightbulbs hanging everywhere, the walls painted black and pinned with plastic . . . *skeletons*. That's the theme of Lost Souls Lounge. There are bones everywhere— from the paintings of skulls behind the bar to the skeletons made from metal mechanical pieces strung from the ceiling. Even the centerpieces at each table contain a skull candle holder.

"Let's sit at the bar." Teal wastes no time stomping in and finding a seat.

I glance around on my way to join her, waving at Olivia and Henry and Dale, all seated in an especially dark corner. Nate's not here yet. I'm not sure if I'm disappointed or relieved. I slide next to Teal, who's chatting up the bartender. Teal's tone is all worried. "But he's *supposed* to be off tonight."

The bartender—a tall woman with short blue hair and dark brown skin—shrugs. "He took an extra shift. Bernard's wife is in labor."

"Dammit." Teal sighs. "I'll start with whiskey then. Neat."

"You got it, babe."

I have a seat and angle my torso her way. "Who's supposed to be off tonight?"

At that moment, a dude walks up with stacks of napkins in his hand. "Sage? That you?"

I blink at him for a moment. "Carter?" I jump up, giving him the warmest side-hug I can without knocking the napkins down. I take a step back. "Wow, you're all grown up."

Carter Velasquez used to live down the street from us when we were little kids. Two years older than Sky, he was often our fourth partner in crime, tagging along for all sorts of Flores sisters adventures. In my mind, he was still this skinny child blended with an even skinnier teenager, but now . . . he's definitely had all kinds of growth spurts. His face is still all the Carter I know, though—pale with dark eyebrows and hair, and brown eyes so light they're almost orange. He grins. "You're back in town, huh?" He clears his throat and glances behind me. "Teal."

Teal downs her whiskey, her eyes darting around as she wipes her mouth with the back of her hand. "Uh. Hi. There."

"Hey." He stares at her some more. "There."

"Carter, I'm almost out of ice up here," the bartender says.

"On it." He picks up the napkins, bumping my hip. "Good to see you, Sage."

"Likewise, bro." I immediately turn to Teal, who's studying her glass with remarkable intensity. I gesture toward where Carter disappeared in the back. "So . . . who saw who naked?"

She groans. "Oh my *God*, Sage."

"Seriously. There were weird vibes just now. Ridiculously weird." My mouth drops open. "Wait. *He's* the one who was supposed to be off. Right?" She's rolling her eyes and signaling for another drink but I keep going. "What's going on? Why do you care so much whether he's working or not?"

She sighs. "Carter and I . . ."

"Did it?"

"No! God. We maybe . . . kissed the other night."

"No." My eyes widen. Carter Velasquez has been in love with Teal since he was nine years old, but she's *never* given him the time of day. Until the other night, I guess. "Well, what happened? Why are things weird?"

She shrugs. "He didn't want to . . . proceed."

"Really? Why?"

"He said I was too drunk."

I mentally calculate things. All that junk that went down with Johnny on YouTube Live . . . that was two nights ago. I wince. I guess that's why she was drinking. "Why do you sound so mad, though?"

"Because I wanted to fuck. And he didn't. He kept talking about *taking me to dinner* and *relationships* and *maybe I'd had too much to drink*." When she imitates him, she makes him sound like a caveman.

I scoff. "Carter's a good guy. You know that. It's not a bad thing he didn't want to when you'd been drinking."

"Whatever." But the word has no bite to it. She knows I'm right.

When Carter reappears, lugging a giant black container, his eyes stay on Teal for so long, he trips and chunks of ice go flying. Teal doesn't even notice—she's on her phone, scrolling through some social media page. I wonder about all the parts of her life I've missed. How long have she and Carter been "maybe" kissing? She was with Johnny for six years, but maybe they were on and off again toward the end, or maybe their relationship was more open than it seemed. I want to ask her. To know her again. But I'm afraid she's going to blow up and shut me out like a million times before.

"Hey, there you are."

I turn around to see Nate there, grinning. In all of a single second, my stomach feels like I'm on a roller coaster. "Oh, hi, Nate." I push a tendril of hair behind my ear and attempt to look as casual as I can. "I didn't know you were here. Fashionably late, huh?"

"My truck wasn't doing so hot for some reason on my way home from work today. I dropped it off at the shop and got a ride here from—" He looks around and points. "Earl. My great-uncle." There's a gray-haired man sitting next to Dale who lifts his beer toward us.

Double date, I can hear Laurel chanting in my head. And with the way he's looking—a dark green button-down over blessedly tight jeans tucked into black boots, his tomato-leaf eyes twinkling in the glow of the skull lights . . . Well. Even without any alcohol in me, I'm already reevaluating my *no* to her demands.

"Oh, I'm sorry to hear it . . ." I say, my voice trailing off as Nate keeps sneaking glances at Teal. She finally lifts her eyes and immediately her gaze goes up and down his form. "Uh," I say. "Have you guys met before?"

Nate thrusts his hand toward Teal. "Not at all. Hi. I'm Nate. I work at Cranberry Rose—"

"Oh, you're Sage's boss, right?" Teal gives me a look like *You didn't mention he looks like* this!

They shake hands for a weirdly long time, and Nate lets his fingers linger on hers right before they break apart. "You live around here?"

"Uh. Yeah. We live by the Cliffs."

"For how long?"

I furrow my brow at Nate. Why's he so interested?

Teal shrugs. "My whole life."

"Wow. I can't believe I've never met you before."

"Well," I say. "It's not like you would've gone to school together. You're . . ." I calculate. "Six or seven years apart."

I was hoping one of them would blink at that information, but it's like I haven't spoken at all. "So where are you from?" Teal asks with a shy smile.

"Oh, well, I—"

"Sage!" There's a clap on my shoulder and I turn toward Dale's smiling face. "Come on over to our table for a minute. I want our newest employee to meet some people."

I turn back to see if Teal's okay with that, but she's turned completely away from me, facing Nate, who's taken up the stool right next to her other side. "Oh—uh. Sure."

Dale laughs and helps me off the stool. The table cheers when they see me—hurrah, the prodigal Plant Whisperer has returned!—and we play musical chairs for the next forty-five minutes as new people come in, each one absolutely desperate to hear my entire life story or to tell me theirs. I keep glancing over at Nate and Teal between snippets like *and that's when they cut out a part of Ned's brain* and *no one's going to accuse my mama of shoplifting turkeys again!* The only movement they've made in the last hour is to lean in so far, they might as well touch their eyeballs together.

I'm not the only one creeping on them. Carter's walked by at least six hundred times. He even waved at Teal once, trying to get her attention, but no go. I'm pretty sure if we could X-ray into his chest right now, his heart would be shredded.

I'm talking to Jada—a lady who, as far as I can tell, is a Cranberry Rose groupie, having never worked there—when Teal walks up, Nate behind her. "Hey, Sage. Nate and I are gonna bounce. You good?"

"Am I good?" I can't hide the panic in my voice. I don't know why I didn't see this coming. I mean, I'm here because Nate was supposed to find out my decision on the job offer. He was supposed to buy *me* a drink. Instead he basically did a cartwheel the second he saw Teal and they've been about to dry-hump since. "Er—" I add when she narrows her eyes. "We came together, though?"

Teal smiles and begins counting with her fingers. "Lyft, Uber, or even a regular old taxi. You want me to order a ride for you?"

"No!" I jump up and grab her arm, pulling her toward the bar. "Just one second," I say to Nate as I go.

Teal pulls back. "What is *wrong* with you?"

"Teal." I take a breath. Considering she looks like she's about to bolt any second, I have to be direct. "Don't fuck my boss, okay?"

She looks at me like I'm crazy. "Why?"

"Because!" I flail my arms. "It'll be, you know. Awkward!"

"No, it wouldn't. He's not *my* boss." When I have no comeback, she huffs out a breath. "Look, you're in no position whatsoever to tell me who I can and can't fuck. You *destroyed* my love life the other night—"

"Oh, wow, I totally forgot that I broke that *pillar* of unconditional love—"

"Stop. You know what I'm saying." She turns back to where Nate's on his heels, hands in his pockets, smiling bigger than I've ever seen before. Teal's got such a sweet smile on her own face when she looks at me again. "Besides. He seems like a good guy."

I swallow. I mean, what can I say to that? "I don't have a ride, though."

Before she can once again list the world's ride service companies, a thick, deep voice sounds from the bar. "I'll give her a ride."

"See?" Teal points. "*He'll* give you a ride."

"Teal . . ." My voice trails off because she bounces toward Nate, grabs his hand, and all but drags him out of the bar.

I turn to see which clown thought he was saving the day there. And of course.

It's Tennessee Reyes.

16

H<small>E'S WEARING A STUPIDLY THIN WHITE HENLEY AND OLIVE</small> corduroy pants with black high-top Converse. I swallow as my eyes linger on the hard lines of his stomach. He's leaned back against the bar, one leg crossed over the other, smirking like he saw me inadvertently ogle his abdomen. Like he knows *I* wanted to go home with Nate. Like he can gaze upon my every insecurity and every wound as though I drew them onto my skin with a ballpoint pen.

I cannot be nice. No matter how kind and endearing he is—or how lickable his stomach might look—I have to remember my earlier lesson. When it comes to Tenn, nice equals dangerous.

"Nope," I announce, walking up to the bar, two stools away from him, throwing my purse on the counter. I dig for my phone. "I'll just do the Uber thing."

"Generally, ride share services are only available during business hours." He turns his body toward me in this languid way, making me too aware of how he's at least nine inches closer now. "If you're lucky."

I stay silent, verifying what he said with the Uber app. "How the—" I mutter. I slide my fingers over the phone screen in desperation. Lyft is the same. No available drivers.

"We used to have a few drivers here and there who'd work any and all hours, but those apps really don't treat their workers good enough for that."

Does Teal know about this? I bet she does. But all she wanted to do was get rid of me as fast as possible, not caring at all how I got home. As long as Teal gets what she wants, that's the only thing that matters. My heart sinks even further.

I hit call for Cranberry Ridez Taxi and Shuttle Services. "Hi. I'd like a ride from the Lounge . . . ? Oh? One hundred and twenty minutes? For the next available—" I glance at the clock on the wall, the big and little hands made of skeleton fingers, pointing. "No, thanks, that's a little long. Uh-huh. You too."

My next step is to call Laurel, but it goes straight to voice mail three times in a row. I consider calling Nadia, but to be honest, I'd probably have better luck with Cranberry Ridez.

I don't even look Tenn's way when I put my phone in my bag. "I'll get a ride with Dale." I turn back to the Cranberry Rose table . . . and of course it's empty. Poor Carter is wiping down the chairs, looking like someone drop-kicked him in the gut. He notices me staring and we wave to each other, but for both of us, it's the sad, pathetic wave of people aboard ships, leaving one another for war.

I turn to Tenn, scowling. "Fine. But we're leaving now."

"I can't even finish my drink?" He's got a half-full beer. At this point, it seems likely that he'd drink it slowly just to irritate me. And I'm tired. I can't spend the evening with *Tenn* on top of everything else.

So I pull out a wad of cash, putting it on the counter for Teal's whiskeys. "You know what? I don't need a ride anymore. Thanks anyway."

I turn and make my way toward the door. It's too far to walk back to Nadia's, but Laurel's place is a hop, skip, and a jump away. A few dozen hops, skips, and jumps, I mean. Before I can push my way out, though, Tenn's there, blocking my way. "You seriously can't wait five minutes?" He folds his arms over his chest. I do not notice the way his biceps strain against the soft fabric. I do *not*.

"Why can't you accept that I *don't need a ride*?" I snap.

He and I stare at each other for a few seconds, until goose bumps prickle up my arms. Finally, he sighs and opens the door, gesturing for me to walk through. "I'm driving you home." His voice is gruff and commanding, so much so that my spine shivers.

"No, you're not."

"Unless you've got someone on their way right now, the only option is walking. And it's too late to walk." He gestures at the sky, so black that not a single star pricks its smooth ink skin. All of the streetlamps have clicked on, moths helplessly flying up, up toward their goldenrod light.

I close my eyes. I'm way too close to tears, so I finally, *finally* relent, for real this time. "Okay." There's nothing but defeat in my voice.

Tenn inclines his head and I follow him toward the back of the parking lot, where a vehicle is parked that I can only describe as a slick, old-timey hot rod.

"You've got to be fucking kidding me."

He stops, and for a brief moment looks almost *unsure* of himself before he gives me that smirk of his again. "You don't like my car?"

It's low to the ground and sleek, and even in this light I can tell it's painted redder than a serrano pepper, with two black stripes shining along its sides. "What is it?"

"It's a Boss."

"That tells me nothing."

He steps up to the passenger side and opens the door for me. "It's a 1971 Boss 351. A Mustang."

I slide in and he gently shuts the door when I'm settled. It smells atrociously good in here. Like the lumber department at Home Depot mixed with Earl Grey tea and magnolia blooms. When he climbs in, I say, "How many cars are there like this on planet Earth?"

He starts the engine, giving me a wicked grin that I feel in my ankles. "When they first produced it, they only made just under two thousand of 'em. Now there's a hundred or so still on the road."

I shake my head and sigh. "I knew it."

He glances at me, his eyes dropping to my bare knees before they return to the road. "Knew what?"

"I figured out your problem. You're . . ." I struggle to find the words. "You're *obnoxiously* cool. It's ridiculous. Of course you drive a beautiful, rare car. Of course it smells like Earl Grey tea on the inside. Of course you've got stubble and corduroy and a white freaking *henley* on. It's like a romance novelist dreamed you up." I close my eyes and laugh. "Oh my God. Your name. Your name is *Tennessee*. You're a love interest! Just like . . . Tyge and Xavier and Dexter and . . . God, I don't know. *Zane*."

"Didn't Dexter, like, kill people?"

"No, I—" I close my eyes. While Tenn might be obnoxiously cool, I'm realizing that I'm sounding like an obnoxious clown. I sigh and let my shoulders fall. "Never mind." I smooth my hand over the door handle, letting idle, useless thoughts come up and over me like a fountain.

I can't believe I was going to ask Nate Bowen out tonight.

I can't believe I thought he might say yes.

"Your name is Sage *Flowers*," Tenn points out.

"It's weirdly poetic. Not cool. Not like Tennessee *Kings*."

"Touché." He smiles as he backs up out of the parking space. "So that's why you don't like me, huh?" Tenn glances my way. "I'm too cool?"

"Maybe." I'm definitely not telling him the stupid truth—that I was in love with him, once, when we were teens, and then he was an ass and I'm way too immature to forgive him even now.

"You gotta tell me how to not be so cool, then."

"That's easy. I know all about that."

"Yeah?"

I glance around. "Wait, why are we this close to Cranberry Wood?"

"Oh, shit." He slows the car down. "Fuck. I started driving home."

I glare at him. "You're taking me *home*? To *your* home?"

"No! I—I don't know. I wasn't thinking. I guess I was nervous. So where do you live?"

I point. "You can take Easy up to the Cliffs down there. I live on Catalina."

"Got it."

We drive the rest of the way in silence. Well, near silence. The rumble of his rare hot rod is ever present, and the wind rushing through the cracks in the windows is there, too. Then there are my thoughts, flying all around like those moths fluttering under streetlamps, looking like little gold leaves in flight.

The look on Carter's face when Teal left with Nate.

How at this exact moment, Teal and Nate are probably doing unthinkable things to each other.

The fact that *Tenn Reyes* is giving me a ride home right now and he smells way, *way* too good, plus he won't stop looking at my legs for some reason.

We finally make it to Catalina and I direct him to Nadia's driveway.

"Thanks for the ride," I mutter, grabbing my purse.

"Wait." He looks right at me. His eyes are somehow even darker now, so dark that I can make out every amber-lit window on this street in them. The scruff on his face frames his lips, making them look plumper. Pinker. Finally he says: "Nate's an idiot."

I rear back. "*What?*"

"You know what I'm talking about."

"No. I don't."

He smiles and it's an arrogant one. "I think you do."

"I think you need to shut up." I open the car door. I'm so flustered, I nearly fall out.

"Hey." Tenn's flung his door open to rush and help me, but I'm already upright.

"Stop. Just go away, okay?"

"Hey. I'm sorry if I overstepped. I just thought—"

I point a finger in his face. "You thought I needed to be reminded that no one chooses me, ever?" He doesn't understand, *can't* understand, but this is especially rich coming from him. "It's not necessary, okay? I may as well be wearing it as a sign on my fucking forehead." Great. Now my voice is breaking. "Now, please go away."

He doesn't look the least bit surprised by my outburst. Instead, he narrows his eyes ever so slightly, like he's scrutinizing me, and I can't stand it. I can't stand the feeling that he can read my face, my history, my pain as though there *are* signs all over me. "I'm not leaving till you're safe inside."

"Of course you're not." I stomp down the path, ignoring how the plants all around me—the roses and the mint, the creeping thyme and the moonflowers, opened up for little light-loving moths—seem to huff and stumble and stomp, too, right along with me.

When I get in, I stay by the window until he leaves. Only then do I cry.

There's *no way* I'm saying yes to that job offer. There's no way I'm spending the summer with a man who sees right through me like I'm made of stained glass, who drives a car stupidly called "Boss," who's just seen me fall apart like a freaking psycho on my great-aunt's lawn without a single drop of alcohol to blame.

Even Sky knows enough to not bother me on my way up the stairs, up into my room, up into my bed, not even bothering to wash my makeup off. I fall asleep immediately, and deeply, and when I awaken, the light's stretching across my room like a long, sharp arrow.

Sky's still around, though she's a little blurry. She follows me to the bathroom. "I don't know if I'd go downstairs yet."

"Why?"

When I turn back toward her, my face dripping from washing it, she's gone.

Hate that for us.

I'm too hungry to heed her warning, but boy do I regret it by the time I get to the kitchen.

There's Nathaniel Bowen, dressed in the same outfit he wore yesterday, bending over my sister, who's in a bright pink bathrobe. He's kissing the back of her neck as she tries to make the coffee. "Stop," she says, giggling, sounding happier than I've heard in years.

This is the second it all comes back to me—how things have been between me and Teal, for as long as I can remember. How when Mom left, Teal started having horrible, hour-long temper tantrums that involved kicking and punching and lightning and hurricane-like winds over la casa de Nadia. How she kept that up because she learned early on that Nadia didn't have it in her to deal with it. It meant that all our lives, we've had to tiptoe around my sister, in case she gets mad.

When I turned sixteen, Nadia said she couldn't afford to get me a car. But two years later, she opened up a new credit card to pay for Teal's brand-new white Malibu. How when Sky died, Teal decided to place the blame heavily on my shoulders, and how everyone apparently thinks that's okay, because not a single soul has corrected her.

How when *I've* been daydreaming about Nate's sunrise smile about once a month for ten years, Teal's the one who went home with him the day they met.

Something cracks deep inside me, like a near-dead seed falling to earth, breaking right in half.

Plant hunting pays a lot more than veg bed tending. Which means I'll get out of Cranberry way sooner. I mean, yeah, spending the summer with Tenn is bad. But staying for months longer than necessary? Watching Nate fall in love with Teal? That's worse.

"My answer's yes." The words are out before I can stop them.

After they're done pretending like they weren't about to make out on top of the percolator, I repeat myself, staring right at Nate, trying as hard as I can to ignore the hickey just under his ear. "My answer's yes. To the job. Plant hunting. I'm taking it."

APRIL 6, 2001
14 YEARS AGO

silvergurl0917: hey

RainOnATennRoof: Hey.

silvergurl0917: no howdy today?

silvergurl0917: . . . hey you there?

RainOnATennRoof: Hey, sorry. My dad's being annoying.

silvergurl0917: oh yeah? that sucks.

RainOnATennRoof: It's fine. It's whatever.

silvergurl0917: so you didn't find me in the yearbook then?

RainOnATennRoof: Ha. I guess not.

silvergurl0917:.. . . . is everything okay? you seem. i dunno. distracted?

RainOnATennRoof: Yeah. Sorry about that.

RainOnATennRoof: My parents are separating.

silvergurl0917: holy shit. i'm so sorry.

RainOnATennRoof: Don't be. Trust me, they need to do this lol.

RainOnATennRoof: It's just that I finally told them I want to live with my mom. And my dad's been pretty pissed. He keeps . . . I don't know, antagonizing me. Getting revenge or something.

silvergurl0917: omg he doesn't hit you does he???

RainOnATennRoof: No! It's not like that. It's more like he starts yelling at me if I so much as leave a textbook out of place. He's so stupid. Anyway. Subject change . . . Tell me about your parents.

silvergurl0917: oh. well

silvergurl0917: my mom's not around. and i never knew my dad. i live with my aunt, actually. she's nice, whenever she's around i mean. she's pretty busy . . . like all the time.

RainOnATennRoof: Wow, I'm sorry about your parents.

RainOnATennRoof: I hope you're not too lonely, living with your very busy aunt.

silvergurl0917: i'm a lot less lonely now. :)

RainOnATennRoof: good. ;)

RainOnATennRoof: Quick tell me your top three favorite things.

silvergurl0917: ummmmmm i love tamales, roses, and

RainOnATennRoof: and?

silvergurl0917: talking to you on friday nights:)

silvergurl0917: ..what about you?

RainOnATennRoof: I love mushroom hunting with my mom, and . . . you said a food so I'll say one too. Spaghetti with garlic bread. and

silvergurl0917: and..??

RainOnATennRoof: and I love talking to you too Silvergurl.

RainOnATennRoof: Literally the best part of my week.

PRESENT

"She *what*?"

I smile, despite the topic of conversation. Laurel's screech of outrage on my behalf just feels so *good*.

I put on my blinker as I exit the highway, my phone rattling in the cup holder. "Yeah. She was with him all weekend and when she finally came home last night, I heard her tell someone on the phone that he was the best she ever had."

"Well, hasn't she just been with Johnny? The bar must've been under sea level."

I snort. "I don't know who she's been with. But . . . she was just so happy. And I'm . . . I don't know. Torn? I like that she's happy. She talked to me this morning. Like *she* initiated the conversation." It consisted of her asking if I wanted the rest of the coffee in the perc, but still. Progress. "But at the same time . . ."

"At the same time, *we* were supposed to double-date. You and me with Nate and Jorge."

"Yeah . . ." I say, though even if I were the one with Nate, I don't think I'd welcome unnecessary time spent with Jorge. "Anyway, I just need to get over my crush."

"But what if they break up?"

"No." I pull off the road toward Cranberry Wood State Park, parking semiclose to the obnoxiously red 1971 Boss Mustang in front of me. "He fucked my sister. Even if they break up tomorrow and she gives me her blessing, I—" I make a face even though Laurel can't see me. "No."

"I get it. Well, guess I'm going to have to find you another eligible man for double-dating."

"Good luck." I snort. "Anyway, I better go. I accepted Nate's job offer and that means I'm meeting Tenn right now at—"

"You're *what*? Sage, you're killing me. You can't just drop that bomb at the *end* of our conversation."

I laugh. "We'll get lunch this week, all right? Wednesday sound good?"

"On Wednesday I'm shooting interiors for a new artisan cheese shop just outside of Baltimore."

"Ooh, cheese."

"I know, right?" I can hear the smile in her voice. "How about Thursday?"

"Thursday works."

"I want all the details. You hear? All of them."

"I hear ya."

We hang up and I take a deep breath, looking around. The parking lot's tucked in a thicket of trees, all tall and looming, a little intimidating, even, on this gray day. At the opening of a hiking path, there's two men talking—a park ranger, I'm guessing, and Tenn.

He's got on a blue button-down plaid shirt rolled up to his elbows, and the bareness of his arms draws all my attention. I don't think I've seen his arms since high school, when I'd spy on him from discreet corners at school, watching him flirt with zillions of girls. His forearms are thick and veiny and *covered* in tattoos. It's almost sick, the way I respond to this revelation. My lower belly warms as I imagine touching the ink on his skin, following it with the tips of my fingers up his arms, under his clothes, down his chest to other aesthetically pleasing spots.

As though he can sense me mentally undressing him, he looks my way and smiles, gesturing for me to join them. I take a deep breath. I haven't spoken to him since my ridiculous temper tantrum Saturday night. I had planned an explanation and everything. I was simply hangry, yes, low blood sugar is the reason why I blurted out one of my deepest childhood wounds. *You thought I needed to be reminded that no one chooses me, ever?*

I wince as my cheeks heat a little at the memory. God, how embarrassing. I mean, yeah, it's true that my mother didn't choose me, Nadia didn't choose me, and Tenn sure didn't, back in the day. Heck, the only one who has chosen me is Sky's ghost, and that doesn't appear to be a choice at all.

But what the hell compelled me to say it to *him*?

So if he's going to pretend like it didn't happen, all the better. Then we're not going to get into why he's so irritating that I end up confessing crap about myself that I've told no one else. Not even Laurel.

I grab my bag and jump out of the van. The door sounds like it might fall off as I shut it. I've driven this bad boy since I was nineteen, using all the money I saved from working summers at Cranberry Rose. It was ancient even then.

"Hi," I say, walking up, willing myself to look anywhere but Tenn's bare forearms. For some reason this means my gaze settles on his crotch (why, brain, *why?*) and I shake my head and opt to stare at the park ranger. "I'm Sage."

"Patrick. Nice to meet you both." He's skinny with pale skin and medium brown hair. He doesn't look all that thrilled to be here, cracking his neck as he lets out an irritated sigh. "So, ah. Nate said y'all were looking at the outskirts of the eastern hiking trail?"

"Yeah, the half acre or so that might get developed," Tenn says, a weird edge to his voice I can't explain. I break my rule to look at him, at his face, but he doesn't look anywhere near as disturbed as his tone indicated.

"So the park does own that particular strip; however, it's not technically part of the park, so it's not under the same protections. So per the Cranberry Wood rules you can take cuttings but not whole plants. The cuttings have to come from healthy, robust plants. Only two per plant. And if there are fewer than twelve of that particular plant in a quarter acre, only one cutting is permitted total."

"Got it." Tenn nods.

"Here, I'll take you there so you don't get lost."

"We can make it ourselves, man, if you've got someplace to be," Tenn says.

"No, I—no. *I'll* direct you there *myself*."

Tenn widens his eyes at me in a wordless *o-kay*, and I can't help my smile. His gaze heats immediately as he stares at my mouth and I turn away, reminding myself of all the practice he got at flirting in high school and beyond. Looks like that must be so second nature to him that he doesn't even know he's doing it.

We follow Ranger Weirdo, stepping through leaf-covered stone still damp from last night's rain. I think this is the main hiking path through Cranberry Wood State Park, unimaginatively named Cranberry Trail. We pass the Welcome Center to our left, and I think of Nadia in there, wearing the same black blazer she's worn to work for thirty years, greeting guests and passing out maps and pouring little plastic glasses of cranberry lemonade.

Although we might not know why or how or when, exactly, Cranberry was settled by white colonists, it's definitely become a tourist town. A humble one, but a tourist town all the same. Cranberry's whole attraction is centered around *nature*—with not one but two state parks, thousands of acres of undeveloped woodlands, and two beaches, one sort of hidden inside Cranberry Falls State Park, and the other, big and busy downtown. Cranberry's whole downtown was developed around that beach, in fact, and something like twenty percent of the town's businesses are based there, from Jorge's architecture firm to the more touristy attractions— ice cream parlors, two competing pizza-by-the-slice spots, and lots of places to buy cheap T-shirts and keychains with vintage-style painted cranberries alongside the town name.

Even Cranberry's biggest church, St. Theresa's Catholic Church for Pilgrims and Wanderers, has become a tourist stop for the religious and/or curious sort. It's got that name, for one, and a rumored mysterious cult dedicated to Mary Magdalene. Nadia brushes all this off as nothing more than small-town gossip, but that doesn't stop the church from stocking Mary Magdalene laminated saint cards, tall prayer candles, and paintings in their gift shop.

I wipe away sweat from the back of my neck. We're hiking a lot farther than I thought. And Ranger Patrick is booking it like we've got zombies on our tail or something. We're all quiet, so I look up and say, "I guess it might rain today."

"Yes," Patrick says. "That is what those dark clouds may indicate."

I blink. Was that intended to be as mean as it sounded? I try again: "What's this mossy smell I keep smelling?"

Patrick's shoulders tense. "It's probably all the moss. In this forest. Where there's a ton of moss."

So. That's awesome.

Laurel says I've got a problem with men and that it all starts with my dad. Me, Teal, and Sky all have the same kind of father: young and just passing through Cranberry. Mom left us only their names and I've never tried to contact mine. I've built him up in my head as this person who doesn't care—if he did, wouldn't he contact me?—and who is an asshole—if he wasn't, wouldn't he contact his child?

So I guess I do have a problem with men, but it's stupid that it's my problem and not the men's, since they're the ones who keep letting me down. Laurel says I don't give them a chance and I don't trust them. But honestly, I think she trusts them too much—her husband is Exhibit A.

Anyway, when Patrick is, yet again, an asshole to me with that dumbass moss comment, I don't even think about it—I just let the pain touch my gift, the part of me that feels plants, that is connected to them as though I had my own white roots and my own green veins—and just ahead, Patrick stumbles on a rock that may or may not have been nudged under his foot by a tree root.

I don't care that I have a problem with men. I haven't yet met one who didn't deserve it.

By the time we reach the strip for plant hunting, a light drizzle has started. "Okay," Patrick says. "Just remember, if you find a plant you want to take a cutting from, let me inspect it first."

I refrain from asking him where in the Virginia State Park guidebook does it say that Ranger Patrick needs to approve cuttings, stopping myself just in time. We don't even need to worry about that stupidity. Just looking around, all I see are plants Nate wouldn't be interested in cultivating for Cranberry Rose. But I walk around anyway, acting like I'm foraging alongside Tenn, pausing to bend and touch a leaf or two. Every now and then, Tenn asks me about a plant, and I have to tell him that it's a common weed, or that it's really difficult to grow, or that it's a protected species and Ranger Asshole would probably jump in front of our cutters to shield it, laying down his life for a plant's, as he seems wont to do.

Just before I suggest we leave, though, I sense something. With my *gift*.

It's hard to explain how this is—like someone's calling my name, but in a voice so soft, I hear it not with my ears but with my hair, my skin, my belly. Like if trees couldn't speak, but the cells in trees could. The atoms in trees. The space inside the atoms inside trees, talking to the space inside the atoms inside me.

I turn toward the sound. *There*. Something pink bobs in the rain on the edge of the woods. I approach it.

It's an iris. A Blue Flag iris, native to this area, and abundant. Abundant in blue, I mean. I've never seen a pink one like this before. I kneel in front of it, taking in more details. It's salmon on its edges, but then it pales to the middle of the petals until it gets to a white, thin stripe. I'm not even sure I've seen an iris this pretty in a bulb catalog before. That's when I know we've found something special.

The last thing I need to do is ask the plant's permission. I know it's weird, but it's important, especially to me, because I can feel the consciousness running through its stems and leaves and petals like a river. I'm convinced that you don't need a gift to feel it; all you need to do is spend time with plants. But for too long, Westerners have measured consciousness by our own, and have concluded that everything else is beneath us. It's a mindset that hasn't gotten us very far, I'll tell you that.

I lean my finger toward the pink of it . . . and it leans forward in return, a water droplet on its petal touching the tip of my finger. That's permission to me.

"Uh. No. Not that one."

I turn around and there is Ranger Patrick, towering over me with a look of disgust that would give Amá Sonya a run for her money. "Excuse me?"

"That one is right in the middle of the line. Most of the plant is in the park, even. So it's protected."

I shake my head. "Why can't I take a piece that's on this side?"

"Because it will kill the whole plant."

I gesture to the iris. It's a four-foot-long clump, the white rhizomes so abundant, they're growing well out of the dirt. At this point, any flower farmer would say it *needs* to be separated. "Do you . . . do you know what kind of flower this is?"

It's a genuine question, because I'm getting ready to educate him on how you can safely split an iris and it would be healthier for it. But he scowls and says, "Look, you need to get the *hell* away from that plant before I issue you a citation."

"Hey, buddy." Tenn's walked up, his arms crossed over his chest. It's too dark and rainy for me to make out any of the tattoos, sadly. "Look, when you were acting like a fucking dipshit earlier to her, I let it slide because I thought, hey, maybe this guy's having a bad day. But there's no excuse for this. You apologize to her."

"You want *me* to apologize to *her*? When *she* was the one . . ."

And while those bozos rattle on, I break off the tiniest rhizome I can. "Thank you," I whisper as I slip it into my pocket.

"It's fine," I say, standing up, interrupting them. "We should just go."

Ranger Patrick looks suspicious. He stomps to the iris, inspecting it, but if the dude didn't know it was an iris to begin with, there's no way he's going to be able to spot the place where a rhizome is no longer connected. "Show me your hands," he says when he turns to me.

"Oh my God. No."

He marches to me, his arms extended. In that split second, Tenn leaps forward, his fist curled, and I shake my head at him.

I've got this, I try to convey with my eyes. He doesn't relax his fist, but he does stop a good three feet away.

Patrick reaches for my arm and I say, "You're gonna assault me after threatening me? What would your boss say to that?"

Patrick falters. "I wasn't going to assault you. I just—"

"You were just going to grab my arms and force my hands open, maybe injuring me in the process? That sounds like it could very well be assault to me."

"You're a fucking liar." He stares at the ground as he says it.

Johnny Miller was the first man I ever threatened with my gift. For some reason, it just didn't occur to me to do that—to wrap vines around legs, to angle a sharp branch over the windpipe—before him. But now I'm hungry with the need for botanical violence. If only Tenn weren't here. Sigh.

I smile and lift my hands, holding them open like I'm the ringleader in a circus, palms up and empty. He checks them both—lucky for him, with his eyes only. "There. No need to assault a woman after all." I drop my arms. "We should go now."

Patrick stares at me and he huffs out a breath. Finally he turns. "We're done here. Let's go."

"Thank you for agreeing with me, Patrick," I say sweetly.

I'm pretty sure he mutters *fucking bitch* under his breath. Tenn's whole body tenses up, so I think that confirms it. After that, though, we're silent all the way back to the parking lot. Patrick stops in front of the trailhead, his arms crossed like the nerdiest bouncer anyone's ever seen. It's clear he's not leaving till we drive away.

"You okay?" Tenn asks softly as we walk toward our cars.

A frisson of anger runs through me. Tenn was kind, today, yes. He was good to me. But the thing is, I'm trying to stay *safe*.

I'm trying to *not* like him. I'm trying to preserve what little motivation I have left to not run away from Cranberry forever, even with my bank account in the double digits. And he's making it so hard.

After all, I have a promise to keep. And I can't make peace with Teal if I'm not in town.

So, my response is much more curt than it needs to be. "Are *you* okay?"

He stops walking. "Uh—"

"I mean, you were going to fight him? For real? You were going to get us fired over nothing?"

"It wasn't nothing." It's the first time I've ever seen Tenn irritated. "He was a belligerent piece of shit. Nate's definitely going to hear about it."

I scoff. "Will you be my knight in shining armor in your version of the story?"

He narrows his eyes at me. "Haven't you ever had someone defend you before? Like, ever? Because I gotta tell you, this isn't how you're supposed to thank that person."

"Oh! Wow! You want me to thank you now." I put my hands in a prayer. "Thank you, Tenn. For saving my *life*."

Tenn blinks, gazing at me for a long time. He takes a breath, letting his gaze run over my frizzy hair, down my face, down to my feet and back again. I suppress a shiver in my spine when he says in a low voice, "You're trying to get me to hate you."

"What?"

"You don't want me to like you."

He's read me so thoroughly, I'm afraid he's going to take one look at my hands and know that I can commune with plants, he's going to see in my collarbone that I don't trust men, he's going to read, on the freckles across my cheeks, that *I* was Silvergurl0917.

"No. That's not what this is."

He steps up and reaches for my hand, like Patrick did, only it's gentle and, to my disgust, entirely welcome. He wraps his whole hand around mine and I can feel his calloused palm everywhere in my body. "You okay? I'm serious."

I close my eyes. They sting with tears. "Yeah. I'm just tired." *Of everything*, I don't say.

He lets go of my hand. "We're going to try something different, you and me."

"Oh?"

He walks backward toward his car, his smile making his dark eyes crinkle. "Yeah. 'Cause I like you a lot, Sage. Sorry to disappoint, but I really like you."

WHEN I PULL INTO NADIA'S, SKY IS IN THE PASSENGER SEAT. Because yes, I cried on the way home. Weird, sad-happy tears at my frustration with men, with my life, and with Tenn, watching me at my worst moments and knowing somehow that it wasn't me. Knowing that I'm better than that. And not judging me for it.

"Sage. You have to make peace with Teal. You promised." Sky's voice is kind, but there is impatience underneath. It hasn't even been a week since she made me promise that. Why is she expecting a miracle?

I sigh. "I introduced her to Nate. That's gotta count for something."

"No. It needs to be like before."

"Before?" I huff out a sharp breath and turn to her. "It needs to be like before, when you were alive." I'm incredulous. "You want me to turn back time so when you ask me, *Hey, Sage, want to come to Cranberry Falls?* I'll say yes instead? Or, you know what I'd need to do is turn back time just a little more to that morning, so that I could tell Nadia, *Hell no, I'm not staying in all weekend to clean Teal's garbage piles.* So I actually could go hiking and prevent you two from being the biggest dumbasses I've ever heard of?" Sky tries to talk but I cut her off. "No, seriously, Sky. Why were you two tightroping the rusted gate *designed* to keep people from falling to their deaths? You were *sixteen*. Teal was *twenty*! You weren't little kids. *Why* were you so stupid?"

"You don't think I ask myself that every day?" Sky snaps. "You don't think as I wander around this earthly plane, as a freaking *ghost*, where no one can see me except you, when you cry. Where no one can touch me. No one can love me or hear me or—" She closes her eyes briefly. "I don't know why we did it. I don't know."

Teal says that as Sky fell, she called for me. *Sage* was the last thing she said. I raised her from when she was two years old. I was the mama, even if she never called me Mama. So my heart breaks at hearing about her suffering like I imagine a mother's would. "I'll do it, Sky. You just gotta give me more than four days, okay?"

She nods. She looks miserable and I wish I could touch her. Hug her. Run my hands through her hair.

Her hair . . . "Sky. Why is your hair so long? You'd just gotten it cut for your birthday before . . . you know."

She looks down, picking up a tendril. "I don't know. Why is it important?"

"Because . . ." *Ghosts do not age.* "I don't know."

"Things are getting fuzzy. I'm fading again."

I'm glad she can warn me. Now, instead of me rolling my eyes or asking a dumb question, the last thing I tell her is "I love you."

She's gone before I can finish the sentence, but I hope she feels the words as deeply as when she was alive. *That's how big my love is for you*, I used to tell her when she was a toddler. *It's bigger than the whole universe. It's bigger than forever.*

18

APRIL 27, 2001
14 YEARS AGO

silvergurl0917: hey there!

RainOnATennRoof: Hello to my favorite Silvergurl;) Is your
sister still bothering you?

silvergurl0917: *sigh* she always is, but thankful her
temper has been better lately.

silvergurl0917: i don't think i ever asked, do you have any
siblings?

RainOnATennRoof: No, it's just me.

silvergurl0917: omg that sounds like heaven

RainOnATennRoof: Yeah, it can be cool. But like now, with my parents and their bs, I sometimes wish I had someone else going through it with me? if that makes sense

silvergurl0917: it makes so much sense. like . . . even though i have siblings, they're younger and they look to me for everything. it's exhausting and i wish there was anyone else to help.

RainOnATennRoof: That sounds so much rougher than this lol.

silvergurl0917: nooo it's not like . . . who is suffering more. that doesn't matter. it's just like . . . you know, i get it.

RainOnATennRoof: I know. You get so much it's like . . .

RainOnATennRoof: . . . how have we not met yet? In person, I mean.

silvergurl0917: hold on, i think i hear my aunt calling me . . .

RainOnATennRoof: nooo Silvergurl. Don't run yet. Please just think about it, yeah?

RainOnATennRoof: I'm going away with my mom this summer and I don't know if I'll be able to log into AOL. I was just thinking of other ways to keep in touch.

silvergurl0917: by meeting me??

RainOnATennRoof: :) getting your number. meeting you. etc.

RainOnATennRoof: think about it. That's all I'm asking.

RainOnATennRoof: So what haven't you noticed today?

silvergurl0917: :) let's see. i didn't notice how good my aunt's tamales were bc my siblings ate them all up. jerks.

RainOnATennRoof: Jerks.

RainOnATennRoof: Anything else?

silvergurl0917: i didn't notice . . . wow. i just looked out the window and the moon is so huge!! and yellow!! and it's not even full right now. i didn't notice that for sure

RainOnATennRoof: Hey, I can see it too. It's beautiful

silvergurl0917: i like that we are under that moon, looking at it at the same time, you know?

RainOnATennRoof: Soon maybe we'll be looking at it together. in person;)

silvergurl0917: i'm thinking about it. :)

RainOnATennRoof: All I'm asking.

PRESENT

It's difficult to repair a relationship with someone when they spend their every waking moment with their new boyfriend. That's not an exaggeration. Teal spends more nights at Nate's place than here. She rushes home to change and go to work, only for her and Nate to make it back to Nadia's or to his place so they can cook and eat and, presumably, fuck, and do it all over the next day.

I mean, I get it. If it were me and Nate, I'd want to be connected to his lean, muscular hip, too. But this is getting ridiculous. It's three whole days when I finally catch her alone. "Hey," I say one afternoon, coming in from plant hunting with Tenn. I'm filthy and sweaty and had just planned on running upstairs to shower first thing, but seeing her drinking tea, I decide to make a cup of coffee first. "How are things?"

"Fine."

"How's Nate doing?"

"Don't you see him every day?"

I inhale sharply. Why does she get like this? Why does she perceive everything I say as some attack against her? I let out a breath, long and slow, and say, "I don't. I'm doing fieldwork most of the time."

"Oh." She blows on her tea. "I didn't know."

Because you didn't ask. Because you never ask. I don't know why the words I want to say come so easily with people like Johnny Miller and Ranger Patrick. With my sister and with my aunt and with Laurel . . . it's amazing my tongue isn't constantly bleeding from all the biting I do. "I'm glad you guys seem to be doing well."

Teal is silent for so long, I think she's just going to ignore me again, but then she sighs deeply. "Sage, would you just stop it? Things aren't going to become a jolly good time between you and me. Not ever again, okay? Not since . . ." She drifts off just long enough for the both of us to finish the sentence in our heads. *Not since Sky died.* "Just stop . . . *this.*" She waves a hand in my direction.

I look around briefly, wondering if maybe Sky would materialize to help me out here. The last time Teal got like this with me . . . I think again of that night. In this kitchen, even. The only light, the microwave's warm glow, lighting up the edge of her and me as I begged her to leave Johnny. Somehow it turned into us fighting about Sky, about the day they decided to go hiking in Cranberry Falls. Teal's words must still be hung around us like the bright-colored Mexican flags Nadia hangs for Día de Muertos. *You were supposed to be there. You were supposed to be there, and you weren't, and now she's dead.*

The thing is, I really was supposed to be there. I almost never let Teal and Sky hike alone because I knew how they could be when it was just them.

But what I told Sky about that morning: it was all true. Nadia had asked me first thing, "Mija, could you tidy the girls' rooms today? They've been so busy with schoolwork. I'm sure they would appreciate it."

What she meant was *You're going to spend your Saturday cleaning Teal's room. It's an absolute dump because Teal would rather bring down a raging thunderstorm than do a load of laundry. And I would rather you clean her shit than deal with her.*

After I saw the state of Teal's room—the dishes stacked on her night table by the bed, the fact that I couldn't walk inside without tripping over a pile of garbage—well. That's why I told Sky no, I couldn't come.

It wasn't just me. Teal always says it was, but it wasn't.

So when she told me it was my fault once again, I couldn't just let it go. My words in response escaped and strung themselves up like twinkling chili pepper lights: *Nadia told me to stay home that day to clean your room because you liked living in a literal garbage dump back then. And you know what? I can play the blame game, too. Because if you weren't too lazy to wash a single fucking dish, Sky would still be alive.*

And boom. Her fist. My mouth. Blood everywhere.

"What's wrong with me trying?"

"It's stupid." She stands, facing me, and we are in almost the exact same spots as that night—me in front of the fridge, her with her arms crossed by the open doorframe. "You're wasting your time."

There's only so many times you can knock someone down before they fight back, claws and fangs out. And I guess this is one of those times, because I say, "Does Nate know about your anger problem?"

She rears back. "Excuse me?"

"Does Nate know you have a really—" I glance out the window where a storm is brewing. "*Really* bad temper?"

"What the hell does that have to do with anything?"

I shrug, trying to act half-bored. "One day you're gonna blow up on him. Hurt him. Shouldn't you warn him in advance?"

Teal's fists are so tight, they're shaking. "Oh my God, *why* are you still here? Trying to make this about *me*? Like you don't fuck up *everything* around you."

"Is it really me who does that?" I step away before the idea of hitting me again becomes way too appealing.

NEEDLESS TO SAY, I'M IN A ROUGH MOOD THE NEXT DAY, WHEN I have to meet Tenn on the outskirts of town at a property that belongs to a friend of Dale's. In addition to Teal making my life so much harder than necessary, Tenn and I have found no plants of interest all week. Well, if you don't count the iris, that is. That one is still a secret because I don't know if Nate would accept that I'd harvested it despite a park ranger threatening me not to, even if said ranger was an asshole. I put it in a terra-cotta pot with bagged dirt mixed with Virginia mud and left it on my little long windowsill, next to the basils.

Other than that, we've come up empty-handed. It's been pretty disheartening to see the wild places Nate's sent us to either just developed, every plant destroyed without a second thought, or full of beautiful, thriving plants that just wouldn't sell for one reason or another. This spot looks no different to me as I park my van in front of the property address. Already I can tell it's full of saplings and boxwood, dandelions and goldenrod and mountain mint. All good plants, mind you—but unless you're a nursery offering strictly medicinal herbs, dandelion's a hard sell.

Tenn shows up behind me after only a minute. I swallow as he steps out of his car in a T-shirt and jeans and Converse. I swallow as those tattoos come into view. I glance away immediately. He hasn't exposed his arms since we had that grand old time with the park ranger. Which means I need to get a grip. The way my stomach and knees feel, you'd think he were sliding his hand down his jeans—or mine.

"Hey," he says with a smile. "How you doing?"

"Fine. You?"

"Good."

Things have been like that, too, since Monday. He said he was going to try something different with me. I guess "different" is a consistent blast of extremely neutral—boring, even—small talk. I mean, we're not fighting. That's good. But I almost want to for variety's sake.

"Ready to head?"

"Sure."

He and I walk around for a bit, as has become our routine. He's getting good at plant identification himself so he rarely calls me over anymore for confirmation.

I'm walking around aimlessly when my foot hits something hard. I glance down—it's a stone. A rectangular stone, half-buried in the earth, and as soon as I start looking for it, I see more. Enough that there is a line of them, indicating that something was here once. "Tenn!" I call. He turns and jogs my way. "What was this property again?"

"It was Violet Earhart's? A friend of Dale's? She said it's been in her family for, like, over a hundred years."

I point. "See this? There was a house here. Or something." I bend down toward the stone, running my hand on it. Tenn does the same, leaning back on his haunches. I glance up, blinking when I see how close we are—I can make out how light his eyes look on this bright day, like buckwheat honey by a window. Said eyes are staring at my lips and he blinks and clears his throat.

I have to clear my throat, too. "You know, I think we might be doing this all wrong," I tell him. "We should be looking for stuff exactly like this." I open my arms. "Old houses. Old places where people kept gardens and a yard. This is where things might've kept reseeding themselves . . . or a long-living perennial still stands."

He nods, his eyes sweeping over me with appreciation. "There are lots of old spots in town."

"Anywhere folks might've grown food, you know? Old-timey farmers and gardeners, they usually kept plenty of flowers, too. They were smart. The more bees—"

"The better pollination." He nods and stands. When he helps me up, one hand on my left forearm, the other at my shoulder, I feel faint. "Well. Let's check out these ruins first. And then we'll come up with a new plan for the rest of the season. 'Cause your idea is outstanding."

I might be blushing a little. "Sounds good."

I follow the line of stones and it gets me wondering about things. Like . . . wow. Over a hundred years of family history right here. Inside these stones, someone lived maybe their whole life. They might've been tucked in bed with a sweet story by their mama. They might've married their first love between these two pecan trees, candles all around, lighting up twilight. Tucked in their own babies, eventually. They stood under this very sun and watched it set with their lover, maybe marveling over the water-colors of orange and pink and purple stretched across the sky like agate ribbons. Did they stand here, like *right here*, where I'm standing now?

I get shivers thinking about the stories these stones hold.

And that's when I see it.

It's a tall bush, but growing sideways like either a hard rain or wind or both knocked it down. And it's got one giant deep violet flower so low, if I weren't looking for bursts of color like that, I'd have missed it.

New England aster. I reach down toward its main root, and it's massive. This is an *old* aster. A long-living perennial, native to the eastern region, and not uncommon, but if, in the Cranberry Rose catalog, we connect it to a story like the one I contemplated just now? Plus the fact that it's native, a butterfly favorite, and is medicinal? Best-seller. Easily.

"Tenn!" I call. When I show it to him, he bursts into this big, beautiful grin that surpasses any sunrise I've ever seen in my life.

He looks like he wants to hug me, or more, and I take a step back and my eyes fall to his forearms. Half sleeves, inked in black and brown with hints of warmer colors, like a sepia photograph. "Mushrooms?"

"What?" he says. Then he looks down. "Oh, yeah. From an old foraging book."

They're soft, like done with watercolor and brush rather than ink and needle. Some caps of the mushrooms are red, some brown, lots white. One looks like a paw of a fox maybe, another, seaweed, white and so delicate, I get the feeling if I breathed too close to it, to that spot before the crease of his wrist, it would undulate.

I don't know what I'm doing. The elation of having just found a gorgeous, ancient aster still electric in me, I reach toward him and slide my fingers over his outstretched forearm, over the old-fashioned illustrations. Goose bumps follow my touch and he makes this sound that might be a swallowed gasp. "Sorry." I step back. "Sorry. Should I grab the supplies?"

He nods, his breath maybe a touch heavy. "Sure."

We don't touch again as we fill our bags with beautiful, beautiful cuttings.

LAUREL AND I MEET FOR LUNCH AT MOONSHINE PIZZA, ONE OF the two competing by-the-slice spots downtown. To be honest, both places' pizza tastes exactly the same to me—that crispy-cornered, chewy New York–style crust with garlicky red sauce and cheese. Freaking delicious. But Moonshine gives away three free breadsticks with any order fifteen dollars and up, and Laurel and I are both motivated by carbs enough to consider that a deal-sealer.

We sit along a bar-style table, facing the storefront window, folded slices of pepperoni pizza in hand. "Well?" Laurel says. "When are you going to tell me what it's like working alongside the man you thought you'd marry back in high school?"

I roll my eyes. "I don't know. Imagine how it'd be if you had to work with the person who you thought *you'd* marry in high school."

"Yeah, but I thought I'd marry everyone I dated in high school. Tim Warner, Deborah Wright."

"Alexa Ramirez."

"Oh, for sure. But I think she's a cop now, right? It would be really weird if I had to work with her."

"Maybe you'd get hired to take pictures of . . . ah. Police vehicles?"

She laughs. "Sounds even more boring than weddings. And stop changing the subject. Seriously. Tell me how work is."

"We've barely been working a week. There's not much to tell."

Laurel raises her eyebrows. "Really."

"Really."

"So, you're telling me you haven't once noticed how much hotter he's gotten? There's not even *that* to tell?"

I take a huge bite of pizza, taking my time with it. Because, yeah. Tenn was gorgeous in high school, but now that he's grown . . . with that stubble along his blade-sharp jaw. His thighs, thick and muscular enough that I can see the line of muscle through his jeans when he squats or walks. That peek of chest hair I saw on that first day in Nate's office, or the botanical illustrations of mushrooms etched into his cut forearms. The way he startled when I touched him there, as though my fingers shocked him with their heat. As though he'd never been touched before.

I swallow. "Fine. He's hotter."

"Told ya!" She points her breadstick in my face.

"Watch it! You almost buttered my nose."

She lowers her voice. "I bet you'd like Tennessee Reyes to butter your nose."

I snort-laugh. "Oh my God. I don't even know what that means."

"Me either, but it sounds filthy, doesn't it?"

"It does." After we're done laughing, I say, in a soft voice, "So, are things any better with Jorge?"

She shrugs. "He's still working all the time. The other day, I walked in on him, and he was on the phone and when he saw me his face freaked and he hung up without saying goodbye."

"Well, that sounds suspicious to me."

"It *is* suspicious, but it's not hard evidence."

"That's what you're looking for? Hard evidence?"

She nods emphatically. "I can't say shit to him without it, can I?"

"And what happens if you find it?"

Laurel gazes out the window, at the folks passing by on foot in front of us. Her long black hair is up high in a ballerina bun, and she's got her classic red lipstick on. High-waisted, acid-wash shorts, a white crop top and boots make her look . . . I don't know. Confident. Beautiful. Way too good for Jorge Jones, even if he wasn't cheating.

Finally, she says, very low, "I'm going to divorce his ass."

I widen my eyes. "Really? No couples counseling or anything?"

"Hell, no. I already know I couldn't get over that again."

I smile and nudge her shoulder with mine. "I'm proud of you, boo."

"Yeah. I hope it doesn't come to that, though."

She looks so gloomy that I immediately stand. "I know." I grab my drink and sip the last of my cherry Sprite. "Come on. Let's go to the expensive home décor stores and mentally design your lighthouse bed-and-breakfast."

Laurel lifts her plastic cup to me in a mock toast before hopping off her stool. "You always know the way to my heart."

IT'S THE WEEKEND, AND I HAVEN'T SEEN TEAL SINCE I BASICALLY implied that her bad temper is what ruins everything. And even though I want to apologize to her, I haven't. Not by phone call, text, nada. Because when I think about it, my whole life, it's been me—and *only* me—apologizing. When I was younger, it was because Nadia made me, and now that I'm older, it's completely out of habit. I'm tired of being the only one. I'm tired of being the person everyone else expects to bend and bend, like a plant under the weight of nonstop hail, so they can go on being nasty and mean. Plants can't bend like that for long without snapping, and neither can people.

So in the morning, when Nadia starts on her bullshit and tells me, "Teal said you picked a fight with her," I don't hem and haw like I normally would do, waiting for Nadia to eventually tell me to make up with Teal.

Instead, I say, "You ever wonder how different things would've been if Teal cleaned up her own messes growing up?"

Nadia didn't say a single word to me after that. And I haven't seen her since, either.

So after all that, I'm unsurprisingly home alone this Saturday, leftover pizza in the toaster oven as I flip through last year's Cranberry Rose catalog. When my phone buzzes, I frown at the number I don't recognize.

You ready to do something different?

Before I can respond, another text comes in. This is Tenn, by the way.

My heart does a triple somersault. What do you mean, something different?

You busy?

I look around. Me, in my satin pajamas. My pizza sizzling in the oven. My only company, an old plant and seed catalog from my place of employment. No, not really.

Good. Meet me at Firefly Mountain in thirty?

Sure.

19

I**T'S A BIT OF A STRETCH TO CALL IT A MOUNTAIN. IT'S MORE** like a rolling hill at the foot of a mountain, though Firefly Mountain is all by itself, between Cranberry Falls State Park and the woods surrounding Pine Stone Lake. It's short enough that you can hike all the way to the top in under thirty minutes, and tall enough that once you're up there, you can see the stretch of downtown Cranberry span as a constellation of twinkling gold and silver orbs. The top is where Tenn leads me once I arrive with my travel mug of tea in hand.

Once we're up there, breathless from the hike, he pulls out a blanket from his pack and sets it on the cool, dew-damp grass. "This is cozy," I say, wondering how I'm going to sit on that, close enough to Tenn to probably smell his delicious scent and then promptly lose my marbles in some capacity.

He responds with a smile I can barely see in this thick night. Then he plops on the blanket and pats it. "Come on, Plant Whisperer."

I sit on the very edge, my legs bent over the grass. We're both facing the downtown view. The headlights of little cars draw fading lines of yellow along the beach.

He clears his throat. "So, Brené Brown says—"

"Hold up." I lift up a hand. "Did you just say Brené Brown?"

"Yeah. Have you heard of her?"

"Have I heard of her?" I snort, thinking of the little pile of Brené Brown books Nadia keeps tucked in a kitchen cupboard. "She's part of the trifecta of white women spirituality."

"Yeah? Who are the other two?"

"Elizabeth Gilbert and Glennon Doyle, of course."

"I haven't heard of them."

"You haven't—" I stop myself. "Well, really, the question is, how do you know about Brené Brown? I can't think of a single cishet man who'd willingly read her work."

He's silent for a long time and I'm afraid I've said something hurtful. But then he says, "My mom le—gave me a couple of her books."

"Ah." I lean back against the blanket, risking closer proximity. I think I can smell Earl Grey, which means I'm getting dangerously close to his body. Oh, well. When in Rome.

"Anyway, Brené Brown says . . ." He's rustling some paper out of his pocket. "Staying vulnerable is a risk we have to take if we want to experience connection."

My spine feels a little funny, like one of those yellow headlight will-o'-the-wisps has made its way down from my skull to my feet. "You're saying you want to experience connection?" I swallow. "With me?"

"I'm saying that we have to in order to do our jobs right. We can't keep . . ." He pauses. "Butting heads like we've been."

That's a really nice way to say that I've been snapping and snarling at him for no reason he's allowed to know. I take a sip of my tea. "So . . . we start over?" I wonder if I can manage something like that. If I can pretend as though I didn't fall in love with him when I was fifteen. If I can pretend he never hurt me two years later so thoroughly, I spent senior year and then some mourning him as though he'd died.

"We have to do what Brené Brown says. Be vulnerable."

"Huh," I say. "That doesn't sound difficult at all."

He senses the sarcasm. "It's not vulnerability if it's not difficult."

"Okay." I sip my tea, looking at where the very last of the sunlight is an indigo line against the ink black sky. "How do we do it, then?" *Do it.* I cough. "Get vulnerable, I mean."

"Well, I've been thinking about it and probably the best way is to tell each other our secrets."

Now my cough is real. "Um." I take a breath. "Secrets?"

I can hear the wry grin in his voice. "Nothing we don't want to tell. Okay? Relax, Plant Whisperer."

Relax. Tenn Reyes wants me to tell him my secrets. That's all. "Okay, you first."

"That's fair. Let's start with sharing something we've never told anyone before. That sound good?"

I bite my bottom lip and furrow my brow. "Sure."

"I can hear you worrying."

"I'm not worrying."

He puts his hand on mine—just for a moment, but it's long enough. Long enough to make me feel warm and tingly in places nowhere near my hand. "Remember, nothing we don't want to tell."

I nod. "Nothing we don't want to tell."

He leans back, his silhouette aligned with the few stars appearing above us. If he lifted his hands, he'd look like the conductor of the universe. "One thing I've never told anyone before . . ." He pauses. "I didn't get out of bed for two weeks when my mom died."

"Tenn. Oh my God." I push up to my knees, tossing my mug somewhere in the grass. "Your mom *died*?"

"Yeah. It was a while ago, though." He pauses. "Did you know her?" There's hope in his voice, probably coming from him not understanding why I just reacted so strongly to the news.

I didn't know her, but I knew he adored her. I knew his favorite meal in the world was his mom's spaghetti and garlic bread and that every summer, they hunted for mushrooms like they were training for the apocalypse. I knew she loved books like Nadia, that she collected seashells from Cranberry Falls beach, that when he was a little kid, he made her "perfume," a concoction of weeds and mud and she dabbed it at her wrists and acted like he'd whipped up Chanel No. 5 from scratch.

I knew that she was, most of the time, his only parent, and it's no wonder he stayed in bed for two weeks. I would have, too.

"No, uh, sorry. I didn't know her. That's just terrible, though. I'm so sorry to hear it."

He huffs out a breath and I can tell it's hard for him to talk about this. "It was an aneurysm. They say she didn't feel any pain. One second she was here . . . the next. Gone."

I don't say anything for a while. I don't know what to say. But finally, my mouth starts going for me. "You started really heavy there. I was going to say no one knows that I once ate two full-sized bags of white cheddar Cheetos for dinner."

His laugh is so beautiful. It just bursts out of him like a song and he falls back on the blanket. "That counts. It doesn't have to be heavy."

"It doesn't feel equally vulnerable, though."

"Doesn't have to be equal. This isn't a contest."

We stay on the light side for a bit, though. He tells me about mushroom hunting and making soup and homemade bread after. I tell him about my sisters, how when we were younger, we thought our names made up a whole landscape—Sage, Teal, and Sky. We're having an argument about who would win in a fight—Storm or Poison Ivy—when he says, "What's your most embarrassing moment?"

I immediately think of Gregory, the department head, and his messy, dark bedroom. "Pass."

"Really? That bad, huh?"

"Yeah. It's the worst, actually." At this point, I'm lying on the blanket next to Tenn. There's enough space to fit a whole person between us, but sometimes—like when he laughs or speaks or breathes—he feels so close it's like he's touching me without actually touching me. We're face-to-face and I don't know why it comes out, but it does. "My sister's ghost is haunting me."

He lifts his head from his arm. "What did you say?"

"My sister. She died in a hiking accident when she was sixteen."

"Jesus."

"Yeah." I take a shaky breath. "She fell off one of the cliffs at Cranberry Falls. They looked for her body for weeks, but it was lost to the elements, I guess." I shrug, as though it hasn't devastated me that we could never properly bury Sky. "Anyway. Her ghost . . . I don't know if you believe in ghosts, but that's why this is vulnerable, I guess, because maybe you'll conclude I'm crazy." I'm babbling now. "But her ghost . . . Sky . . . she says she needs to move on. And I need to make up with Teal, my other sister, who hates me, in order for her to do that."

"I'm sorry about your sister, Plant Whisperer." There's sincere sorrow in his voice.

"Thanks."

He's silent for a moment, and then says, "I've got one that you might think is crazy."

"Yeah? Like a vampire?"

He laughs and I can feel his warm breath on my forearm. "Like *one who got away*."

Something pinches me uncomfortably in the heart area. "You? Have one who got away?"

"Sure. A friend from way back." I about breathe a sigh of relief at the word *friend* when he slaps me with this: "Were you ever on AOL back in high school?"

Oh. Oh God. "Sure. Me and my sisters all were."

"Did you, like, IM and shit?"

I chuckle and try to make it sound casual. "Sure."

"Yeah, well, when I was sixteen, one night, someone IMed me. Someone who went to our school. We started talking. And she was smart and funny, and always knew the right thing to say."

I kind of want to punch this girl in the face, even though she is, in fact, me. "Oh?"

He pauses, like he wants to say something more. But instead, he settles for: "But we lost touch. She ghosted me, I guess you could say." It's not a lie. After what he did, I wanted nothing to do with him. Until now, apparently, sharing a blanket with him during a summer night so beautiful it feels like we are, in fact, conducting the universe somehow, moonstone planets and sunstone stars swirling at the tips of our fingers, right here on the top of Firefly Mountain.

He shifts and I feel the blanket pull from under me a little. "I've always wanted to try to figure out who she was. To see if she's still around Cranberry. Maybe talk to her again."

"Mm-hmm. Yeah. Makes sense."

There's silence for a moment—uncomfortable for me, and

maybe companionable for him. And then he turns toward me, his eyebrows raised. "Hey. You know, y'all were in the same year. You and this girl."

"Were we."

"Yeah." He takes a quick, deep breath. "So I have an idea."

Uh-oh. "You do?"

"What if you helped me find her?"

I have visions of internet sleuthing and hiring private investigators, all for them to announce that the true identity of Silvergurl0917 is . . . Sage Flores. "You . . . want *my* help?"

"And maybe I could help you, too. You need to . . . make up with your sister? To help the other sister's ghost?"

"Yeah . . ."

"What if I helped you with that?"

I shake my head. "I have no idea how you could, but . . ." His expression is so full of hope, *so* endearing, that I can't stop the words that come next. "I mean, I guess." The faster I can help Sky move on, the faster I can get away from Cranberry. That's all I want, right?

Tenn bursts into a bright smile and seems so excited that he has to jump up. He pulls on my hand, helping me to my feet. "Okay, so we have a plan, then. I help you help your ghost. And you help me find my ghost."

"A ghost deal," I say. "Is that vulnerable enough for Brené Brown?"

He chuckles. "I think she'd approve."

Not if she knew I was lying by omission.

He holds out his hand for me to shake. And though I don't want to, it's like a string drags my arm up and out, like the chance to touch him is more important than a deal done in bad faith.

As soon as my hand reaches his, and he clasps me, I notice a blinking light behind him. "Woah, there's a firefly!"

He turns. "They're out early this year, then? Or . . . one is, I guess."

We watch the lightning bug like the universe must see the lives of stars, until it blinks one last time, and then is gone.

MAY 11, 2001
14 YEARS AGO

silvergurl0917: so where are you going for the summer??

RainOnATennRoof: Why good evening to you too:)

RainOnATennRoof: I'm going to Santo Domingo. Mom and I will be staying with my uncle.

silvergurl0917: he doesn't have internet?

RainOnATennRoof: No, he does, I checked a couple days ago w him, but it's Earthlink. No AOL chatting unfortunately.

silvergurl0917: oh, okay

RainOnATennRoof: Did you think about it? Us meeting?

silvergurl0917: yeah

silvergurl0917: i'm not ready.

RainOnATennRoof: Oh.

silvergurl0917: i'm so sorry. it's just that every time
i think about it i feel like i might have a panic attack
and vomit

RainOnATennRoof: you know I don't bite, right?

RainOnATennRoof: I would never hurt you.

silvergurl0917: i know. . . . it's just

RainOnATennRoof: Let's change the subject.

silvergurl0917: oh

silvergurl0917: okay

silvergurl0917: Is your mom from Santo Domingo?

RainOnATennRoof: Nah she was born here. 2nd gen.
My dad too. But both their families are Dominican.

RainOnATennRoof: Listen . . . I know you're not ready
but I'm still pretty bummed. not good company right
now

RainOnATennRoof: So I think I should go, Silvergurl. I hope you have a good night okay

silvergurl0917: no no no wait please. please

silvergurl0917: i know this isn't the same as meeting but

silvergurl0917: 943-4246

RainOnATennRoof: Is that your number? Your actual number?

silvergurl0917: it's the place i will be this sunday at 10:45 am if you want to call at literally that second (otherwise someone else might pick up)

RainOnATennRoof: Wow

silvergurl0917: i know it's not the same as meeting in person but

RainOnATennRoof: Hey. Are you sure you want to talk on the phone?

silvergurl0917: yes, i am.

RainOnATennRoof: okay. I will call you at 10:45 on Sunday.

RainOnATennRoof: Can't wait to hear your voice.

RainOnATennRoof: Have a feeling it's going to get me
thru this summer:)

PRESENT

I'm supposed to be meeting Tenn at a to-be-demolished home after lunch today. I'm rushing, trying to get my food done quick, when I get a call from Laurel.

"Hey, woman," I say when I pick up. The only thing I hear in response is hyperventilation. "Laur? What's the matter?"

"I'm in my car. In the Townhall parking garage." She sounds like she's been crying.

"What happened?"

"Nothing! Not yet anyway."

"Laurel. What the hell is going on? I'm totally freaked out."

"I need you, Sage. Can you come quick?"

"I'm on my way." I turn the stove—with my half-cooked macaroni and cheese—off, grab my keys, and jolt myself out the door.

It takes me a while to get to the top of the garage, but I pull up next to Laurel's sedan, jumping out and then rushing to the passenger side of her car. "What happened?" I ask when I get in.

Her face is pink and her eyes are swollen. She's in a big, ratty T-shirt and sweatpants and flip-flops. If Jorge's responsible for this, I'm gonna—

"It's Jorge."

Yup. A murder is gonna happen today. "What did he do?"

"He . . ." She takes a big, shuddering breath. I grab her hand. I don't know what else to do. "Every Wednesday, he goes to Merida for lunch."

"Okay . . ."

"It's kind of a new spot. Venezuelan. Best arepas in Virginia, supposedly." She shakes her head. "Anyway, I got into online banking. That's how I found out about the lunches. I hadn't checked it in like a year or something, because you know Jorge likes to take care of the bills."

He likes control, I want to say, but don't.

"And every Wednesday, since that receptionist was hired, there's a charge for Merida. And it's almost a hundred-dollar check, every time. Sometimes over that."

"That's a lot for a lunch."

"That's what I thought. I . . . I went on the menu. Their most expensive dish is almost forty dollars. Unless he's chugging drinks, what else could it be?"

I nod. "And today's Wednesday."

"Today's Wednesday."

"Did you go to the restaurant?"

"I did not. I just . . . look at me. I drove here in a fit of . . . I don't know. Rage, I guess. But when I parked, I froze and I started crying and I couldn't stop. And that's when I called you."

I squeeze her hand and then let go. "Do you want me to come with you to the restaurant?"

She shakes her head. "I don't know, Sage. What am I gonna do . . . if . . ." Now she's crying again. I search my purse, and when I find a little pack of tissues, I hand her one.

"What am I gonna do?" she asks, but I can't answer. Because . . .

"Laur . . . Is that Jorge down there?"

"Shit! It is! Quick! Hide!"

She and I crouch down, the tops of our heads just above the windows so we can see.

"Is that . . ."

"Yes. That's Cynthia fucking Peterson."

They're standing pretty far apart. It doesn't look improper. And I really want to help Laurel. I want my beautiful friend to stop crying over that piece of shit. So I start theorizing. "Well, look. Maybe he met a client for lunch and bought *their* meal. Maybe Cynthia comes to assist. Look, they're not even . . ." My voice trails off as he wraps an arm around Cynthia's waist. ". . . Touching."

We stare in silence as she puts an arm around him and they walk just like that toward his car. Cynthia laughs, and then Jorge presses his face to her neck. Kissing it? Nuzzling it? I can't tell from here, but even without that detail, it's pretty clear what's going down.

"You've got to be fucking kidding me." Laurel slides down her seat, her hands over her eyes. "Fucking stupid *fucking* cheater, cheating on me, out in the open like this? How many people in town know? How many people laugh at me behind my back?"

"Are we going to confront him?" I'm imagining all the ways I can make Jorge pay for this, starting with running him over good with my van.

"No. No. I need to think first."

Jorge and Cynthia disappear into his car and drive off, slowly passing us but not looking once. No one else in the world exists but those two assholes, I guess. I turn to Laurel. "What do you need right now?"

She sighs, curling and uncurling her fists. "I think I need to visit the lighthouse. And be alone for a bit."

I think of her at the very top, looking down with all this grief inside her like boulders, like planets, trying to burst out, and I ask, "You're not . . . in a bad way, are you? You don't feel like . . . hurting anyone physically? Including yourself?"

Laurel smiles at me through the tears. "I'm good, Sage. I'm glad you were here when . . . when I found out for sure."

"You sure you don't want me to tie him to a tree and torture him?"

"Although I admit that's not the worst idea in the world . . ." She sighs. "I just need to be alone. I need to think about this. About what I should do next."

I nod. "If you need me, though . . ."

"I know. You'll be there."

When I drive by the architect firm on my way to the property, I narrow my eyes, trying to see inside the mirrored glass. I don't understand why people like Jorge . . . like Johnny Miller . . . why they just hurt the people they supposedly love for no good reason. I mean, Jorge is *obviously* not into monogamy. A part of him must've known he couldn't keep his dick to himself forever. So why beg to marry Laurel? Why waste her time like that?

Tenn's leaning against the fence of the front yard when I pull up, his eyes full of worry. "Hey," he says when I jump out. "Is everything okay?"

"Yeah? Why wouldn't it be?"

"You're twenty minutes late. Didn't you see any of my texts?"

"Oh." I frown, fishing my phone out of my pocket. There's four messages from him. "I'm sorry. I . . . it's been a stupid day."

He looks at me for a moment. "You need to talk about it?"

His thick, black eyelashes look extra curly today and I have a brief, dumb thought about how those eyelashes would feel against my lips. And then I stop myself. *Who* fantasizes about kissing someone's eyelashes? I shake my head. "I'm good."

He raises an eyebrow in a silent *if you say so* and then opens the gate for me.

The property is tiny, with a sliver of a front and back yard.

The bank's going to demo this house sometime in the fall, and they gave Nate permission to save any plants beforehand.

"Roses," Tenn says, pointing.

I glance over at the beetle-eaten plants, mostly dead brown twigs. "Knockouts. They're modern, not heritage roses."

He picks one of the few pink blooms and puts it to his nose. "Wow. It doesn't smell like anything."

"Right. Sometimes when you breed a plant for one thing . . . size, color, disease resistance . . . you lose another trait. Modern tulips and petunias are a good example of this, too. They smell like nothing."

"How do you know all this?" Tenn asks. He's leaning against the little porch—or what's left of it, anyhow. This house was probably cute once, but sometime in the last few years the roof's caved in, the windows have cracked, and Virginia creeper has steadily been eating the rest alive.

"Know what?"

"All this plant stuff."

"Oh." I lift a wild violet from the neglected lawn, one of the rarer ones, pale purple in color. "I was going to be a botanist. Once upon a time."

It was a deal me and my sisters made when we were younger. Nadia was always saying we shouldn't expose our gifts, but we could share them. We thought we'd share them to make the world better. I'd be a botanist, traveling the world to save near-extinct species. Teal would be a meteorologist, learning how to control her gift so she could cure drought and wildfire. And Sky would be the wildlife rehabber, calming animals enough so they let her heal them.

"What happened?"

I sigh. "My sister died. I couldn't be home anymore, so I

dropped out of college and lived in my van for a while, trying to figure my life out." I think of how I couldn't stand the sound of Nadia crying all the time. I couldn't listen to Teal blame me for Sky's death for another single second. *What about your gift?* Nadia had asked when I shoved all my belongings in the van. *I gave it up*, I told her. What I didn't say was, communing with the plants just didn't feel the same. This gift—it was the only thing I shared with my sisters that I shared with no one else in the whole world. I mean, sure, Nadia *knows* things and Sonya will occasionally admit she can sense a ghost. But through our childhoods, what bonded me and Teal and Sky the most was our deepest and most beautiful secret—that we were literal magic. For a long time after Sky was gone, connecting with that magic just didn't feel right.

That's why Nadia was so shocked to see me show up a couple weeks ago with pots and pots of basil. Truth is, I couldn't give it up. Not forever anyhow.

"You lived in your van? Badass."

I smile at him as he bends over goldenrod, not yet flowering. "Yeah. Well, I figured . . . when I was in high school, I was obsessed with making jewelry. I mainly did wire work, but it was . . . the only thing in the world that I could get lost in, you know?" *Besides talking to you on AIM.* "Anyway, I found a metalsmith outside of Philly who took me on as an apprentice. She was an adjunct at Temple, and in the middle of my apprenticeship, she passed away. In a series of weird coincidences, I got her job, and I taught intro to silversmithing and wax casting, with the occasional gem-setting class, for . . . oh, almost five years."

"Then you quit?"

"Budget cuts."

"Ah."

I startle a little, because he's found his way directly in front of me somehow without my hearing his footfalls. He's . . . well. He's just big. I can't help but gaze at the tattoos on his arms, leading up the curve of his biceps toward his thick shoulders. He's studying me, too—his eyes roaming over my ears, my hands, then back up to my neck, glancing once—just once, fast enough for me to question it—at my chest before grunting, "You're not wearing any jewelry, though."

"Oh." I take a step back. "I . . . Well, it was a little traumatic, leaving my job. I *loved* it. I mean, I loved everything about it. Teaching was the freaking bomb dot com. And the fact that I had access to a studio all day . . . I was even designing on my lunch breaks. Toward the end, I was developing my first line of jewelry, to be showcased at this little boutique down the street from the school, all featuring labradorite and white bronze, and then, you know, my boss let me go and I couldn't make rent and . . ." I trail off, realizing I've started rambling. "And I haven't unpacked all my stuff from there yet. Not my projects, my supplies. I haven't worked on anything jewelry related in . . . God. Months. Anyway, it's hard to look at my pieces, much less wear them right now."

"I get it." He glances down my neck once more. "When my mom passed away, basically all I got were her books. My dad sold anything of value, and that left the books. And I couldn't bring myself to read them for, like, a year. Thinking about them hurt too much." He swallows. "And then I picked one up and I couldn't stop. I read them all in two or three months. And it was a *lot* of books."

"A lot of Brené Brown?"

He smiles, his face lighting up. "Some." He brushes his fingers on my sleeve, and it feels like he touches my skin, the way it tingles underneath. "You'll get to your work again, too. When it happens, it's going to be like my books."

"I'm going to start quoting Brené Brown randomly to my coworkers?"

He grins. "You're going to get lost in something you love again."

This conversation is a bit intense. In order to distance myself a little, I bend to grab another violet, but when I stand, my head throbs. I touch my temples, wincing.

He regards me for a long moment. "You okay?"

"I'm—" I rub my eyes. "I'm fine. I just skipped lunch today and I think—"

"You didn't eat?"

I shake my head. "There was a family emergency." Laurel's family, so that's not a lie. "Do you mind if I run down the road and grab a burger? I'll be ten minutes."

He starts to nod, but stops himself. "I got a better idea." He inclines his head toward his car. "Come on."

"Come on what?"

"Let's get some food in you, Plant Whisperer."

"But what about—" I gesture to the house.

He waves it off. "We can always come back." He gestures for me to follow him to the Boss.

I fold my arms. I don't know why, but deciding to get in Tenn's Mustang . . . it feels like something there's no turning back from. Like right now, I'm on the edge of the dark, wild woods. Inside are mysterious things. Treasures. A circle of fairies, their edges lit with firelight, inviting me to dance. And dangers. Mystical footprints that are not quite human, surrounded with dusts of gold.

And I could *so* easily turn around and pretend like there was never something new and maybe awful, or something maybe *precious*, right there, within my grasp like a rare jewel. Like tanzanite or a chunk of an orange sapphire, bright as a lantern, floating just beyond the tips of my fingers.

I could turn away. I could go grab a burger from Pal's. I could go home and finish my mac and cheese.

"Sage. Come on." He gives me an attractive, crooked smile, his eyes crinkling up. "Let me feed you."

"HOLY SHIT. ARE MY EYES DECEIVING ME? IS THAT A TACO truck?"

"Your eyes do not deceive." Tenn parks off the side of the road, right in front of the lake. "Best damn tacos in Cranberry."

"Maybe the only tacos. Didn't Holy Guacamole shut down a couple years back?" It was the only Mexican restaurant in Cranberry for over a decade, and then the owner, Milagros, one of Nadia's friends, retired to Arizona. I'm pretty sure it's a hardware store now.

"They sell tacos at the barbecue place on the water."

I make a face. "At Jack's Grill? White people tacos, you mean."

He laughs. "Yeah. They really have no flavor, do they?"

"I'm pretty sure last time I was there, they had one with goat cheese and raw corn." I shudder.

"How was it?"

"You think I ordered that shit? I ate a whole rack of blackberry bourbon ribs that night, thank you very much."

"A *whole* rack of ribs, huh?" He gives me a smile, his eyes running all over my face like he's seeing me for the first time. "Marry me."

"Shut up," I say, opening the car door fast so he doesn't see any pink in my neck or cheeks.

I order two blackened chicken tacos stuffed with Oaxaca cheese and lime-drizzled avocado slices. On the side, a slab of grilled corn, drenched in butter, crema, and cheese. Tenn grabs a steak quesadilla and gets us both waters and we sit on a picnic table right on the water.

These lakes are called God's hands because they reminded some white settler with lake-naming power of Michelangelo's *Creation of Adam*, the lazy, pointed, pale hand of God and Adam's own hand pointing in return. And although one is known as the larger hand and the other, smaller, I can never remember which is which. Either way, they're the most popular lakes in Cranberry. Even now, in the middle of the day in the middle of the week, folks are everywhere, dotting the sand with purple and red towels, yellow-striped beach umbrellas, blue coolers full of Subway sandwiches and Coronas and cake pops.

"Oh my God, this is so freaking good," I say through a full mouth.

"Told you. It's real sabor. Real ajo y chile."

"Real carne, también."

"Sí." He laughs.

"So what's Dominican food like?"

He swallows a bite of quesadilla. "How'd you know I'm Dominican?"

Shit. I wasn't supposed to know that, was I? He told me over ten years ago . . . when he was RainOnATennRoof and I was Silvergurl0917. "Uh . . . you told me? Small town? I don't remember. I'm sorry, I—"

"No, you're good. I'm just . . . not used to people being so specific about it. Most folks in this town assume I'm Black, and I never know whether I should correct them and say I'm Black *and* Latino. If they're going to take offense or something. Or if they're even going to understand that's *possible*. It's fucked up that I never know what to say to them, when . . ."

"When they're the ones making assumptions."

"Yeah." He shrugs. "Anyway. Dominican food. You know, my mom didn't cook a lot of it. She made a lot of dishes from like, Betty Crocker and Nigella Lawson cookbooks. We ate spaghetti, we ate coq au riesling."

"You made mushroom soup."

"Oh, yeah. We made mushroom soup from summer to winter every year. I told you before that she made bread, fresh, like she'd let it rise all day, too. Once in a while she'd make pollo guisado con tostones—"

"Mmm . . ."

"And sometimes on weekends, for brunch she'd make mangú."

"Mangú?"

"Mashed plátanos, eggs, fried meat, and cheese."

"Oh my *God*, that sounds good."

"It was. It was." He wipes his mouth with a napkin. Then his eyes twinkle and he turns to me. "Hey. I got an idea."

"Yeah?" I got an idea, too, and it's all about Tenn taking me to the beach, a cooler full of tostones and soup. Or taking me home and cooking coq au rivers or whatever the hell he just said. Us eating at his dining table. By candlelight. In bed.

"About making up with your sister."

At the mention of Teal, I deflate on the inside. On the outside, I smile and raise my eyebrows and say, "Oh? Do go on."

"Y'all must've had dishes like that. Food from when things were good. Things you don't make anymore."

I nod slowly. "Yeah . . ."

"What if you surprised her? What if you made her favorite dinner?"

I think of happiness on Teal's face when I pull out a platter of cheesy enchiladas from the oven. For some reason, it's hard. It's much easier to imagine her spitting in the food or taking the whole tray and throwing it out the window. "I could try that. This weekend." It's much better than any other ideas I have.

"So dinner is your plan for your ghost situation. As for my ghost . . ." He fishes a notecard from his pocket. "I wrote down a few things I remember from when we used to talk." He hands it to me.

- *a ton of little brothers and sisters*
- *lives by (or used to live by) a streetlamp*
- *went to St. Theresa's (?)*
- *one year younger than me (c/o '04)*
- *snorts when she laughs*

"A ton of brothers and sisters?" I sound incredulous. I know I never told Tenn I had imaginary brothers back in the day.

He shrugs. "She said 'siblings' a lot, so I assumed. And she took care of them, like, all the time. It sounded like there were a thousand of them by how busy she was."

Well, that sounds about right. And now I do remember saying "siblings" a lot, because I was terrified if I revealed I had two little sisters he'd somehow figure out it was me. "Okay." I glance back down at the card. "And she lived by a streetlamp. This is really narrowing it down, Tenn."

He snorts. "I just wrote all I could think of. I'll add more as they come."

"She went to St. Theresa's?"

"Once she let me call her while she was there."

"Yeah?" It was when I had rejected his offer to meet in person and I knew he'd be super disappointed. And I wanted to offer some part of me, even if that part was a phone number to church, and a time I'd be there, so I wouldn't have to give my real landline.

In an instant, I'm transported there. The walls around me wood paneling, the carpet might've once been blue or violet but over time has faded to a mud gray. The books on the shelves are titled things like *Jesus Takes the Wheel: Twenty-One Stories of Catholic Compassion in Modern Times*. His voice, so deep on the phone that it vibrates. *Is this my Silvergurl?* he asks. *I'm* the *Silvergurl*, I say in return, giggling. The sound of him makes me even more nervous than I am, sneaking a call from a boy in the religious education director's office.

"Yeah. We talked for, like, five minutes before she had to go. But she laughed a lot. And in one of her laughs, she—"

"Snorted."

He laughs now. "It was cute."

Was not. I went home and cried; I was so embarrassed. "So what would you like me to do with this?"

"Well, you're class of '04, too, right? Can you just think about it and see who might fit these criteria? Or look at a yearbook? I've looked myself, but I really didn't know a lot of people in the year behind me."

I nod slowly. "I could do that."

"Here." He pulls out a thick navy book embossed in gold letters. Cranberry High School, 2003, his senior year. "I brought one of mine just in case you didn't have it."

"Thanks. I honestly couldn't tell you where any of my year-books are." Knowing Nadia, they're tossed on some bookshelf or another, under a hundred other books and candles and stones. I flip through it after he hands it to me, not really looking or reading anything. "Tenn, can I ask you something?"

"Anything." His gaze flits to my lips so fast, if I'd blinked I'd have missed it. I have to turn away or I'm going to lose all train of thought.

"Why do you want to find her so bad?"

He inhales sharply, then turns to face the lake. It really is a perfect lake day. The water is so still, it looks like a piece of polished Paraiba tourmaline. The sky is full of clouds like whipped cream and cotton candy, set against a blue that reminds me of butterfly pea tea.

"I left college, too," he finally says. "I never finished. It broke my mom's heart. An education—it was all she ever wanted for me. And . . ." He sighs. "I guess like you, I spent some time wandering. I bartended, I worked as a tour guide for caves out west. I sold Himalayan salt lamps in a tourist shop in Sedona." He smiles and I can't help but smile in return. "I didn't like coming home and seeing that heartbreak in her eyes. I told her school wasn't for me—not then, at least. But she didn't like hearing that."

"I can imagine," I say softly.

"And so my trips home happened less and less. And then she—well. She died. And after something like a month, I tried to remember back to when she and I were happy, like really, really happy with each other. And it was senior year. It was when I was talking to this girl. And as stupid as it sounds, I wonder if finding her will feel like maybe I can get that back again."

I blink. "Get what back?"

He looks at me, right in my eyes. "The feeling like . . . everything was going to be okay." He shrugs. "I miss that feeling. A lot."

I close my eyes for a moment, then take a breath when the tears have made their way back inside. "Yeah. Me too."

21

WHEN I GET HOME, I CHECK IN ON LAUREL. SHE DOESN'T want to talk about catching her husband sucking neck like a vampire in a parking garage; instead, she asks, Are y'all doing anything for Nadia's birthday? It's soon, isn't it?

"Shit," I mumble, pulling up the calendar app. Nadia's birthday is three days away, on Saturday. She's gonna be . . . I close my eyes, calculating. Seventy-four.

For her last eight birthdays, I had flowers delivered, I sent handmade earrings of little gatos that I sculpted to look like Vieja, her old cat who passed a few years back. One year I beaded up a rosary of pink quartz. I sent gift cards for the Olive Garden and Logan's and Corrina's, her favorite bakery supply shop. I did everything I could to try to make up for the fact that I rarely found my way back to Cranberry again.

I think of Tenn's suggestion of making a special dinner to win back Teal's good graces.

Okay. Two birds, one stone, then.

Yes, I text back. You wanna help?

Abso-fucking-lutely.

TENN AND I MEET UP AT THE IVY-COVERED PARKING LOT IN front of Persimmon Graveyard, Cranberry's oldest cemetery. I haven't been here since I was a teenager, joining Laurel and a couple friends to share a bottle of sangria someone snuck out of the fridge without their parents noticing. That night, the sky was so clear, I felt like I could reach up and touch the milk white of the stars. All around us, wild rabbits hopped and jumped, scattering when we started making howling wolf noises once the wine got us tipsy enough.

Now, it's the middle of the day, the sunshine so thick, my skin feels like it's burning through my thin white T-shirt. Tenn's not here yet, so I push through the rusty iron gate, feeling like I'm stepping through layers and layers of time. Time and *stories*. Most of these graves are so old, they're unmarked. The only indication they're here is the blocks of sunken moss-earth, all in a row like carefully set emeralds.

Amá Sonya never goes anywhere near graveyards or funeral homes. I wonder if it's that she sees or hears or feels the ghosts there, fuzzy-edged, roaming, desperate for human contact they're not going to get, except, perhaps, through her. I guess I can understand a little better the way she denies her gift. I've only got one ghost and that's more than enough.

"Hey."

I startle, jumping back, nearly twisting an ankle over a white rock I think might be a headstone. "Shit. You scared me!"

Tenn walks up, his eyes dropping down to my feet. "I'm sorry. You okay?"

"I'm okay."

He doesn't say anything for a moment as he draws his eyes back up slow, over my legs, bare because I'd worn midthigh cutoffs. He turns away, his cheekbones maybe a shade pinker than normal. "Sorry I'm late. You find anything yet?"

"Just got here, myself."

"Right. Let's get to it, then."

He and I wander toward the far end of the graveyard, searching. It extends deep under the trees, where barely any light reaches. There's a swath of deep-forest Indigenous plants—trillium, all blooming in deep bloodred, and in between, jack-in-the-pulpit, only a few blooms, with their elegant, lilylike flowers the color of peridot. I ask for their permission, leaning in, my hand extended, and a handful lean back toward me. God and the creation of Adam. (The plants are obviously God.)

"I think we could harvest a few of these," I say. "There's so many, and native plants are becoming really lucrative." I realize how fucked up that sounds aloud. Native plants. Lucrative. Capitalism. Sigh.

"Sounds good."

We grab trays and hand shovels from the back of my van and get to work, being mindful of not clearing house in any one square foot.

"You've got a lot of books in your van," he says as he packs dirt around an unflowering trillium.

"Yeah . . . you should see my house. Nadia could make furniture with the number of books she owns."

"Nadia, that's your grandmother, right?"

"My great-aunt."

"Ah."

I sit back, remembering that as much as Nadia wasn't there for us, emotionally, physically, she was always there through books. "When we were little, she'd read to us June Jordan and Sandra Cisneros. Poetry. She'd read us creation myths and cookbooks and novels featuring women who'd had enough and moved to the other side of the world." That last genre, it was like a premonition for me.

"So no children's Bibles or lions, witches, and wardrobes for y'all, huh?"

I laugh. "No. I didn't even read anything like that till I was in college." I spread dirt out over pulled roots, topping it with forest floor leaves. "Well, come to think of it, maybe a little, with the witches. Nadia had—and has—lots of books on magic, too. Some of our nighttime stories were actually spells." I can't help my smile as I remember it. "She called us her little wild brujas. I was the witch of wild things. Teal was the witch of wild lightning." And Sky was the witch of wild criaturas—creatures.

Nadia hasn't called us her little witches since before Sky died. I won't say my smile falls as I consider this fact, but it certainly dims.

"The witch of wild things," he repeats with a half smile. "I like that."

I look down before he can read my face. How I enjoyed hearing it from his lips.

"And your mom? What did she call you?"

I shrug. "I was seven when she left. But I remember *querida*. She said *querida* a lot." So much that if someone calls me that now, even if it's some old man saying good morning at the grocery store, it feels like a knife in the gut.

"I'm sorry. That must've been difficult."

I almost say the normal script. *It's fine. It was worse for Teal.* But that's not true. Teal was just the one who was allowed to feel what she felt. I was the one who had to learn how to soothe her—not that I ever could, really.

"And your dad?"

I shrug. "Never knew him. Don't want to, either. What about your dad?"

He pauses, sitting back in the dirt. We're both filthy at this point, but honestly it's just part of the job description. "He—well. He's . . ."

I wince, remembering what he'd told me about his father back in the AIM days. That guy . . . didn't sound like a great person.

Before Tenn can finish his sentence, though, a cackle of thunder booms so loudly, it rattles the ground. Then the dark clouds I hadn't even noticed gathering overhead like a cloak—they break. The rain is so immediate, so thick, I can't see my hand reached out in front of me through sheets of gray.

"The van!" I shout, and we balance the trays in our arms and run toward the parking lot.

I open the back door as fast as I can, and we shove the trays in and then, as though we'd exchanged an unspoken agreement, we both climb in ourselves, each sitting cross-legged, facing the back, the door overhead acting like a little awning.

Tenn turns to me and glances at my shirt. He flips his face back toward the rain so fast, I furrow my brow, glancing down.

Black bra. White shirt. Pouring rain. Great.

His T-shirt is pretty thin, too, though. And I'm noticing cuts of muscle where I didn't even know muscles were supposed to be, the baby blue fabric clinging to them in a way that makes me jealous. Jealous of a shirt. That's who I am now.

Crossing my arms over my chest, I say, "Um. I wrote down a few names of girls who might be your AIM friend."

"Yeah?" he says, cautiously facing me. Once he notices my arms covering my bits, he relaxes.

"I'll text them to you. But I'm warning you now, you didn't give me a lot to work with. Adding in the fact that I wasn't some social butterfly in high school . . ."

"Right. You said you knew all about being uncool a while back. Was that from then?"

I freeze for a moment, racking my brain, trying to remember . . . right. It was when he'd given me a ride home from the Lounge and I'd accused him of being way too cool. Obnoxiously cool. "Oh. Well, I've never been cool, actually."

He snorts. "You? The woman who made a park ranger nearly piss his pants by just talking to him?"

"I—that's—"

He leans in further. "The woman who can look at a dormant rose and somehow know what exact shade and color its flowers are?" He's so close, his voice vibrates in my sternum just like thunder. "The woman who can touch a seed and know where it was found, even if it was in a fucking convenience store on the Florida Panhandle?"

I suck in air in what could be described as a gasp. "Well . . ."

"The woman who can carve metal and set gemstones and shit?"

He's leaned in even further, his face delighted with whatever's written on mine. Being revealed on mine.

"My van isn't cool. Not like your Boss." I manage it out in a whisper. He smiles, crinkling up his dark eyes in this mischievous way that makes my stomach flip and my heart speed up.

I think he knows I want to kiss him.

I think he's known I've wanted to kiss him since I saw him in Nate's office three weeks ago. Since I was fifteen years old. And even knowing this, he doesn't lean back. He stays still, suspended in a universe made only of possibility.

It feels as though the lightning out there has made its way in here, with the air between us charged like the single moment before an inevitable strike.

He hasn't moved away, I think. *He's only gotten closer.*

Like a plant, reaching for my hand. Saying yes.

So I lean toward him, in return. And then I kiss Tennessee Reyes.

22

THE FIRST THING I NOTICE IS HOW SOFT AND WARM HIS lips are. The second is the sound of surprise that comes from his throat. I jump back. "I'm so sorry," I gasp. "I thought—"

"No, you thought right," he says, his voice unbearably husky, and he cups my face in both hands, and this time he presses his mouth to mine.

I'm hyperaware of his heat, of his stubble scraping me over and over as he puts his closed lips on my mouth, on the line of my jaw, where the contact ripples out like a stone in a lake, pleasure mounting so fast I don't know what to do with myself. He takes my bottom lip in, touching it with the tip of his tongue. I return the favor, doing the same, except I run my teeth over him in a gentle, quick bite.

Instantly his hands run down my shoulders, to my waist, and he pulls me over his lap, lying back. Two trays of plants knock over but neither of us cares. I bend toward him and this time when we kiss, we open our mouths. When our tongues meet, I moan, and he involuntarily lifts his hips, only a little but enough. Enough that I feel him, big and hard, against me where I'm already wet. Enough that I pull back because I am *this* close to coming.

"Is this how it normally is?" I say in one big gasp.

He pushes on his forearms, his breath heavy. "How what normally . . . wait." He blinks. "Was that . . . your first kiss?"

"No." I shake my head. I don't know how to explain it. "It's like . . . I've never felt so . . ." Wired. Electric. Near orgasm so *soon*. "Intense before. This isn't normal for me. It's not normal . . . is it?"

He gives me a half smile, his eyes dropping slowly down my neck, to my breasts, to my core, still against where he's hard, and he gives me a rough shake of his head. "No. It's not." Then he leans up and we keep kissing.

I run my hands over his chest, putting my weight on his pecs as I grind, one, two, three times. He grabs my waist tight, grunting in a way that makes my stomach sizzle. When he slides his hand up my chest, over my shirt, over my breast, I break the kiss and moan. When his thumb runs over my nipple, I swear I tingle and contract in a small orgasm, a little preview of what could happen if I keep going like this with him. I am wearing all my clothes and I came just a little bit, within what? Seconds of kissing this man? And it kind of scares me. I jerk back, off his hips, scrambling to pull my legs in front of me as some kind of armor.

"Shit. Did I hurt you?" He pushes up, looking me over.

I shake my head. I don't know how to put what I'm feeling into words so I burst out with "I didn't have sex until I was twenty-eight."

He opens his mouth like he's going to say something, but closes it when there's no obvious response.

"That's my most embarrassing moment. I didn't have sex for the first time until last year."

He pulls himself up, slowly, sitting cross-legged, facing me. I make a point to not look anywhere below the waist, and even then I can see . . . things.

"That's not . . ." He pauses, like he's trying to shake himself out of a reverie. "That's not embarrassing, Sage."

"It was, though. It was the most embarrassing moment of my life."

"Oh," he says, taking in the tears filling my eyes. "It's not that you were twenty-eight. Something happened that embarrassed you."

I nod miserably. "Something . . . lots of things . . . happened."

"Do you want to tell me about it?"

I shut my eyes tight. Thick tears spill out, but when I open them and glance around, Sky isn't anywhere to be found. I don't know how she does it or where she goes, but she knows when to respect my privacy, I guess. "You're not mad that we stopped?"

"Hey." He reaches for my hands. "I'll never get mad over anything like that. Got it?"

I nod. "Got it."

He stares at my eyes for a few seconds and says, "I think you need pie."

"I do?"

"Yeah. Why don't you follow me with your van? I've got pie at my place."

"Oh. Your place." My heart leaps a little. "You're sure you're okay with me coming over?"

He smiles at me and it's kind and wicked at the same time. It makes me feel better instantly. "I'm sure. Come on, Sage. We both need pie."

"WOAH," I SAY WHEN I GET OUT OF MY VAN IN FRONT OF AN A-frame home made entirely of stone. The grout between the stone is a blue I can only describe as storybook, don't ask me how that is, but it's true. It's got skylights built into the moss-green roof, and big open windows all around. There's no porch, but that's not necessary, not with floor-to-ceiling windows like that, open to the layers and layers of woods. "Your home is beautiful."

"Thanks, but it's not mine," he says. "My best friend is letting me stay here while he's having archaeology adventures on ships and icebergs."

"Best friend," I murmur. I follow him up the stone steps toward the golden, carved front door. "You mean Abe Arellano?"

"Yeah," he says, giving me a smile as he opens the door. "How'd you know it was him? You know Abe?"

Again, a fact of his life I know from my stint as Silvergurl. This time I have a good cover. "I saw a lot of pictures of you together in the yearbook."

"Ah. Yeah. He's like a brother to me."

It's as cozy as you'd think on the inside, with green walls mounted with drums and art and masks. On every piece of furniture, there's like a dozen throw blankets and pillows in all patterns and textures, from purple falsa to deep blue and brown Navajo patterns. The floor is a mosaiclike tile, cold under my socks after I slip my shoes off. "It looks like a Pinterest board exploded in here."

"He hired his sister to decorate. So don't be too impressed. With him, I mean. Iris's the one who did the work."

"Consider me impressed," I say. "With Iris."

He leads me to the open kitchen, where a breakfast nook is tucked into a bay window, overlooking a pond in the back filled with orange, shimmering fish. "Wow. Did Iris do the water feature, too?"

"Yeah. She's good, huh?" He pulls out a container from the fridge and places it on the counter. "I hope you like chocolate."

"I love it, in fact." As I watch him cut slices, I say, "So do you always have pie stocked up, or—"

"Ha, no. Uh. There's a lady at the bakery . . ."

"Oh." I say. "Like . . . you're dating her?"

"No! No. I'm not dating anyone." He pauses, licking chocolate off his thumb, making my stomach somersault. After he washes his hands, he brings me a big slice of pie. "She just likes to give me free stuff."

"Is that it? It doesn't have anything to do with the fact that you're beautiful and tall and sexy?"

His eyebrows drop as he surveys me. His cheeks are pink and I'm pretty sure mine are, too. "You're beautiful and *short* and sexy," he concludes with a grin.

"And yet there are no free pies in *my* fridge." The way he's looking at me, I'm afraid I'm going to jump on him any second. I shatter this impulse with, "So, about my embarrassing moment."

"Yeah?"

"His name was Gregory."

"Hate him already."

I snort. "Yeah. Anyway, he was my boss, where I taught. Department head." I take a bite of pie. "Wow, this is rich."

"You like it?"

"I do. Tell your bakery girlfriend thanks for me."

"She's not—" He laughs when he sees me smiling. "Go on."

"Well, I thought he was so . . . I don't know. Romantic. Not that he ever did anything romantic, mind you. But he was this absent-minded, mad professor, always talking about theories and recommending books no one had ever heard of."

"And sort of laughing at you when you said you hadn't heard of them? Yeah, I know the sort."

"Right? I didn't realize he was laughing *at* me until it was too late. I thought he thought I was endearing." I shrug. "Anyway. I always had this fantasy, right? Of my first time. There would be candles and like, mystical music, and okay, maybe it wouldn't blow my mind—"

"It should have. Just saying. You should've expected to have your mind blown."

"Well, I was trying to be realistic." I put my fork down and place my hands on my knees. "And, like . . . *he* needed to feel right. The guy. That's why I was a virgin for a while. With the men I dated—not that there were many—none of them felt right to me."

"But this guy did?"

I shake my head. "In retrospect, no. I just convinced myself he did. I think I got tired of waiting, to be honest. Anyway. He knew about my . . . inexperience. He knew what I wanted. For my first time. And he said he had it all planned for me."

I look at Tenn, where he's patient, watching, his pie all finished.

"And . . . well. He took me to his place. He took me to the bedroom. And I kept thinking, okay, now he's going to do what I want. Now he's going to put on music. Now he's going to pull out the candles. But he didn't. He kept undressing me, and kissing me, and finally it was about to happen. And I said . . . *What about the candles?* It was all I could think of to say to address . . . the inadequacy. He was confused—I mean, we'd had a *whole* conversation about it—"

"He didn't listen."

"Right. That's something about him I figured out too late, too. Greg *never* listened." I sigh. "Anyway he jumped up and rummaged and found a candle. It was dirty. It smelled like vieja perfume. Thick and florally and eye watering. And then he fucked me." I clasp my hands together, tapping my fingers. "It felt horrible."

"He didn't—" Tenn pauses. "He didn't . . . prepare you? Like with his fingers? And other things?"

I shake my head. "He . . . did not. I was so nervous, I was shaking. I wasn't . . . prepared at all, to use your word. And after it started, after I realized it wasn't going to get any better, I just watched that candle the whole time." I look out the window, where it's started raining again, the leaves and branches of the elderberry and pine dancing under it. "It's so weird that's what I remember most vividly from my first time. I kept thinking, *Where did he get that thing? Did his mom get it for him a thousand holidays ago? Did he dumpster dive?* And before I knew it, it was over." I shrug. "He rolled off me, took a shower, and ordered pizza."

"No cuddling?"

I shook my head. "None. Not that I was in the mood for it." I take the fork, dragging it across the plate, putting the crumbs of crust in a little pile. "Anyway, we did it one more time. He kept pushing it and pushing it and finally, I was like, okay. I figured it wouldn't be any worse . . . except it was."

Tenn's jaw tightens. "Did he hurt you?"

"No. Not like that. He . . . well, in the middle of it, I started to feel sick. It felt really bad again, and I asked him to stop. He said, and I quote, *Wait, I'm almost finished*. And I said, I yelled, *Stop it!*" I look back up at Tenn, who's frozen except for that muscle in his jaw. "And he got mad at me. He started *condescending* to me. He said I was acting like he raped me, and I was delusional and deranged, and finally I said, no, I don't think I like sex very much." I look down for this next part. "And he said, some women aren't meant to be good in bed."

That was the most embarrassing part. That somehow, he'd

made it my fault, and the shame touched me so deeply, my cheeks felt like they burned for hours afterward.

"That fucking . . ." Tenn's growl startles me. "Sorry, Sage, but I can't think of a strong enough word for him."

"I appreciate the sentiment." I smile at him but he's all puffed up, his fists tight, his shoulders tense, his eyes shiny and sharp like daggers. "Uh—well. At the end of the semester he fired me. Said it was budget cuts but I'm pretty sure the unofficial reason is I was bad in bed." I swallow. "The worst part wasn't even how bad the sex was, or that he blamed me for it. It was having to leave my job. Teaching silversmithing was like a literal dream come true, you know?"

Tenn sighs, running a hand over his five-o'clock shadow. The almost-beard thing, Laurel had called it. "It fucking kills me, knowing he did that to you." He looks at my face. "You know he was projecting, right? Only a guy who's absolute shit in bed blames the woman."

"Well, I'm not that experienced," I say, looking back down at my hands.

"No, Sage. No." He scoots his chair over and puts his hand under my chin, gently lifting my head up. All I can see is the gold flecks in his eyes when he says, "You asked me if that intensity was normal, back there in your van?"

I nod.

"It's not. You've got to know, it's not. When I kissed you, I felt like my spirit left my body. I want you to know that. I felt like I had died kissing you, it was so good. I know we haven't gone to bed, you and me, but I already know it's impossible that you'd be bad at it."

I swallow when he wipes away two tears with his thumbs. "You probably say that to all the women you flirt with."

"There's only one woman I've even wanted to flirt with in

years, Plant Whisperer." He whispers this so close, I feel his breath warm on my cheek.

"To be clear, you're talking about me, right?"

He chuckles. "I mean you. Yes, Sage. You."

I know I said I wasn't going to fall for this sweetness again. But when I look into Tenn's eyes right now, all I see is sincerity. And the thing is, we're not teenagers anymore. Maybe his interest in me actually means something now. It sure feels like it does.

"Are you going to kiss me again?" I ask.

"Do you want me to?"

"I do."

He puts his lips to mine, soft as the leaves of cosmos. And then he pulls back just a touch and says, "Just kissing, okay?"

I understand immediately. He wants me to know he's got no expectations. He wants me to know I'm safe with him. "Okay," I say. He takes my hand and leads me to the sofa, where for the next twenty minutes, we make out like teenagers, the rain softening all around us until there's only the drips from trees like ink, writing stories across this whole landscape.

"YOU ASKED ABOUT MY DAD, EARLIER," HE SAYS AS HE HOLDS my hand, walking me to the van.

"Yeah?"

"I've actually got a meeting with him Saturday night."

"Oh, really? I was going to ask if you wanted to come to Nadia's party that night, but . . ."

He smiles. "I wish I could, but you don't cancel or postpone things with my dad."

I'm leaning against my van, barely noticing the wet seeping into the back of my shirt. "Where are y'all going to dinner?"

He laughs. "My dad doesn't do dinner. He does meetings. Everything is . . ." He sighs, running a finger over my knuckles. "You asked about him and the easiest way to explain it is everything is transactional for him. Everything. Even the love of his child." He gives me a sad smile. "I'm meeting him for the first time in years because he's got something I want really, really bad."

I want to ask what it is but I'm not sure if it's my place yet. If we're there yet. "Do you think he'll give it to you?"

"I don't know. I guess we'll see."

I squeeze his hand. "I hope he does."

Tenn looks at my face, from my eyes to nose to mouth to back up again. "I hope so, too."

23

W OW, LAUREL WENT ALL OUT," SKY SAYS, HER ARMS crossed as she surveys the bags covering the dining table. Inside are streamers and banners, extra-fancy paper plates and plastic cutlery. We watch through the window as she rushes back in the house, her arms full of balloons.

"I asked her to grab cake," I say. "That's it."

"Looks like she's distracting herself from that cheater-cheater-pumpkin-eater," Sky responds. I say nothing because she's not wrong.

Laurel comes in, breathless, handing me the balloons. "Okay. Last thing to grab. The cake."

"You sure you don't want help?"

"I'm good! You start on those enchiladas, woman! It's almost time!"

We have two hours, but okay. I start mincing onions when Teal appears on the stairs, rubbing her eyes. "What the hell is all this?"

I glance at Sky, who's looking longingly at a photo of the three of us when we were tiny. Framed in hammered brass, hung over the table. Me, seven, Teal, five. Sky was two. We're cheesing it up something awful, smiles bigger than our faces, Sky in my skinny arms. She didn't remember Mama at all. All she knew was me and Nadia and Teal and sometimes I wonder if that was anything close to enough.

I look back at Teal. "Nadia's birthday, remember? I texted you and you said you'd be there?"

"Oh, right. Shit. I forgot."

I close my eyes and take a deep breath. I've asked this woman for next to nothing in our whole lives and yet . . .

"I'll get Dawson to cover my shift."

I blink, my jaw dropped in shock. "Really?"

"Yes," she says, already annoyed.

Laurel plops in. "Oh, hey, Teal!" Teal says hi and then stomps back upstairs. Laurel places the cake on the counter. "Cinnamon breakfast cake covered in churros." She turns to me. "Now what? You need me to do the beans? The meat? Chop cilantro?"

She's so breathless, I say, "Why don't you take a break and have a cup of coffee? You've done enough."

"Not nearly enough. The enchiladas are barely started!" She grabs the knife from my hand and starts slicing the red onions like she's a contestant on *Chopped*.

Laurel loves organizing, planning, and prepping. Always has. That's why she's going to be awesome at converting the abandoned lighthouse to a sweet and cozy B&B. The problem is, when she's stressed, she turns up the dial to an eleven, and it's all you can do to get out of the way before you're covered in Post-its scrawled with self-help affirmations and holding a planner in which the rest of your year is penned for you.

"Laur," I say, gently putting my hand on her arm. "You're doing it again."

"Doing what?" She turns around. "Oh. I'm Martha Stewart on Unholy Amounts of Caffeine?"

I nod.

She sighs. "Okay. I'll take that coffee. Or, er—tea?" I hand her some chamomile with a wink.

Once I have the sauce simmering and the tortillas rolled and stuffed with cheese, I sit down next to her. "You ready to talk about it?" I've texted her a hundred times since that day we spied on Jorge and Cynthia Peterson, but she always changes the subject.

She places her mug on the table. "Every night, I square my shoulders and march into his office. I have the words ready. I know what I'm going to say about her, about him. About the fact that I've already packed his suitcase and he's failed to notice." Her voice breaks and she takes a breath. "But once I get in there, I freeze. If he happens to see me at all, he says, *Hey baby, you mind grabbing me a drink?*" She shrugs. "That's as far as I've gotten with confronting him. By getting him a fucking beer."

"Confronting who?" Teal's appeared again, in an off-the-shoulder hot pink dress, her hair in a cute, messy bun.

Laurel and I look at each other. I don't know how to read her face—is that panic? Confusion? "Oh—" I say. "Laurel has an issue—with the lighthouse . . . and—"

"It's okay," Laurel says. "You can tell her."

"Tell me what?"

I glance at Laurel again, and she nods. "Jorge's fucking his assistant."

"He's *what*?" Teal's mad voice is so loud, it almost echoes.

"He's cheating *again*? After all that bullshit he put you through when you were dating?"

"Granted," Laurel says. "I haven't confirmed the fucking part, but he did try to suck her neck off in a parking garage in the middle of the day, so I think it's a safe assumption."

Teal looks at us for a moment, then nods a little, like she's decided something. "You need something much stronger than chamomile." She turns and flings open the freezer door, digging and digging until she pulls out a frosted bottle, *MOONSHINE* scrawled on it in Sharpie.

Laurel dumps her chamomile in the sink and holds the cup toward Teal. "Fill 'er up."

Teal grabs two more mugs. "You too, Sage?"

I freeze. "Me?"

"No, the *other* Sage." She's staring at me, her hand on her hip, and even though she still kind of looks like she hates me, for the first time, I get a sense of something more nuanced. That Teal's in pain. That if she hates *me* enough, she won't feel that pain so acutely, like she's drowning in it. That maybe that hate isn't a thing in and of itself—maybe it's inextricably linked to something she can't bear to look at. Like she's afraid looking at it would kill her.

"Take it." Sky stands behind Teal. Her hair at her waist, her face nowhere near sixteen anymore. *Ghosts don't age.* "Take the drink, Sage." Sky nods. "It'll help."

I look to Teal. "Sure. Pour me one."

BY THE TIME NADIA ARRIVES, WE'RE ALL WARM AND TOASTY. "Surprise," we yell, nowhere near in unison, and there are a few giggles mixed in. Nadia's delighted—Teal and I are in the kitchen at the same time, *not* pointing steak knives at each other—and soon she finishes off the moonshine. We eat the enchiladas, siz-zling from the oven ("Wow, I haven't eaten this in a while," Teal says with an *actual smile*—score for Team Sisters Getting Along Again!), and after thirty minutes of drinking, Laurel's trying to teach us how to belly dance.

"Jesus! No!" Laurel screeches. "Nadia, I said no air-humping!"

"How am I supposed to 'pop' and 'lock' without—"

"This needs to stop!" Teal yells, her hands over her eyes. "No more!"

"What, like it's hard?" I say, swirling my hips around and around.

Laurel appraises me and says, "You're just moving your chest in a square, Sage."

"What?" I look down. "Oh. Where are my hips again?" I press my hands to them. "Oh. There. Okay."

"We need water *now*. Water and cake. Otherwise we're going to have such bad headaches tomorrow." Teal's grabbing bottles from the fridge and directing us back to the kitchen table. Sky's in the living room, on the outside, looking in. Her hands folded behind her, mostly in silhouette, her face unreadable. I raise my eyebrows at her, but she just shakes her head.

"How about some coffee for the birthday vieja?" Nadia calls, and Laurel grabs the perc to get it going.

"So, Sage," Laurel says. "How are things going with a certain Tennessee Reyes?"

"Who's that?" Nadia asks.

"My partner. My *work* partner."

I stare at my slice of cake so hard, Laurel immediately shouts, "Something happened, didn't it?!"

"What?" I scoff, throwing an arm lazily her way. "No. Between me and Tenn? *No*. Of course not."

"Oh my God. You're the worst liar," Teal groans.

"Spill. God knows I'm not getting any anytime soon." Laurel places four cups of coffee at the table, each one sweetened and creamy to our liking. When she sits, she makes a get-on-with-it motion. "Is he good?"

"Good at what?" I take a sip of coffee.

Teal rolls her eyes. "At dicking you down."

"Language," Nadia says with a fake frown.

"Fine. Laurel's asking if he's good at *fornication*."

"Oh my God." I cover my eyes. "All we've done is kissed."

"I knew it!" Laurel raises her fist. "I called it!"

"We just kissed," I repeat. "No down dick or whatever you just said." Teal snorts and briefly we smile at each other.

I glance over at where Sky is, leaning against the opening of the kitchen. I thought that she'd be thrilled. Clearly, I'm closer to our mutual goal of helping her move on, right? But instead, Sky looks devastated—curled in on herself a little, like she might cry. I give her a questioning stare, and then Teal asks, "What the hell are you looking at?"

"What? Nothing." I shake my head and say the first thing that comes to mind. "Tenn wants me to help him find this girl he used to chat with in high school on AIM."

Laurel tilts her head at me, her eyes narrowing. Shit. I drunkenly forgot she knows *exactly* who Tenn used to chat with in high school on AIM.

"You used to do that AOL chat box all the time, Sage," Nadia says, and my lie floods around me so thickly, I pull my hand back from my fork like I've been burned, knocking over my coffee in the process.

"Crap," I say, jumping up for napkins. But before I can cross the room, Sky walks in, right in front of me. She reaches between

Laurel and Teal, her finger dipping into the spilled coffee, drawing it across the table.

"Why is the coffee moving like that?" Laurel asks, her voice full of awe. They can't see her. As far as they know, the coffee's currently moving itself all over the table like autonomous ink.

Sky's writing something. *I . . . M . . . I . . .*

"Is this a joke?" Teal asks, glaring at me. "Is this *your gift*, Sage?"

"Since when could I do *that*?" I ask. "Do you see a tree attached to the liquid there?"

Meanwhile, Sky's still drawing. *I MISS TH—*

"It's her, isn't it?" Nadia asks with a low voice. She's looking at me. Why is *everyone* looking at me?

"I don't know what you mean," I say, my voice so unsure, the lie is immediately apparent. I want to ask Sky what on God's green earth does she think she's doing—doesn't she know she's messing *everything* up?—but then she finishes with a flourish.

I MISS THIS.

And then, after, in her cursive signature: —*Sky*

"What the fuck," Teal says, standing up so fast, her chair almost knocks over. "That's *so* not okay, Sage."

"I didn't do it!" I yell. "Why are you *always* blaming me for shit I never did?"

"Because it *always* comes back to you! Whether we're talking about Sky, or the fact that you abandoned us a *week* after the funeral, or, or that bullshit that went down with Johnny, or—"

"Girls." Nadia's voice is forceful. "Sit."

I sit. Teal sits. We glower at each other.

"Sage," Nadia says. "How long has Sky been haunting you?"

I close my eyes and look down. The silence is so visceral, it presses in on me like a vise. "Since she died." It's so vivid in my mind, the memory pours through me like rain. How when I finally, *finally* could cry, weeks after the funeral, it happened on Nadia's red couch, right there in the living room. How it was evening, late summer, the light pouring through the window in sheets of green gold. And when I looked up, there was my dead sister, looking just as confused as me. *I think we're connected somehow*, she'd said, before she faded away that first time.

There's a moment of shock in my admitting it. Teal, of course, is the first one to explode. "And you didn't think to tell us? You didn't think that was important information? You didn't think that we might like to *know*—"

"Teal." Nadia makes her tone gentle.

"Whatever." Teal stomps to the porch, grabbing her bag and keys on her way out.

After the front door slams, Nadia asks, "Is she here, now?"

I glance to the right, where Sky's perched on the counter. Papers rustle under her. *Ghosts do not affect the physical world.* When she bends forward, her chin on her hands, her hair's nearly at her knees. *Ghosts do not age.* "She only comes when I cry," I say. "And she sometimes brings me coffee. Chocolate raspberry coffee." It was the coffee she and Nadia re-created, right here in this kitchen, to avoid Starbucks prices. Two pumps of chocolate, one of raspberry, and lots and lots of cream. Sky was always the little kitchen helper, back when Nadia still baked flans all the time.

Nadia sighs. "Can't say I'm not disappointed in you. Teal's right. You should've told us."

I close my eyes and take a breath. When I open them, I say, "Nadia. There's something I've been needing to say to you for a while now."

Laurel puts her hand on mine. "I'm going to make a couple

calls in my car." I can tell she knows what I'm gonna say, the words that need to be heard by Nadia alone. The letters, the sentences, they're underfoot like pine straw, like beetles, like serpents. They slide up my legs, over my belly and lungs and throat. They're on the tip of my tongue and when I nod, even before Laurel's out the door, I tell Nadia, "My whole life, I've been alone. And I'm going to try as hard as I can to explain what I mean." I take a breath. "Since I was seven years old, I made the girls every meal—for two years, standing on the little wooden stool because I couldn't reach the burners. I measured their medicine in the little plastic cups when they were sick. I didn't even notice when *I* got sick, I was so immersed with taking care of *them*."

The hurt is already evident on her face. "I took you in, mija. And you know I worked a lot, to provide—"

"I know, Nadia! God. I'm not saying I'm ungrateful. What I am saying is you disappeared a lot. What I am saying is I didn't have a childhood. You didn't even let me cry when Mama left, because you said Teal was younger and she needed *me* to hold her when *she* cried."

Nadia blinks. "I don't remember saying that."

"That's awfully convenient." It's always that way, isn't it, though? It's so easy for the person who's done you wrong to forget, meanwhile you're the one stuck with the lifelong trauma.

Nadia looks around. Her eyes are a little shiny. I think I might be finally getting through, so of course she begins, "It's getting late, Sage. This isn't the time—"

"The reason why I didn't tell you about Sky is because I have learned, over and over again, that you won't help me. You'll run off to church, you'll scold me for upsetting Teal, but you won't help *me*, Nadia! *I* needed help." I'm crying now. "I was a child and I needed help."

Nadia looks at me for a moment. "This isn't how I wanted this birthday to go."

I scoff. Guilt-tripping, that's just such a great move. "Oh, and you think I planned for this? For Sky to write us messages in coffee from the grave to upset everyone?" I glare at Sky. "Great idea, by the way. For sure you're *well* on your way to the afterlife now."

Nadia stands, moving slowly, her eyes roaming over Sky's direction—looking but not spotting. "I took all of you in," she repeats. "No hesitation."

"Is that what you told yourself when I was in the hospital with the pneumonia I got from taking care of the girls when we all had the flu?" I ask. "Is that what you told yourself when I potty-trained Sky? Is that what you told yourself when I skipped meals because I was too busy making theirs?"

I stand. "Is that what you told yourself when you made me stay home the day they went hiking? So I could clean Teal's room?"

Her only response is to walk to her bedroom door, shutting it so gently, I have to admire the restraint.

LAUREL UNLOCKS HER CAR DOORS WHEN SHE SEES ME WALK up. "How'd it go?"

"Well." I sigh. "I finally told Nadia Flores that she neglected me for most of my childhood."

Laurel nods. She was one of the first to point it out to me. I think her mama knew before either of us, packing extra food for me for lunch throughout high school, sending over casseroles and roast chicken whenever she could so I didn't have to cook another box of mac and cheese for us three while Nadia taught, like, three Bible studies in a row. "I'm proud of you, girl. How'd she take it?"

"Yeah, well, she didn't like it. That summarizes that."

"I'm sorry, love."

"It's fine. It needed to be said." I sigh and look out the window. "Though it would've been nice if the shenanigans had waited till after her birthday."

After a beat, Laurel says quietly, "You didn't tell me about Sky."

I sigh and nod. For some reason, I couldn't tell anyone about Sky. Not even Laur.

"I . . . I was afraid that if I told anyone, they'd think I was to blame for her . . . you know." I blink, and one tear escapes. "What Teal always accuses me of."

"It wasn't your fault, though. You know that, right? It wasn't anyone's fault."

I sigh. "I know. Just let Teal know the next time you see her, all right? She could use the reminder."

There's a beat of silence, and then Laurel says, "What are you lying to Tennessee Reyes for?"

"Oh my God." I lean back against the car seat. That was a weirdly abrupt change of subject. "Because! He asked me to help him find this person, and if I'd said, *Oh, yeah, that was me,* then he'd have to . . . we'd have to discuss . . ."

"The way he hurt you junior year?"

"Yeah. That." I groan. "And I just want to move on, Laur. I'm so tired of blurting things out that are true and uncomfortable and pissing everyone off. From Johnny Miller to—" I wave my hand at Nadia's place. "This. I just want a break from reality. I want to kiss. I want to maybe, eventually, have an orgasm, even."

Laurel laughs. "Wouldn't we all." I laugh, too, and she puts a hand on my shoulder. "Just promise me, if you two start to fall for each other, like for real. For real. That you'll tell him." She turns away. "You don't want to start a relationship on a lie, you know?"

I grab her hand and squeeze. "I know. And I promise. If I fall in love with Tenn Reyes—again—I'll tell him the truth." My heart lurches around uncomfortably, as though it knows I'm telling a whole mess of lies right at this moment. And I really can't think about that right now. I turn to Laurel. "Come on. Let's pack you up some cake."

24

AUGUST 24, 2001

14 YEARS AGO

silvergurl0917: omg. you're back!!?!

RainOnATennRoof: Hey, there's my Silvergurl. And yeah, we just got in yesterday.

silvergurl0917: how was it??!?!

RainOnATennRoof: Good. Hot. Best parts were my tía's cooking, and so much dancing. So much fucking dancing, and every abuela on the block HAD to dance with me

silvergurl0917: omg that sounds adorable

RainOnATennRoof: Wait until you're forced to merengue

with your family's 90 year old neighbor, then we'll see how adorable it is.

silvergurl0917: omg i cannot stop laughing

RainOnATennRoof: ;)

RainOnATennRoof: Missed you, Silvergurl.

silvergurl0917: ;)

silvergurl0917: i missed you too, Tenn Reyes <3

PRESENT

Promise me if you start to fall for each other for real, that you'll tell him.

I'm folding foil paper over the enchiladas, a little annoyed at Laurel. I mean, I get it. Her marriage started on one big fat lie titled: Jorge *Can* Keep It in His Pants. And now she's hurt and projecting. But this . . . is so different. We're not even together. We made out only exactly twice. He touched my nipple *through* my clothes. Those events do not a love match make.

After the dishwasher's rumbling, I sit back at the table, phone in my hand. I told Tenn that I'd text him some names that may be his AIM girl. It's not exactly a lie, is it? Any one of them might be his Silvergurl. They're not, but hypothetically, they *could* be.

I think of the promise I made Laurel and groan. I begin typing.

Hey. There's something I need to tell you about the AIM friend.

And suddenly, a memory seeps in, and I don't see my phone anymore. I'm seventeen, wearing a brand-new cerulean dress, the prettiest one I could find at the mall. *Wear blue so I'll know it's you.* I'm climbing the beige carpet stairs of a stranger's home, the walls vibrating with bass, and I'm so scared, my heart feels like it's on the outside. *I'll be waiting for you, Silvergurl.*

He wasn't waiting. Not for me, anyway.

I delete the whole sentence and list Joan Watson, Farah Zapata, and Tabitha Williams. Boom. Sent.

Hope this helps, I add.

After, I run a soapy cloth over Sky's ghost scrawl of *I MISS THIS —Sky*, erasing it all back into the crisp white of the plastic tablecloth.

AFTER I WASH MY FACE, THE SMEARS OF GLITTERY VIOLET AND magenta, once carefully applied smoky eye and lip stain, circling down the drain, I lift my face and scream.

Sky stands behind me in a classic villain-in-a-horror-film stance. "Jesus *Christ*," I sputter. "Are you *trying* to give me a heart attack?"

"I'm sorry, Sage."

"It's fine." I run a towel over my cheeks. "Just don't do it again, okay?"

"Not about that. Though I didn't mean to scare you."

"Okay." I grab my nighttime moisturizer.

"I'm sorry for screwing everything up."

I sigh. "Honestly, the way things just magnificently imploded, it was going to happen sooner or later anyway. Don't get too hard on yourself."

She's quiet for a bit. Then adds, "I just couldn't stand it. Being here but not being here. You all . . . laughing. Celebrating. I felt like I was dying all over again."

My heart breaks, just like it did every time she scraped her knee or hit her head when she was little. "I wish I could hug you."

She smiles miserably. "Me too."

I click the bathroom light off and move to the bed, and Sky settles next to me, both of our eyes on the full, silvery moon. It's perfectly aligned in front of my basils, making them look like the ink-blue silhouettes of trees in the distance.

"Sky?"

"Yeah?"

"Remember when you told me how you sometimes dream about Cranberry Falls? Even now?"

"Uh-huh . . ."

"Tell me more about that. Like, what happens in the dreams?"

Sky traces the moon with her finger extended in front of us. The whole room is shades of deep green and teal blues, all except the moonlight lining us, chipped moonstone inlaid along our edges. "Well, up high, sometimes I can see the moon, or daylight."

"Like a skylight?"

"I guess. And sometimes there are animals . . ."

"Animals."

"Wolves. Foxes. Owls." She smiles. "Not a bear. Not yet."

"What else?"

"Um. It's cozy. There are leaves piled all around. Oak, I think. And . . . sometimes there's someone there."

"Someone." I don't know why this alarms me, but it does. They're just dreams, right?

"Yeah. They take care of me."

"How so?"

"I don't know. I just feel it, I guess."

I knit my brow. She's not giving me a lot to work with here. "Well, what do they look like?"

"I don't know. Like I said, it's fuzzy. I can't even picture a face. All they do is sort of shimmer around me."

"Shimmer?"

"Yeah. Like that one tiger's-eye necklace you gave me?"

"Set in gold-fill wire." I'd saved my own birthday money to make her gift.

"Yeah. That shimmery, sparkly effect. It's like they're made of tiger's-eye, set in gold." She finally tears her eyes away from the moon to look at me. "Why do you want to know?"

I shrug. "Because . . ." *Ghosts do not age. Ghosts do not affect the physical world.*

Ghosts do not dream.

"It's nothing. Just curious."

25

NATE'S WORKING AT CRANBERRY ROSE THIS MORNING, overseeing some shipment or another. He stops to say hi while I'm unloading all of the trillium and jack-in-the-pulpits.

"You and Tenn are doing amazing work," he keeps saying, taking trays out of my hands. We walk to the nearest hoop house together. "I mean, I know this was pretty experimental, sending you two out to see if our town had anything special hiding here and there. But you've blown me and Gramps away."

I frown. "We haven't found a whole lot or anything . . ."

Nate grins, and to my surprise, it does nothing for me. He's still handsome, of course, but that smile—it's definitely not a sunrise anymore. It's more like a lamp—real pretty but I'm not going to sit down and write it an ode or anything. "What you've found is great, don't get me wrong, because as awesome as the plants are, we sell stories here. Native New England aster from an old homestead? Woodland flowers from an ancient cemetery? Folks are going to clamor to buy *these* stories if Instagram is any indication."

"Instagram?"

"Oh, yeah. We posted about the aster when y'all found it, and it went semiviral. It got us almost three thousand new followers!"

"Holy cow, Nate. That's amazing." I keep looking at him from the corner of my eye. I mean, he's dating my sister, who currently hates me more than ever, which I wasn't even sure was possible until last night. He's acting pretty normal, though. I clear my throat. "Hey, how are you and Teal doing?"

He smiles as we walk back toward my van. "Good. I think? I hope. I really like her."

"That's good. I mean." I cough. Am I really going to squeeze information about Teal from her new boyfriend? I guess so, because I keep talking. "I'm sure she's told you how she and I haven't gotten along lately. Last night, we had a fight and I didn't know if she—"

"Really?" He's stopped and his brows are furrowed. "No, she didn't mention it."

"Oh," I say.

"Sorry, I'm just a little startled. Teal's always saying how she looks up to you."

"She *what*?" My eyes are wide, but he just laughs.

"Yeah. She really does—look up to you. She's always saying how she wishes she could be more like you."

"More like *me*?" As in spineless? Always saying the wrong thing? Ruining everything around me?

"Yeah. Kind. Independent." He smiles again. "That's one of the things I love about her. She's so honest."

Is she, though? Because based on this conversation alone, Teal's been lying a hell of a lot—either to my face about how shitty of a human I am, or to Nate's face, about how much she doesn't hate me. My instinct is that it's the latter.

We resume walking, rounding a corner, and there, leaning against my van, is Tenn. I can't help it. I smile a smile bigger than any sunset on any planet, and he does the same to me.

"Oh, hey," Nate says with a wave. "How you doing, man?"

"I thought I'd come and help unload, but it looks like y'all have got it."

"I told you that I had it," I say, that same smile on my face. "When I texted you earlier."

"Yeah? Maybe I just wanted to see you."

Nate points behind himself, walking backward, like he knows any closer would be immediate electric shock from some wild sexual tension brewing between me and Tenn. "I've got to help unload a mulch shipment here. Holler if you need anything." Tenn and I both say goodbye without taking our eyes off each other.

"So," he says, putting his hands in his pockets.

"So." I lean on my hip. "How was the meeting? With your dad?"

"Not great." He sighs. "How was Nadia's birthday? With your sister's favorite dinner?"

Now I sigh. "Not great."

He looks at me, up and down, then walks over a few steps and opens the passenger side of his car. "I've got an idea," he says. He gestures inside.

I walk past him, sliding into the car seat. "What's the idea?"

He winks. "It's a surprise." He leans down and gives me a long, gentle kiss.

"Mm," I say. "I like this surprise already."

He winks again and shuts the door. "I think you'll like the rest of it, too."

As we drive, Tenn hands me his phone. My heart sinks a little when I see what's pulled up. The Facebook profile of Tabitha Williams.

"I did some looking into the other two, and they all have lots of pictures with their moms and dads. I can't remember exactly, but the AIM girl didn't have either one or both parents around . . ."

"Ah." My stomach is a mess right now, like I'm climbing to the top of a roller coaster with bare feet. I slide through Tabitha's pictures. She's got one praising someone named Aimee Decker, the woman "who helped raise her." There's only a handful of profile photos, one with her and a dog, one with her and I'm guessing her husband—she's in white and he's in a tux. I click back to her profile, scrolling, but everything is set to private. I can't see her friends, or comments, or posts at all.

"Go back to the one of her wedding," Tenn says.

"Got it."

"See where her husband is tagged?"

"Yeah . . ."

"Well, I was wondering if you wouldn't mind doing me a favor." He grins at me. "Seeing that we're helping each other with our ghosts and all."

"Sure." The fake enthusiasm is so bitter on my tongue. "Anything."

"Assuming you're on Facebook, would you mind messaging her husband from your account? She's got all the privacy settings turned on for her profile."

I click on her husband's profile. She married Daniel Jagger. "His profile's private, too."

"Yeah, but he's got his Messenger open."

It's true. "What do you need me to say?"

"Just let him know you're an old friend of hers. Just curious how she's doing. You *were* friends with her, right?"

I frown and shrug. I might've had lunch with Tabby, like, twice. She sat behind me in biology freshman year. "I guess so. I mean, we weren't enemies or anything." I clear my throat. "Why don't you message him?"

He laughs. "If I were married, and some dude messaged me asking about my wife, I'd ignore the hell out of that shit."

I nod. "Yeah, that makes sense." I wiggle my toe against the floorboard of the Boss. "But . . . I mean. I get that you're trying to get back to that feeling. That's what you said before. The feeling that everything was going to be okay. But isn't this"—I hand his phone back to him—"a lot? What if she's not the girl? I mean, are you going to message the partners of everyone in my year? When does it end?"

His jaw goes tight and he knits his brows together. "You don't have to do it, Sage. It's not a big deal."

"It's a big deal to you."

He doesn't say anything for one long minute. We're on the highway, the sound of rushing air and tires on gravel closing in on all sides, and somehow I haven't felt anything this silent ever. Not even eight years ago when Nadia called me to tell me there had been an accident—that quiet, gut-punching second before she said it. *Sky fell.*

Finally, he sighs. "You ever fuck something up so bad, you spend years and years coming back to it?"

Sky, kissing my cheek. *You sure you don't want to come with us?* I swallow. "Yes."

"I messed up with this girl. And I feel like I owe it to my mom to make my life right, you know? Going back to that feeling I mentioned? Me owning up to the mistake I made back then is an important part of that." He pulls the car to a stop in front of thick, dark woods. He turns to me, his eyes flashing with heartbreaking honesty. "I *know* there's a good chance I won't find her. But I'm going to try anyway."

I nod. I can barely keep eye contact, so I grab my phone from my purse. "I'll message him now."

He smiles. His shoulders relax. "Thank you."

He gets out of the car before I can fail to say *you're welcome* in return.

"WHERE ARE WE?"

I've followed Tenn on a little path in these woods. The more steps I take, the louder the crickets get, until it feels like they're touching the skin of my neck and cheeks and hands. It's dark, the trees so thick it feels close to twilight in here. It's peaceful, too, the wind rustling the trees, the dapples of sunlight running over our bodies like warm, gold silk.

Tenn extends his hands. "This is . . . the reason why I moved back to Cranberry." He drops his arms. "This is my mom's land."

"Yeah?"

"Yeah. Thirty-one acres of woods. She had a dream to build a house here but . . . life got busy."

I look around more closely. This is a *gorgeous* piece of land. It's full of pretty, fine-leafed pines, and flowering dogwoods and red-bud, but there are also hundreds-of-years-old oaks here and there, their trunks spread wide like a car, their branches thick and low enough to put a tablecloth on and have dinner. I immediately think of what a house would look like here, right smack in the middle of all this wild. I imagine a screen door open to a pink dogwood in spring. I imagine looking out a bedroom window at one of these ancient oaks as the moon stretches across one of its limblike branches like a lit-up coin.

My heart aches for this woman. Alba Reyes. I looked up her obituary yesterday. She was *such* a good person. She deserved her dream house in the woods—in *these* woods. "So you're going to build a house here, then?"

"Nah." He's stopped, his eyes on the trees. "My parents, they never finalized their divorce. They were separated for over ten years before my mom finally got the paperwork together, and then my dad decided he wasn't going to sign it. He made it so difficult, she just gave up."

"Why? Did he still love her?"

Tenn laughs. It's hollow. "No. He wanted to punish her for leaving him." He moves on fast. "Anyway, because they never divorced, he inherited all her assets. Her belongings, bank accounts, and property." We're walking again, going at a slow gait. "So this all belongs to him now. And last night, I was supposed to convince him to let me buy it. But instead, he told me it was already sold."

I stop and gasp. "To whom?"

"To a bank. This is prime real estate. The beach is only a twenty-minute drive away. And they've developed everything else between here and downtown. I knew they'd been bugging Mom for a while to sell, but she wouldn't."

"And why wouldn't he let you buy it? I mean, no. That's not how it should've gone down. You're his son. Her son. He should've *given* it to you." I'm so angry, my fists are tight.

"They made him an offer he couldn't refuse. He said he'd give me a cut. But I don't want anything from him. From this." He takes a breath. "I put her ashes here. Mom didn't have a will, but I knew she would've wanted to be in her land. This was her life goal, you know? To retire here. To sit on her big, wraparound porch and watch her grandbabies play in nature. That's what she was always saying to me, like, *Hint hint, Tennessee, find a good woman and make babies.*" We laugh a little, but it's rough going. "And now they're going to build a gated community right over it.

Over *her*." He shakes his head, his eyes shiny. "It's the perfect metaphor for what my dad put her through in her life, to be honest."

I don't know what to do, so I take my arms and wrap them around him. "I'm so sorry," I whisper. He hugs me tight in return, one hand splayed across my back, the other on my hip. He leans his head down and kisses the top of my head.

"They're going to tear the woods to pieces in about a week. That's all I have left of this. Of her dream."

And now I'm crying. Sky appears instantly, sitting on a tree branch in the distance, her face telling me she's heard it all and understands how messed up it is. She puts her hand on her heart before turning away, giving us privacy.

"This is all so horrible," I say after a few minutes, pulling my shirt up to wipe my face.

"Hey," Tenn says softly. "I didn't bring you here to cry, Plant Whisperer."

I sniff. "Yeah? What did you bring me here for, then?"

He grins, and it's back—Tenn's sparkling eyes, his wide mouth, his eyelashes looking thicker as everything crinkles with that smile. "We're going mushroom hunting."

26

JANUARY 1, 2002
13 YEARS AGO

silvergurl0917: hey there. happy new year:)

RainOnATennRoof: Happy New Year, Silvergurl.

RainOnATennRoof: You got any resolutions?

silvergurl0917: ;)

RainOnATennRoof: Oh man. What does that
mean?

silvergurl0917: i made one.

silvergurl0917: it's to get the courage to meet you.

RainOnATennRoof: Really?

silvergurl0917: yes

RainOnATennRoof: For real.

silvergurl0917: yes. i'm going to work on my anxiety and fears first, tho

RainOnATennRoof: like what kind of fears?

silvergurl0917: i dunno. like maybe i'll disappoint you.

RainOnATennRoof: No offense, but that's impossible.

silvergurl0917: okay sweet talker. that's nice and all but my fears didn't just magically evaporate, reading that just now.

RainOnATennRoof: :) How do you think you could ever disappoint me?

silvergurl0917: well

silvergurl0917: lol

RainOnATennRoof: Silvergurl . . .

silvergurl0917: i . . . i don't look anything like the girls you always hang out w/

RainOnATennRoof: what do you mean??

silvergurl0917: **deep breath**

silvergurl0917: i'm not exactly cool, you know? i don't have name brand jeans or anything. my hair is a mess. it's . . . oh my gosh, when it rains, it, like, explodes, you don't understand

RainOnATennRoof: I don't care about brand names. And I think explosive hair is hottttt;)

silvergurl0917: omg Tenn!!!

silvergurl0917: i am lol-ing so hard right now my aunt's going to hear me

RainOnATennRoof: :)

silvergurl0917: seriously, my . . . i'm super short. my shape.. i don't look like a model, okay? low-rise jeans do not work on me. neither does anything baring the midriff. i don't really know how to do my makeup right . . . and i know it's dumb for me to be jealous but . . . it seems like everyone you flirt with . . . is perfect, looks-wise. &they prob do not watch their little siblings w all their free time, you know?

RainOnATennRoof: Wait, everyone I flirt with? lol who do you mean?

silvergurl0917: you know . . . girls . . .

RainOnATennRoof: Listen, Silvergurl? I . . . there's only
one girl I'm interested in right now. And I don't give a
fuck what kind of jeans she wears or how she does
makeup, ok? I literally do not care about any of that.
I care about you. :)

silvergurl0917: omg. now i'm sobbing

RainOnATennRoof: Stop crying, Silvergurl:)

silvergurl0917: hahaha okay, okay. it's more
sniffling now.

RainOnATennRoof: :) OK how about this- you work on
your fears, I work on our perfect meeting spot.

silvergurl0917: :)

silvergurl0917: sounds like a deal <3

PRESENT

"It's a bit late to find morels," Tenn says as we stomp through the
brush. "And I don't much like chicken of the woods."

"I don't think I've ever eaten either of those."

"No? You and your family never went foraging?"

I think of Nadia and my mom, when she was little, trekking
through Cranberry Falls, stopping once a year or so for humanoid

footprints, pressed into the mud, gentle as a prayer. "Not for food, no."

Tenn pauses, and then points to what looks to me like a regular, wide portobello-like shroom, surrounded by baby ferns. "Don't ever eat one of those, or anything that looks like it."

"Why? Would I trip balls?"

He grins at me and my heart feels warm and big and thrilled. "It's a part of the *Amanita* family, and it's very difficult to tell which is edible and which will, as you say, make you trip balls . . . before dropping dead."

I bend next to him, waving my hand over the mushrooms. My gift isn't mushrooms, but mushrooms and plants live so close together that I can still feel it, its consciousness, like the thrum of the heartbeat hidden in its cells. Thump, thump. Not poisonous.

He stands and we keep walking. "But you can tell the difference, right?" I ask.

"Yeah. That one's not toxic. But it's also not what I'm looking for."

"Your mama taught you all this?"

"Yeah. She was a master forager. But even now, after years of experience, I stick to what's easy to ID."

"Like chicken of the corn—"

"Of the *woods*," he says with a laugh. "Though 'chicken of the corn' sounds like a hilarious horror film."

"A poultry nightmare," I say in a deep, movie-narrator voice, then feel elated when Tenn belly laughs. "So what are we looking for today, if not chicken mushrooms?"

He gives me a half smile. "I'm not telling."

"Why not?"

"I want you to use your plant-whispering powers when we find it."

I trip a little. "Yeah?"

He grabs my hand and helps ground me. He's so warm. And big. And wonderful. "Yeah."

We walk in silence for a few moments, and an owl hoots in the distance. That reminds me of what Sky had told me, about her dreams. How animals come to visit her. I'd planned on seeing Amá Sonya today, to ask her more about these ghost rules Sky seems to keep breaking, but this—hiking with this beautiful man through these beautiful woods—is much preferable to sitting in that cold, marble home, filled with signs yelling at me to be *THANKFUL*, *GRATEFUL*, and *BLESSED*.

"Hey, Sage," Tenn says. "How do you do it?"

"Do what?"

"You know. How do you sense all those details about seeds and plants? Stuff no one, not even the most trained and decorated botanist, could know?"

Laurel's the only one who knows about our gifts for sure. Johnny Miller might have an inkling now that I've threatened him with vinery, but he's dumb as shit to not have figured something out every time lightning strikes when Teal's pissed off. It would've required him to do things like care about someone's feelings and pay attention, so, yeah. He didn't know a thing until I pinned him to a dogwood tree.

"My family . . . the women in my family . . . are gifted."

We stop, and Tenn pulls two water bottles out from his backpack, handing one to me. He's quiet. Listening. I take a sip and say, "My sister Sky, her gift was animals. She could coach a hawk onto her shoulder like a parakeet. Teal's is the weather."

"Like Storm from *X-Men*?"

"Yeah, except she can't control it. Stay clear of lightning rods when she's angry."

He laughs and then looks at me, up and down, down and up, in a way that makes my face as well as other parts of my body heat and tingle. "And yours is plants."

"Mine is plants."

I wait for him to laugh, or to call bullshit. But he doesn't. He nods, like I've said the most natural thing in the world. *I was born in Cranberry*, or *My favorite color is indigo mixed with milk, like periwinkle but not quite.*

He takes the water bottle from me, and when his fingers touch mine, it morphs my whole hand into an erogenous zone. He places the bottles in his pack and takes a step closer to me, his eyes so dark now, they mirror this whole forest in night.

I panic. "What was your first time like?"

He blinks and leans back. I'm pretty sure he was about to kiss me, and God, why didn't I let him instead of asking a personal and probably invasive question? "To be clear, you mean sex, right?"

I nod.

I think he sees how nervous I've gotten, because he glances at me once over again, with a quirk of a smile, and then tilts his head forward, urging me to walk with him.

"It was my first year of college. She was a friend, and we went to a party, and we kissed. She said we should go back to her place, so I did."

I'm . . . not prepared for the jealousy that rushes through me. I mean . . . this was when he was eighteen, nineteen. I was still in Cranberry, crying my eyes out over him. I definitely wasn't in the dart-to-the-portrait phase of mourning his friendship. I take a breath as he goes on.

"It lasted a good thirty seconds," he says, laughing. "She was nice about it, though." I don't expect him to, but he keeps going. "I dated around here and there, and then I lived back in Denver for a while, and that's where I met Pia. She was my longest relationship at almost three years. We moved in together, the whole shebang. But when my mom died, she kinda bailed."

"*Why?* That's a brutal thing to go through alone. Jesus."

"Things weren't going well between us, and it was the final nail. I started taking more and more trips out here, trying to get my mom's shit sorted, and she stayed behind. Met someone else."

I try to imagine what kind of person would be lucky enough to have Tenn Reyes and choose someone else. *While* he's in the middle of grieving the biggest loss of his life. I can't help hating her.

"Hold up," he says gently. He cuts into a more bushy part of the woods, off trail. I follow.

There, growing out of a gnarled, knocked-over tree trunk, is a collection of mushrooms. They look like a series of little tables, stacked all over one another, like something Alice would've skipped over while tiny in Wonderland. "This," he says, with a tone of awe. "This is what I'm looking for." He gestures for me to come closer with him, and he starts pulling supplies out of his pack.

I hover my hand over them, letting my thumb fall to graze the top of one.

A long time ago, as teenagers, Teal and I were fighting and she said something she'd intended to really hurt me with. *Talking to plants is gross. It's not natural.* You're *unnatural.*

It didn't sting as she intended, and not because I knew that it had come from jealousy. She's always hated that she can't control her gift and took that out a lot on me, like it was my fault or something.

No, I didn't care about what Teal thought because "talking to plants" feels like the most natural thing in this whole universe. Hearing the songs of plants (and dirt, and mushrooms), being able to reach their cells with my mind, with the tips of my fingers, sensing what can only be described as their consciousness, because yes, plants are conscious, they know what color you're wearing, they know if you're blocking their light, they have nervous systems and can feel pain. Talking to them is as easy as the inhale and exhale of breath.

We literally share an evolutionary ancestor with plants. At some point in our lineages, the lines converge into one. How can speaking with them be unnatural?

"What are you?" I ask the mushroom in a reverent whisper. And then I listen.

"Oyster," I announce a few seconds later. Edible, too.

"Holy shit," he says. He reaches his arm out, where the hairs all over the mushroom tattoos stand straight up. "You just knew that, huh? With your gift?"

He's got the same awe still in his voice. He's looking at me with that sparkling, black heat in his eyes, and he clears his throat, glancing down. I think he doesn't want me to freak out again. "If we could see through the forest floor," he says, "we'd see fungal threads—called mycelium—every-fucking-where. These mushrooms, they're sort of the fruit. The rest of it, the parts we can't see, are the body."

I sit on the forest floor and close my eyes, placing my hands on the dirt. When I connect—when I sense what he's talking about—there's a click in me. It's like I'm plugged into the Matrix, only it's not lime-green code everywhere—it's those white veins of mycelium, connecting everything in this forest in miles and miles of microscopic strands of silk.

"The plants use the threads to exchange resources. And to communicate with one another."

His voice is nearer but I don't open my eyes. "I can feel it." I say it as a whisper.

"You can?"

"Yeah."

"What's it feel like?"

I shake my head, keeping my eyes closed. "It's like . . . I don't know." I blink my gaze open. "No, I do know. Sometimes plants get extra chatty. Some old trees especially." I look around me, at the big oaks, wide and tall and ancient. "Once I heard from a tree, what connects everything in this world is story. Stories hold the universe together. And that's what I see, this . . . mycelium . . . that's what it feels like. It feels like stories, connecting all plants, like the most complicated and beautiful spiderweb of all time."

He's close to me now, sitting next to me. I see the whole forest, the whole world, in his eyes again, and me there, too. I don't lean away when he comes even closer. "Sage," he says, his voice husky, and he kisses me.

My whole body is alive with my own veins, veins that have been created and connected to the veins of mushrooms right here in town, which are created and connected to the veins and webs and threads of mushrooms the world over. Everything electric with life. With stories. One might say that mushrooms are older than story, but only if they believe mushrooms didn't also tell stories.

This is my story right in this moment: Tenn, kissing me so gently, his tongue touching mine, coaxing my mouth more open. Tenn, who I loved at fifteen. Who I've loved since fifteen.

All we do is kiss, and that's more than okay, in these woods destined to be destroyed, which breaks me every time I think about it. But for now, they hold stories and dreams and dappled sun poured between the trees, poured all over us as we kiss, like sweet sunflowers made into light.

27

TENN MAKES ME MUSHROOM SOUP. HE DOESN'T LET ME lift a finger—no. He takes me to the A-frame cottage, sits me down with pistachios and a chocolate bar, since my stomach was growling, and then he lets me watch as he dices onions in the food processor and slides them into a big cast-iron Dutch oven. He adds cloves of garlic, and while that all sizzles in butter, he washes and slices the oyster mushrooms, adding them soon after.

As he grates cheese, he says, "You said your family didn't forage for food."

I'm so warm and lazy. I lean my head on my arms against the surface of the table. "Yeah."

"So what did you forage for? Herbs?"

I smile. "It was kind of a joke."

"Yeah? Tell me about it."

I think he likes hearing my voice as he cooks. I wonder if this is how it was when his mom cooked for him—two people spending time together while making something delicious.

"Nadia says that in the beginning there were gods. Gods and this world."

"Holy shit," he says, tasting the cheese. "I wasn't expecting a creation myth."

I snort. "Well, we didn't forage for those."

"That's too bad. Because that sounds awesome."

"It does." I slide a piece of chocolate in my mouth, thinking for a moment. "Nadia always said our family moved here because we could feel the old gods still inhabiting these mountains. She says that if you go deep enough into Cranberry Falls at the exact right time, you can find their footprints."

"Really?" He doesn't sound incredulous—just excited. "And you've seen them?"

I shake my head. "No. The last time anyone saw them, it was my mom and Nadia. I guess they used to go 'foraging' pretty regularly until I came along."

He's silent for a moment, and then he says, "Why did your mom leave?"

I blink, lifting my head up.

"Don't tell me if you don't want to. I understand if you can't."

"It's okay." I shrug. "It's just . . . she was only sixteen when she had me, eighteen when she had Teal, twenty-one when she had Sky. Every one of our dads left after the positive pregnancy test. They didn't want to deal with a child. And then Mama met someone." I sigh. "He was up front with her, I guess. He didn't want kids. But he didn't just mean his own kids with her, he also meant us. And I guess, between us and him, Mama chose him."

"Assholes," he mutters, and then his eyebrows drop. "No offense."

I laugh. "No, I agree. Mama left when we needed her the most."

The tears sting at my eyes and I glance around—no Sky in sight. I imagine her exploring the woods, or maybe talking to wild cats. The other night she surprised me by saying Old Man Noemi down the street was sick. She's been snooping in all the neighbors' homes, probably because she was getting bored watching my bullshit all the time. "I can't imagine having babies that young. But I can't imagine leaving my kids, either."

"You haven't contacted her since?"

I shake my head. Mom's gift was disappearing. Don't get me wrong, I've searched for her on the internet since we got the family desktop when I was in high school. Looking for what, I don't know—a wedding announcement, maybe. An obituary. I never found a thing.

He looks at me for a moment before he returns to stirring the soup. "I don't like seeing you sad."

"Sorry."

"Don't be. I'm just saying."

And then I get real happy, because Tenn sets a bowl of mushroom cheese soup in front of me. Over the top, he grates black pepper and then drizzles a little olive oil. He grabs his own bowl and a loaf of soft Cuban bread, and rips us both giant pieces. "Bon appétit," he says.

It's the best soup I've ever had in my life. I couldn't even say what was in it besides mushrooms and cheese and pepper and olive oil, but the combination is foodgasmic for sure. I have to make myself slow down so I don't get it all over my shirt.

"Have you ever heard of literal reincarnation?" I ask. He shakes his head, his mouth full of bread, and I smile. "Teal was never one for organized religion. But she always liked this idea. How when someone dies, they go back into the earth, and then the atoms and molecules that made them up become the earth. They become dirt, and plants, and they nourish the living, just as they were nourished when they were alive."

Tenn gives me that wry grin of his. "Are you telling me we're eating the body of my mom here?"

I snort so big, soup almost comes out. "Oh my *God*, Tennessee, *no*. Jesus. No!"

"Well, I did put her ashes in her woods. Where we got these mushrooms . . ."

"That's not what I'm saying. I just thought it was a cool theory. Dios."

He laughs. "My mother would smack my head for saying that *while* we're eating."

"She would have every right."

We're silent for a few moments while I soak up the last soup in my bowl with a piece of bread. "Ugh," I say, putting my head in my hands. "I don't want to go home." This day has been so perfect. Too perfect to end it with Nadia's hurt glances and Teal acting like I never existed in the first place.

"So don't." He says it so casually. As though it wouldn't be me and him . . . *alone* . . . in this *house* . . . at *night*.

"You . . . don't mind me staying here?"

He shakes his head. "There's a guest room. I don't have women's sleep clothes but you can borrow one of my shirts if you want."

I sit back. "Do you have any extra toothbrushes?"

"I do. I buy them in five-packs."

I take a breath and nod. "Okay."

"Okay?"

"Yeah."

I reach for the bowls but he shakes his head. "I'll do dishes. Why don't you shower?"

"Oh—"

"Unless you don't want to shower?"

"No, God." I look at the dirt on my arms and legs. "I do."

"So go ahead. There's clean towels and washcloths stacked in the bathroom. You'll see it. For one of my shirts, go ahead and look in my dresser. It's the bedroom on the right, down the hallway there. You can wear whatever you want."

I nod, like this is totally normal. Me, about to get naked in Tennessee Reyes's bathroom. Shower using his soap. Put on some of his clothes to sleep. Just another day.

"Hurry, woman," he says with a grin, as I stand there with an apparently dazed look on my face. "I really need to shower, too."

I don't need him to read my face as I think about *that* scenario, so I hustle.

Tenn's room is dark, so I push open a curtain. I feel like I'm intruding a bit, but I do glance enough to notice that this room, of all the rooms, feels most like him. The walls aren't lined in art, but there are two landscapes, loosely painted in various shades of blue, both featuring moons, one a thumbnail and the other, full. There's two dressers, one tall and one short and long. The shorter one features a couple of lamps and a closed laptop. In the middle of it is a midnight-blue blown-glass tray where he's put his keys and a leather cuff. I pick up the cuff, entranced—I've never seen him wear it, or any jewelry before. It's about an inch and a half wide, and its outside is carved into intricate spirals. Inside, there are words printed: *SANTO DOMINGO*. It's meant to be held together with a glass orange button, but it's broken, only half the button still sewn on. It feels well-worn and well loved. I place it back carefully. Reverently.

The bed is large, with oatmeal-colored sheets that look like satin. There are a few pillows, which is a step up from most men's bedrooms I've seen. And there's a soft-looking throw tossed right in the middle, knitted in what looks like merino wool the color of wheat.

Everything in here is simple and cozy. And, yes, deeply cool. Like him.

I hear something banging in the kitchen and I'm afraid I'm going to get caught snooping. So I throw open a drawer—oh God, boxers—and keep on going, until I find a black ribbed tank top and blue cotton pajama bottoms.

In the bathroom, I roll up my clothes, including my bra and underwear, into a little ball, and pray he's got a washer and dryer in-house. I sweated a lot today, and so those aren't going back on until after some aggressive agitation and detergent. His soap—ohhh. It's scented with leather and bergamot—no wonder he smells like Earl Grey tea. His conditioner is, thank the old gods, silicone-free. I don't see a comb, so I detangle with my fingers. There's a big bottle of unscented lotion, but no hair product. That's okay, I keep a little bottle of whipped shea butter in my purse, for curly emergencies. After I slip on his clothes, I floss and brush my teeth and feel like a whole new woman.

There's something to be said for a man who owns plenty of soap, washcloths, and lotion. I know, I know—low bar. Even so, it makes me like him even more.

I step out, my arms folded over my chest, and walk down the hallway. He's in the living room, on the sofa, a game on the television. When he sees me, his jaw goes slack. His eyes roam over my wet hair, down to my hips and my thighs and back up again. "Hey," he says, and his voice is hoarse.

"Hi." I'm blushing. I can't remember the last time a man reacted to me like that. I mean, yeah, Tenn's looked. He's even touched a little. But there's a whole new level of heat in his eyes right now. Maybe he can tell I don't have underwear on, I don't know. Or maybe it's all about desire. Maybe he just wants me that much that it comes through his skin like molten metal, red as azaleas and hot as chile.

"Oh shit," I say, naturally breaking the moment. "I left my dirty clothes in there. Balled up in my towel."

"I'll throw the whole thing in the wash."

"No, I can, if you'll show me—"

"Sage." He smiles, his eyes crinkling up. "You're my guest. Make yourself comfortable, okay?"

I nod. "Okay."

"I'll take a shower, too. I won't be more than fifteen minutes."

"Okay."

I'm a little too jittery to get comfy. I sit down and flip through a few channels. Then I get up and pace the perimeter of these two rooms, the living room and the kitchen, stopping to look out the massive windows every few laps. There's the sunset, clouds reaching around the whole sky like arms, dipped in hot pink and violet. There's the trees, swaying in the wind like they're hearing some cosmic music we cannot. I even spot, deep in the bush, a doe, two babies behind her, their fur still spotted cotton white.

"Hey."

I turn toward him, and now I'm the one staring. His hair is wet—I don't know why that's hot, but it is. The waves and curls are a little darker. His stubble is still there, framing those full pink lips. He's got on a white shirt and black cotton pants, both materials thin as can be. His hands are in his pockets, pulling the fabric between his legs taut, and I have to will my eyes to stay above the collarbone with the mental note of *Don't look at his crotch, please God, don't let me look there.* The way he's smirking, though, tells me he hears my every dirty thought. "Ready to see your room?"

"Yeah. Sure."

He takes me to the guest room, which is more feminine than his—the bed covered in a bright yellow comforter, the walls painted field green, the art a collection of tree prints. "It's cozy," I say, my voice tight, because I am in a *bedroom* with *Tennessee Reyes*. I repeat, I'm in a bedroom with Tenn Reyes. My inner sixteen-year-old is dorking out so hard right now.

He nods and clears his throat. "It's ahh—getting late—" I glance up. Uhh, is *not*, I can see on the clock right there that it's just after nine. "I'll just . . . be over there. You let me know if you need anything." His cheeks are pink. He won't meet my eye.

"Oh—thanks?"

He nods. "You're welcome. Good night, Sage."

And then he shuts the door behind him.

28

That's it? I want to scream. All that eye-fucking and all I get is a *good night* at *nine p.m.*?!

Tears sting at my eyes and I angrily wipe them before any can fall. Not because I want to be "dick downed" that badly, as Teal would put it. But because I can't help but think, what if my wildest fear is true—that Tenn doesn't really want me. That all this mushroom hunting and flirting and kissing that meant so much to me didn't mean anything to him at all.

I turn and then almost scream for real, because Sky is at the window. She's pressing her face into the glass, and then she sees me and steps in, right through the pane.

"What the heck are you doing here?" I hiss.

"You're the one who's been crying," she whispers back. "What do you expect me to do? Climb trees all day? The nearest house is, like, four miles away!"

I sit on the bed in a big, sad plop and sigh. "Whatever."

"What are you upset about now?"

"Shh," I say. "We need to whisper."

"He knows about me, though, right?"

"Yeah, but it'd be nice if he didn't hear me talking to a ghost he can't see, Sky."

She snorts. "Fine."

"If you must know, I'm a little bummed because I thought he was going to make a move." I shrug. "But it's fine. He's probably not that attracted to me, so. It's whatever."

"Oh my God, Sage, why are you so dumb?" Sky rolls her eyes. "He's waiting for *you* to make a move."

I shake my head. "Why would he do that?"

"Uh, because your last guy traumatized you? And Tenn's a good guy who doesn't want to push you into anything you don't want to do?"

"How do you know this?" I lift a hand. "You're supposed to give me privacy when I'm doing things like kissing and spilling my secrets."

"I do. But . . ." She sits on the bed next to me. "It's like you said. There are stories everywhere. I can sense them all around me, like this. Like as a ghost. I can feel histories. And I can feel your conversations you've had. I can feel when you're thinking about them." She gives me a side smile. "I can feel his, too, and he was *totally* giving himself a pep talk in the bathroom."

"Really? About what?"

"About you, you clown. He keeps telling himself to go slow. He doesn't want to hurt you."

My heart. Oh my God. My eyes fill up with tears so fast, it hurts. "I've never had a man not want to hurt me before."

Sky's face and hair and whole body get more vivid and solid as I wipe away tears. When I move my hands away from my face, she smiles. "So, what are you waiting for? Go get what *you* want, Sage."

I give her a sideways look. "You're not going to watch, are you?"

"Oh my *God*, you're *sick*. No. I'm going to go sit on the roof for a while."

She stands and starts leaving the way she came. "Go," she hisses, pointing toward Tenn's room, before she slips through the window and disappears.

It takes me a good ten minutes to get to his door. I spend most of that time fussing with my hair and applying lip balm. Finally, I'm there, and I spend another two minutes trying to make out octagons in the woodgrain of his door, and then, *finally*, I brace myself and knock.

"Come in."

He's in bed, over the covers, his phone in hand. He puts it on a nightstand as I walk in. "You okay?"

"Yeah."

"You need water? Tea? A glass of wine?"

I shake my head, moving closer to him. I can do this. I can.

I make my way to the bed, and then I climb into it. Tenn's mouth makes a soundless *oh* as I crawl over, straddling him. He doesn't move at all—he's frozen. Tense. The lines of muscle under his shirt tighten. It takes less than thirty seconds for me to sit on him but when I'm there, his breath is rough and he's already hard under my ass. "Sage," he says. His voice is low. Husky. "Tell me what you want."

"I want you."

He smiles, and finally he lifts his arms up to touch me, to slide his hands over the sides of my ribs, falling to rest on my hips. "You want me how?"

I can do this. "I want you on me. All over me." I gaze at his chest and place my hands there. "Inside me."

His grip tightens on me and I whimper. I'm so warm between my legs already. He slides a hand over my breast and I close my eyes with a gasp.

"Wait," he says. With his hands on my hips, he helps me onto the bed.

"Was that not okay?" I ask as he stands, the tent in his pants making me think about telephone poles.

"Are you kidding? That was—this is—" He shakes his head. He can't put it into words, and it makes my heart feel so warm. "Just—lie back for a minute. And keep your eyes closed."

"Uhh—okay." I obey him, placing my hands over my eyes. "Is this a kink thing?"

He laughs, and it's so deep, I feel it low in my belly. "Maybe."

I hear him rustling. There's a clank of metal, and what sounds like paper being crumpled up. "Are those the condoms?" I ask. "Is my surprise, like, a thousand condoms?"

He laughs again. "Just wait. Be patient, Plant Whisperer."

I'm so relaxed that I let my arms fall, my eyes still closed. I sink into the bed—the comforter is so soft, and it smells so good. All Earl Grey and leather and something else that's just him, all warm and sweet around me.

After about five minutes, he says, "Okay. You can look now."

And when I open my eyes, I rush a hand over my mouth as I sit up. My jaw's dropped. I can hardly breathe properly.

It's dark in here. All dark except for candles.

They're everywhere. On the dressers, nightstands. There are even a few on the floor, wedged into the corners of the room. They're in all shapes and widths, making me think he bought sets and sets from someplace like Williams Sonoma. They're a combination of medium gray and white, and the wicks flicker, drawing him in an orange-yellow glow that dances. He's standing in front of the bed, hands in his pockets, and he asks, "Do you like it?"

I nod. It's all I can do. I'm speechless.

He leans toward the nightstand and grabs his phone. "As for

music. I don't know what you like—" He opens an app, sliding his thumb over buttons and words. He hits play, and the guitar twang from "Let's Get It On" by Marvin Gaye starts. I laugh so hard, I snort, falling back onto the bed. "That wasn't what you were thinking? Okay, okay." He presses more buttons, and then "I'll Make Love to You" by Boyz II Men comes on.

"Oh my God," I wheeze. "That's even cornier!"

He grins at me as I lose it, and when I'm calm, I say, "I don't need music. Really. The candles—" I look around, at their glow. "And you. That's all I need."

"Yeah?"

"Yeah."

He puts his phone down and swallows. "I'm not going to lie. I'm actually nervous."

"Why?"

He smiles. "I want it to be good for you." He bends over me, kissing my forehead, kissing my cheek, my lips. His tongue slips into my mouth and he smiles, pulling back for a moment. "I'm gonna make this so good for you." The gravel in his voice gives me shivers.

And . . . that's exactly what he does. He pulls off our shirts and when we line up together, when I feel his scratchy chest hair against my bare breasts, goose bumps slide up and down my arms. He kisses me, long, lazy, and then it becomes hurried and needy. We lose the rest of our clothes and then things go from hurried to frantic. He kisses my breasts, his tongue flicking my nipples before he sucks, and then I reach for him, hard and slick, and he does the same for me. We touch each other as we kiss, and I start to get sloppy because I'm so close but he doesn't care. In fact, I think he likes it. I think he likes that it's been four minutes and I'm just about there.

"You ever had someone lick your cunt?" he asks in a growl, pulling my hand from his cock.

I shake my head as a slight, full-body shiver runs through me. "That's kind of . . ." I'm breathless. "An obscene way to put it."

"Is there another phrase you like better? Eat you out? Eat your pussy?" My muscles tighten with every dirty word that comes out of his mouth, and then he tops it with, "Perform cunnilingus?" And then we both laugh.

"I don't know if I'll like it, but you could try." I frown. "If you're okay with it."

"I'm okay with it, baby."

And he's not lying. He wraps his arms around my thighs and jerks me toward his mouth, and we both groan when he laps me up. He's so okay with it that he doesn't stop moaning, the deep of his voice pebbling into my skin. And I'm so okay with it, with the hot wet of his tongue concentrated right where I need it the most, that it's only one minute before I buck my hips up and grab his hair and moan, "Oh my God, I'm coming." He softens the pressure as I dissolve into shivers, and he kisses me once, all soft and sweet, before pulling back.

"You good?" he asks when he lifts his head with his smirk, and okay. He can smirk all he wants. He just made me come harder than I've ever come before in my life.

He grabs a condom and slides it over himself, and I just sit back and enjoy the view. His body is beautiful, his brown skin mixing with the gold of candlelight. Everything about him is beautiful.

He climbs over me and says in a half whisper, "If you don't like something, tell me."

I nod.

He slides inside me and we groan against each other's faces

before kissing—one sweet, slow, syrupy kiss before he starts thrusting.

And the thing is, I like everything.

I like how full he feels inside me.

I like that he keeps checking in, either looking at my face or outright asking, *Is that okay? Is this okay?*

I like that he maneuvers me, one leg over here, or tilt my hips over there, until he gets what he wants—me gasping and curling my hands over his shoulder and arm so hard, my nails scratch till he hisses.

"You like that, huh? That's the spot, isn't it?"

I guess I do, but it feels too good to confirm. He knows, though. He knows not to change a thing, to keep thrusting, hard and slow, and then he slides his hands between my legs, swirling slick over me, and just like that, I'm coming again, and so is he, and it lasts so fucking long. And then we collapse and then the only sound is the wild rhythm of our heavy breath.

He disappears to the bathroom, I guess to get rid of the condom, and then I have to pee, and we smile a little at each other before I shut the door, and after I wash my hands, I stare at myself in the mirror for a minute.

My hair is mostly dry by now, though it's frizzed up thanks to all that action.

My eyes, bright. Happy.

My lips, swollen and red.

And then I frown.

What am I doing?

Before fucking, before even kissing, I told him a lie by omission. I let him think I'm not Silvergurl.

It shouldn't matter. It was over ten years ago. We should've moved *on* by now. I should've forgotten RainOnATennRoof, and he should've forgotten me.

My breath is still too fast. I put my hand on my thumping heart. I think I'm having a panic attack. *Shit*.

I lied to this man I'm pretty sure I still love. I'm pretty sure that puppy love never went away—it was like a seed, and then he had to go and water and nurture it until here I am, coming on his cock, thinking he's the most beautiful and gentle and kind man I've ever known.

I take a long breath and wipe back two tears.

Thing is, he doesn't *need* to know. Right? He'll forget about her, his mythic Silvergurl, and then he'll focus on me. On what's right here, in front of him. And then this will all be behind us.

There's a light rap at the door. "Hey, you okay?"

I swing it open. He's got his cotton pants back on, the deep *V* of his hips sliding out from under the waistband. His brows are knitted.

"I'm good," I say.

He doesn't buy it. "What's wrong?" He grabs my hand and pulls me to bed. He slides us under the covers and wraps his arm around me as he studies my face.

"Are we . . . together now?"

He smiles big, and I can't help but smile back. "Yeah. We're together now." He frowns. "Unless you don't want that."

"I do!" I say it kind of too loud and close my eyes with a sigh. When I open them, he's back to smiling. "I do want that."

He's looking at me again, close, and I'm scared of what he's going to see. The piled-up lies, stacked till they resemble Firefly Mountain, solid and full of stories. Stories I don't want anyone to find, to spread out, to read. So I say, fast, "When did you buy all those candles?"

He laughs and leans back and I breathe a silent sigh of relief. "The day we kissed. And you told me about . . . your teaching job, and what happened." He lifts his arm to rest his head on his hand. "I was so fucking pissed, Sage. If it weren't illegal I'd find that guy. Lay one or two or three on him." He shrugs. "I didn't know what to do. I went for a run, I lifted, I made a cup of tea. None of that worked so I went to Bed Bath & Beyond."

I snort-laugh. "You knew it was going to happen, huh?"

"I didn't *know*. But I wanted to be ready if it did." He's serious now as he gazes at me. "You deserve so much better than that."

And you deserve so much better than me.

Tenn can't know this, though, so he thinks my tears are about my past. He kisses them until they're gone, and then he's hard and I'm wet and we tear at each other, going fast, hard, and it feels so good I let myself forget about everything enough to sleep after, to sleep deeply, wrapped in Tennessee Reyes's arms.

MARCH 1, 2002
13 YEARS AGO

RainOnATennRoof: I've got it.

silvergurl0917: you got.. . . . . what? did you & your mom finally find that bear claw mushroom?

RainOnATennRoof: Hey. That's bear head tooth mushroom, thank you very much. And no. It still eludes us.

silvergurl0917: :(no lobster mushrooms for you then

RainOnATennRoof: Hey. We can still totally find it. No losing hope now

silvergurl0917: :) so what did you get?

RainOnATennRoof: I got the perfect spot for us to meet.

silvergurl0917: oh?

RainOnATennRoof: You know Sebastian Song? He's throwing this epic spring break party. Next weekend at his place on Shore Springs

silvergurl0917: oh i think i heard about that

RainOnATennRoof: I'll be there. And now you'll be there. ;)

silvergurl0917: but there's a problem with this plan

RainOnATennRoof: yeah?

silvergurl0917: . . . i wasn't invited to Song's epic spring break party on Shore Springs

RainOnATennRoof: hell yes you are. this is me, inviting you, right now.

silvergurl0917: :) yeah?

silvergurl0917: but how. . . . do we meet tho?

RainOnATennRoof: Wear blue so I know it's you.

silvergurl0917: any sort of blue?

RainOnATennRoof: Any kind. idc.

silvergurl0917: okay. how about a blue dress?

RainOnATennRoof: Really?

silvergurl0917: really:)

RainOnATennRoof: Really, seriously really?

silvergurl0917: yes! really seriously really-really-really

RainOnATennRoof: Holy shit. Okay.

silvergurl0917: guess i'll be seeing you next saturday;) literally

RainOnATennRoof: I'll be waiting for you, Silvergurl.

PRESENT

When I awaken, there's a light drizzle, but the clouds must be thin because sunlight's also coming through the trees. It makes me think about Tenn's mom's land. Us kissing there, between streams of yellow echinacea light. The very woods that won't exist in a week. With that thought, grief comes through slick, like a sharp blade at my chest, at my throat. Our town has several neighborhoods that need fixing up. Why can't the bank work on that? Why do they have to take something precious, something increasingly rare, and hack it to pieces? And why does everyone pretend this is somehow civilized?

I sigh. It feels useless to grieve over the lost wild because I feel so powerless. Instead, I swallow it back, the rage, the sorrow, and then I get up to wash my face, making my way out of the bedroom after.

Tenn's voice is coming from the kitchen. "Yeah, of course," he's saying, phone to his ear. "I'll let her know." When he sees me, he smiles and winks. I breathe out a big, soundless sigh. I guess a part of me was worried he'd regret what had happened last night. Based on how his whole face has lit up, though, there was no need.

He says goodbye and clicks off his phone. He hands me a big cup of coffee.

"Thank you." The mug's warmth instantly comforts me.

"You feel good?"

I nod. We smile at each other like that for a few seconds, and then he bends to kiss my cheek. "I like the way you look in the morning."

"How do I look?" I ask.

He looks at me, up and down. "Well fucked."

I laugh till I snort and then say, "Who was that on the phone?"

"Nate. He's got an adventure for us."

"Oh?"

"Yeah. He wants me to let you know about a tip he got."

"On a plant?"

"Yeah. There's this couple down by Dogwood Hills. Say they've got a rose."

"A heritage, I'm guessing?"

He shrugs. "They say it's blue."

"Blue? That can't be."

"Yeah, Nate didn't think so, either." Tenn drinks from his mug. "What's so wrong with a blue rose?"

I take a sip of coffee, giving it a double take when the flavor hits me. Chocolate raspberry. "Uh." I take a seat at the dining table. "They're . . . impossible. That's the main thing. Roses, genetically, aren't able to make a true blue. Plant breeders and hybridizers and geneticists have been throwing millions—maybe even billions—to create a blue rose for decades, but the closest they've come is a cold lavender."

He leans on the counter, sipping. "I'm pretty sure I've seen blue roses before. In bouquets at the supermarket."

"Yeah. That's not natural. If you put a white flower in water that has food coloring in it, it'll turn its blooms any Skittle color you want. You'll see that with bouquets of mums a lot, too—hot pink, neon yellow."

"So you don't think this rose is blue?"

"Nah. If it is, Cranberry Rose would be the most lucrative plant company in the world in short order. But like I said, it's impossible. But of course. We'll check it out. I'm definitely intrigued."

"After breakfast, then?" He opens the fridge, bending to inspect it. Yes, I take a long look at his backside. I'm only human, here. "Sorry, I'm kind of low on groceries. Would mushroom soup be a weird breakfast?"

I give him a smile. "It would be the best breakfast."

And it is. He toasts more Cuban bread with butter and between that and the soup and the way he puts me on the counter and kisses me like I taste better than any soup or bread or coffee— it may well be the best breakfast of my life.

"I'VE BEEN THINKING ABOUT WHAT YOU CAN DO TO HELP WITH your sister," he says, when we're on our way to the so-called blue rose.

"Yeah?" The clouds have come on strong, making it a little

cooler than usual. In the distance, sunrays burn through with a bright rose gold. It gives the landscape a dreamy feel.

"Yeah. Maybe you could make her something."

"Make her something, eh?" I frown thoughtfully. "But not food." Lord knows that ended up being a disaster, though that certainly wasn't the idea's fault.

"Yeah. Make her something that reminds her of who she was when she liked you."

I try to think about what that something might look like. But the truth is, I can hardly remember a time when Teal even liked me. Tolerated me, sure. Let me take care of her, yes. But I always had this weird feeling that she blamed *me* for Mama leaving. Like she resented me for making her cinnamon butter toast, or for making sure she finished her homework, because I was the one doing it instead of Mama. And that comes through even today. I can't do a single nice thing for her without her acting like I stabbed her back somehow.

No wonder making peace with her has been impossible.

"Did Jagger write back yet?" Tenn asks. Daniel Jagger . . . right. Tabitha's husband. Who I contacted on Facebook, based on a lie I told this guy for whom I have developed Strong Feelings. If I could go back in time and punch myself in the face, it would obviously be when I declined hiking with Sky and Teal through Cranberry Falls eight years ago. However, agreeing to this ghost deal a few weeks back is a close second.

I pull open the app on my phone. There's a direct message notification, and along with that, there's dread in my belly. Now I'm going to have to lie some more. This is a tornado of never-ending lies, and I'm stuck here, useless as the letters and words swirl around me, thicker and thicker, *unless* I decide to tell the truth and do what Teal says I always do—ruin everything. Which shall *not* happen, namely due to my cowardice.

And then I read the message. My dread turns into something sharper. I try not to gasp and fail.

"Sage? What's wrong?"

"She's dead." I look over the message again. Hi Sage, thanks so much for asking about Tabby. Unfortunately, almost one year ago . . . "It was a car accident."

Tenn's jaw is hard. He scrubs a hand over it, and all the muscles tighten even more.

I take a shaky breath. Lie. Just keep lying, it's what I'm awesome at, apparently. "Do you want me to say anything specific back to him?"

"Just the usual. If you want. Condolences. Et cetera."

"I'm sorry, Tenn."

"It's—" He shakes his head. "No, I'm sorry, too." He bites his lips, releases. "It doesn't matter if she was the AIM girl or not. She was too young."

Just promise me, if you two start to fall for each other, like for real. For real. That you'll tell him. Laurel's voice is strong in my ears. *You don't want to start a relationship on a lie, you know?*

It takes me five whole minutes before I can summon the courage to try.

I take a deep breath. "Tenn?"

"Mm."

"About your AIM girl. There's . . . there's something—"

"Sage." His voice is firm as he shakes his head. "Sorry, but I can't. I can't talk about this—about her—anymore. I thought this would be fun or cathartic or something, but . . ." He sighs and turns the Boss down a gravel road. "I just can't right now."

He's all drawn in and closed off. Armor up. Swords aren't out, but he's clutching some hilts. I don't know what to say, so I say nothing.

He parks the car in front of a tiny log cabin. It's rustic and gorgeous, the wood warm and red. There's an old woman sitting beside a pile of chopped firewood on the porch. She wears a bright yellow, flower-print dress, her white hair contrasting beautifully with her brown skin. Her smile sparkles as we get out of the car.

"Hi there," I say.

"How do you do?" Her voice rings like a bell.

We walk up and introduce ourselves. Her name is Loretta, like the country singer, but this Loretta insists she couldn't carry a tune in a ten-gallon bucket. Loretta invites us in, and soon both Tenn and I sit in her little breakfast nook, eating cookies and drinking what she calls "coal miner's coffee," meaning the grains settle at the bottom of the mug like tea leaves. The little tin cups, they remind me of Nadia, pouring that thick hot drink into the dirt. Into the earth. Into the footprints of old gods.

"Seems like the rain won't make up its mind," Loretta's saying.

"Mm," Tenn says into his cup.

I furrow my brow at him and turn to her. "Yeah. We've been getting a lot of rain this year." I have no idea if that's true but between Teal losing it in la casa de Nadia, calling forth all kinds of lightning and thunder, and Tenn and I kissing for the first time in diamond-gray rain, my memories feel like this summer has been one giant, wild storm.

And now, next to me, Tenn continues the storm. His jaw is still tense, his shoulders tight. He loves chatting with folks, normally, or, at least, chatting with me, but he hasn't said a single word since we got inside. The news about Tabitha really battered him, I guess.

Jealousy flares deep in my belly. And I *know* it's all kinds of wrong. It's *me* he's looking for. It's fucking unfair as fuck that Tabby died at the age of twenty-eight. The fact that she's even involved in any capacity in this ghost deal is my own fault for lying. But I'm having such a hard time compartmentalizing my feelings. It's all boiling over, the water spilling into letters just like when Sky drew into spilled cream and coffee.

No one chooses me.

Not Mom, not Nadia, not Amá Sonya, and not Teal.

Tenn *has* me. Right in the palm of his hands. That's pretty certain after all we did last night. I know he's not interested in her like that. So why can't he let Silvergurl0917 go? He said it was to touch happiness again, right? But why aren't *I* the one who makes him happy again? Why aren't *I* ever enough?

I shake my head and keep small-talking with Loretta for another ten minutes or so. Tenn doesn't contribute a single word. "Well, I guess I better show y'all the rose," she says. She ushers us out the back door. "Go on," she tells Tenn as he walks ahead. "It's up there by the tree stump." She turns to me and lowers her voice. "You're that plant whisperer, aren't you?"

I nod. "Yeah. I did that for a little while."

"You know, my great-granddad said he could hear plants talking to him. They like stories, don't they?"

I blink in surprise. "Yeah. That's true."

"The reason why I called y'all out here is because this rose has been giving me trouble for ages. I don't think she wants to be here anymore. I think it's too cold or some such."

"Oh . . ."

"She doesn't want to be cut up and sold, though. I'll tell you that much. She's been on this mountain for as long as my family's been here, and no one even remembers when that was. She needs a new home. I blame climate change. And I like Dale. I know he'll be good to her over on the farm."

I don't point out that Dale's technically retired, especially considering I'm not sure Dale's gotten that memo yet himself.

"Sage!"

I guess Tenn's found it. And he sounds excited.

"I'll just—" I say to Loretta.

"Go on ahead. I'll be right here. There's too many rocks and roots up there for my frail bones."

I walk up, taking care over the forewarned giant, gnarled rocks and roots. There's a little bit of fog about, pouring over the top of the mountains around us, falling through distant trees until they dissipate into nothing.

"Sage, look."

Tenn's bent over the rosebush. It's covered in dead branches, but there's good, lush growth near its bottom. And he's pointing at its only bloom. It's tiny and barely open, but . . . holy shit.

It's blue.

It's not the blue of delphinium or bachelor buttons or California bluebells. It's the blue of a sweet summer sky over Virginia. It's the blue of a robin's egg that came out just a little light. It's the blue of Montana sapphires, of aquamarines, of blue lace agate, each lit from within like impossibly blue lanterns.

"Jesus," I whisper. "That looks like a true blue."

"Yeah?" Tenn's grinning up at me, and my belly feels like it goes inside out.

I hesitate, and then nod. "I mean, we'd have to see how its other flowers look. Variation can exist even within a single plant. But . . ." We look at each other for a pause and then I gesture behind me. "Loretta said the whole plant needs to be moved."

"Like she's giving it to us?"

I hesitate, then nod. "Yeah."

Before I can say anything else, Tenn's up. "I'll grab the shovel."

I bend down over the rose, lifting up my hands. I imagine taking it to Nadia's, adding it to her collection she keeps for Cranberry Rose. And then as gentle as a water bird, one of its leaves lifts toward me . . . reaching. I smile.

And then I think about taking it to the farmhouse, to Nate, to Dale. The rose leaf snaps back so fast, the whole plant shakes.

Shit. Loretta's right. This rose doesn't want to be cut. It doesn't want to be sold. It just wants a new home, that's all.

Tenn digs it up and I lift it, roots and all, placing it into doubled-up grocery bags. We don't have our usual supplies because I don't have my van, but we make do.

Loretta's thrilled. I think the rose's decline was really weighing on her. "I can't thank y'all enough. I know you'll do right by her."

"Of course we will," I say.

She hugs us both goodbye, making us promise to visit for honey biscuits and blackberry jam any time we're in the area.

When we're in the car, Tenn gives me the biggest smile, his dark eyes crinkling his lashes into thick curly fans. "Nate's going to be so pumped."

I swallow as he backs out onto the main road. "Tenn . . ."

"You said this is lucrative, right?" Tenn glances at me. There aren't dollar signs in his eyes—but there are stars. "You said this could be worth millions? Right?"

I know of at least one biotech company that threw a reported forty-five million dollars to create a blue rose . . . and this was in the *nineties*. Since roses aren't genetically capable of making a blue color on their own, the researchers took a rose, inserted blue genes from a pansy, and then tried to suppress the rest of the colors, which failed. Red still made it through, which meant the highly anticipated, decades-developed blue rose ended up looking . . . well, purple.

Blue roses are an impossibility. That's why, if we are able to clone this plant, with cuttings or any other method, it may be worth way more than millions. I don't say any of this, though. I'm not sure he would hear me. I don't think he even realizes he's driving well over the speed limit.

"Hey. Slow down, okay?" I mean it not just with the car, but he doesn't get it yet.

"You think Nate would be down for an advance? I know this isn't going to go on the market for a while. But if—"

"Tenn. We can't take the rose to Nate." It's on the floorboard right now. I've got its branches between my knees. When he drives over potholes, the thorns dig a little into my legs.

"What do you mean?" He doesn't hide the dismay in his voice.

I shake my head. "It . . . the rose . . . doesn't want to be sold. It doesn't want to be made into cuttings."

"What do you mean, it doesn't *want* to be sold? Since when do plants *want* anything?"

Ouch. "Well, for starters, plants want to be healthy. They want water, and light."

He rolls his eyes. "I mean, since when can a plant even know what being sold is? And have an opinion on it?"

I'm silent for a few moments. Then I say, "Don't you remember? My gift is plants. I can sense them. I can *feel* them."

"That's bull—" He stops himself. But I blink, my heart in my throat. He was about to call my *gift* bullshit. He was about to call *me* bullshit. He tries another route. "Why wouldn't it want to be made into cuttings and sold? That means its survival is more ensured."

"If we cut this plant up and try to cultivate it, it will die." I say it quietly. "Because it doesn't want that."

"Jesus Christ, Sage. You're not making any sense."

He's driving too fast still. "Slow down, Tenn." Finally, he lifts his foot from the gas so we're only five over the speed limit rather than twenty.

He runs a hand over his jaw. "The only reason it would die would be if someone killed it."

Now anger rises up in me. "Are you accusing me of planning on killing this plant? What the *fuck*?"

He throws up a hand. "Why wouldn't the cuttings work, then?"

"*Most* cuttings don't make it. You know this. That's why we take a million and a half every time."

"So we let it grow in the hoop house. It's safer from pests in there. When it's bigger, we can take cuttings."

He's not listening. I refrain from banging my head against my window, and my voice is clear as I emphasize it one more time: "If we take this rose to Cranberry Rose, it's going to wither up and be gone. Simply because that's *not what it wants*."

"Yeah? Well, what the hell *does* it want?" He's pulled into Rosy Lane and I blink. How did we get here so quickly? Oh, right. Because Tennessee likes to speed in his dumb hot rod when he's mad. He pulls up next to my van, parking so fast I jerk against the seat belt, and sighs, repeating himself. "What does it want?"

I shrug. "It wants a new home. In Nadia's yard."

He barks a mean, hollow laugh. "Well, that's convenient. You want to put this *extremely* valuable plant in *your* yard? So you *won't* then take cuttings from it?"

I can't take this shit anymore. I burst out of the car, not even blinking when thorns tear into my legs on my way out. Tenn's right on my heels.

I turn to him. "I thought you believed me when I told you about my gift."

"I do believe you." He crosses his arms.

"No, you don't." If he did, I wouldn't still be explaining this to him.

I march up in front of my herb spiral. I've been coming every few days to make sure it's watered, to thin the seedlings, to arrange in a layer of mulch. It's still not much to look at, but I point my finger, anyway. A plant reaches back in a soundless *yes*.

"Look," I say to him. He walks up, his eyes hard, his hands in his pockets. "Look," I repeat. And then I place my hand over that plant—lime basil. Yes, it smells just like limes mixed with basil, and I imagine it'd make a killer mojito. Under my palm, its leaves reach toward me. I push on. And then it starts to *grow*.

It grows larger, leaves forming out of its stems, one after the other, right before our eyes. Soon it pushes out flowers—tiny, white, delicate, lining a long, thin branch like baby popcorn garland. I run my fingers over the flowers—they open, wilt, and then brown. I shake a few of the seeds into my hand and then I take a step toward him. I hold my palm open, and he watches, his eyes wide, as the tiny black seeds sprout, their little white roots reaching out, and then, the small, rounded first leaves, emerging from what's left of the seed shells.

Tenn's jaw has dropped.

"Do you believe me yet?" My voice is hard.

"Sage." He runs a hand over his stubble. "What is happening?"

"*This* is my gift. This is what I've been *trying* to tell you. I can hear plants. I can feel them. Like they're a part of me. And if you'd get your head out of your ass, you'd know that what I'm saying is the truth. That blue rose doesn't *want* to be cultivated." I place the sprouts back in the dirt of the herb spiral.

He groans, taking a step back, his hands up in false surrender. "You don't get it." He takes a shaky breath. "If this is as big as you say it is, I could get enough money to buy my mom's land back."

I close my eyes briefly. I make my voice as gentle as I can. If there was something of Sky's out there—something significant and sacred, like his mom's land—I'd probably speed down the freeway for it, too. But he's not thinking rationally about this. What he thinks is possible just isn't. "Tenn. That's not going to happen. Do you know how much money you'd need? And in less than a *week*? The bank's not going to sell it back for whatever they paid your dad. They're going to make a killing on it. Your words."

"Like *we* could make a killing on that rose."

The fact that he's *still* not listening. Same way that Johnny Miller didn't listen. Same way that Gregory didn't listen. "Stop it!" I yell. "That rose will *die* if you leave it here. And moreover, it isn't going to bring your mom back. That land won't bring your mom back. Finding Silvergurl zero-nine-one-seven isn't going to bring your mom back. You can choose the people who are around you now, you know. You can choose those of us who are here, standing in front of you, *loving* you right now."

I've basically declared my love for him, right here in front of the herb spiral I first made when I was brokenhearted over him. It seems like it should come full circle, right? Like he'd soften up. Tell me I'm right. Give me a hug, a kiss, my happily-ever-after.

Instead, his back straightens. His jaw tics. His eyes narrow. "What did you just say?" His voice is so low, I take an unintentional step back.

"I said—I lo—"

"No. You said Silvergurl. You said all the numbers. I never told you her screen name."

Oh, *shit*. "Sure you did. I can't remember when, but—"

"No, I didn't. I didn't tell you on purpose."

"Why would you do that?" It's a whisper now. I'm trembling.

He laughs and lifts his arms. "Because I was afraid we'd find her too quick. I wanted to talk to you longer than that. To get to know you. To help you, with your sister."

I shake my head. "*You* said you wanted the feeling of everything being okay back. You said this was about doing right by your mom."

He throws his hands up again. "It can be both, Sage. Humans are complicated. You should know that. And it *is* both. I wanted to make things right, for a lot of reasons. *And* I wanted to get close to you." He takes a step forward. "How do you know her screen name? Right down to the number sequence?"

I shake my head. My mouth won't open. The truth is there, pressing on my lips, but I can't let it out.

"You know who she is."

I shake my head again. It's my last attempt at pulling the tornado of lies back around me.

"Wait . . ." I can tell the second it comes to him. The second the truth lands on his shoulders like the weight of an eagle, wide winged and seeing everything I've tried to hide, as though it were flung from my throat like a song of confession.

"Seriously?" he breathes. "Was it you, the whole time? Were you Silvergurl?"

Finally, I open my mouth, but nothing comes out. My voice doesn't want to work. The words slide down into the dirt under my shoes. Instead I nod, staring at his legs.

He huffs out a deep breath. "Why did you lie?"

Now I meet his eye. "Because you *broke my heart*. Because when I climbed the stairs in Song's house during that spring break party, you were *making out* with someone else. You had your hands around her waist. And then you . . . you took her hand and you pulled her into a *bedroom*." My voice breaks. Tears run down my face now—big ones. Fat ones. I don't see Sky, but I'm sure she's nearby. The memories are nearby, too. "I bought a blue dress covered in a blue hibiscus print. It flared a little, like a mermaid, at the skirt." *Wear blue so I know it's you.* "I wore a new perfume, too. Vanilla Fields, from Kmart. I thought you"—my voice doesn't want to work but I make it keep going—"you said you liked the smell of cookie dough, remember, so I thought you would like that." *I'll be waiting for you, Silvergurl.* "You said you'd wait for me, but you *didn't.* You said you didn't care that I was short, that my hair was frizzy, that I wasn't model-thin. You were with another girl, and she was so much prettier—and, Jesus, Tenn! She was *everything* I wasn't. I *mourned* you. Because you found someone else, just like that. Someone *perfect.*"

He is speechless for a few moments, his jaw slack, his wide eyes looking me over as though for the first time. "That's because I thought she was you!"

"*What?*" I cry out. "Why the hell would you think that?"

"*She* wore a blue dress! She came to me, all giggling, and I asked her if she was my Silvergurl, and she said yes! I kissed her because I thought she was you, Sage. All we did was kiss in that room. And two or three minutes later I found out she had no idea what I was talking about. That she was wasted. And then I went back out and waited for you for the next *four hours* before going home."

"She looked nothing like me, Tenn. She was tall, she was—"

"Sage." He shakes his head. "You've got to know how nervous I was. My hands were literally shaking. I barely noticed how she looked. I only cared about meeting you, get it? *I only cared about you.*"

Oh my God.

I have spent the last decade hating this man over a *misunderstanding*?

Am I *seriously* that dumb?

I shake my head, backing up until my back hits the stones of the herb spiral. "That's . . . what happened that night is in the past. We can let it go."

He huffs. "You *lied* to me. That's *not* in the past. You lied to me every day for the last few weeks, and even up till today, over Tabitha—"

"I didn't know she died," I say helplessly.

"Is that supposed to make it better?"

I say nothing. Because, of course not. I can't think of a single thing that would make this better.

We stare at each other for a few seconds. Then Tenn shakes his head. "I'm done. *We're* done." He stomps back to the Boss, jumps in, and before I can blink, he's off.

Taking the blue rose with him.

30

MARCH 15, 2002
13 YEARS AGO

RainOnATennRoof: silvergurl

RainOnATennRoof: . . . I know you're there. you logged on like thirty seconds ago.

RainOnATennRoof: did you even come to the party?

silvergurl0917: yes. i did.

RainOnATennRoof: what happened?

RainOnATennRoof: Why didn't you say anything to me?

RainOnATennRoof: Unless . . .

RainOnATennRoof: shit

silvergurl0917 has logged off Messenger.

PRESENT

I'm hyperventilating when I get in my van, but not so much that I can't call Laurel.

"Sage?" I can barely hear her even as she shouts my name. The sound of music drowns her out. After a minute, it quiets down. "There, that's better."

"Where are you?"

"Wedding. But everyone's eating, so it's good timing. I can chat for a few minutes. What's up?"

I take a deep breath so my voice stops shaking so much. "Tenn found out I lied to him about the AIM thing."

Laurel lets out a long sigh. "You didn't take my advice, did you?"

Even though she can't see me, I shake my head. "To be fair, I didn't know I loved him until the lie had escalated and spiraled out of control." I think of his face, not five minutes ago. The tears in his eyes, the hard line of his jaw. *I'm done. We're done.*

"How could you not know? You've been in love with him since, what? Fifteen?"

There's a harshness to her tone that makes my head rear back. "Uh—"

"And you just lied to his face. From, what, day one?"

"No—"

"And now he's what? What the hell is he going to do now? Skip town? All because you couldn't do something as basic as tell the fucking truth?"

"What the *fuck*, Laurel?" I'm breathing hard again. "You called me a week ago for help with *your* crisis, and that's what I'm doing now. I didn't contact you for a lecture. I need support."

"I already supported you by telling you to *not* do the thing you ended up doing!"

So she wants to go there? Fine. "You wanna talk about liars? How long have you known Jorge's been cheating?" I don't give her time to respond. "A whole week? And how is that going? You sitting down for dinner with him. Grabbing him a beer. Saying fuck-all. We could call that a really big, fat lie, couldn't we?"

"This is not the same. This is nowhere near the same."

"Isn't it? So when are you planning on telling him, then?"

"Telling him what?"

I throw up my hand even though she can't see me. "That you're getting a divorce." There's silence for a long moment. "Laurel. I thought you were getting a divorce."

"Some of us can't just leave every time things get difficult, Sage."

Whatever knife Tenn just stuck in my heart, Laurel took the handle and twisted.

"Sage, that didn't come out right."

"Sure it didn't." I hang up and turn my phone off.

I'M DRIVING WITHOUT A SINGLE CLUE AS TO WHERE I'M GOING. I follow random roads, passing groups of brown cows lazing under pecan groves, and then the mountains, little old homes visible on their tops, until I'm on the scenic highway, through downtown, all slow because it's Monday.

When I was little, this walkway was filled with mom-and-pop shops—a kitchen supply store called Smitten, a tiny boutique where an elderly couple sold yarn. Even Cranberry Rose used to have a storefront selling rose water, wine, and jam. Now instead there's a Banana Republic, a White House Black Market, and a Starbucks that has squeezed into where the yarn store used to be, trading hand-spun merino wool for chocolate chip frappuccinos.

It gets me thinking about the history of this land, of this whole world, even. How someone got it in their head that ripping down thousand-year-old trees was a-okay. How people who grow gardens are crunchy; how people who grow their stock portfolios are sophisticated. How Tenn's mom's land, with its birdsong and dappled light and ancient mushrooms, will be destroyed in just a few days because a few rich people want more money and there's nothing any of us can do about it.

I street-park in front of an old brick building, its windowpanes wide and well lit, displaying amber necklaces and ruby bracelets. Brass bells chime when I make it inside. There's a single employee whose presence I'd recognize anywhere: Brian Saleh, a big newspaper opened in front of his face, the familiar scent of black coffee in the air.

He lowers the paper and smiles. "Sage! Heard you were back in town. I was wondering when you'd stop by."

Brian is a lapidary—meaning he cuts and polishes gemstones. It is, frankly, a ridiculously tedious process and requires a ton of skill. And that's coming from me, a person who's trained in things like soldering and gem setting. Once I bought my van, I basically lived in this store, my nose pressed to the glass as I imagined what I'd design around sapphires the color of hawthorn berries or blue lace agate with veins so fine, it resembled ancient sediments you sometimes see in highways carved through mountain rock. Even before the van, I came here after my birthdays, cash in hand, and bought wire and rough stones and made it my personal life goal to transform the materials into something beautiful and precious.

We small-talk for a bit. Brian somehow hadn't heard I'd been teaching design classes. And then he asks, "You looking for anything in particular?"

I don't know why, but this question makes my eyes water. "No, not really."

"Hey, is everything okay, little leaf?"

That's Brian and his wife Mia's nickname for me. Or, it was. I haven't heard it in years and I wipe back the tears that fall. "I'm fine. It's just been kind of a bad day."

He stares at me for a moment. "Would coffee help?"

"Sure."

"Let me make a fresh pot." Brian disappears into the back. I'm sure I freaked him out, so I take a breath and try to calm myself down.

The display of unset jewels has always been my happy place. I lean over the glass, marveling over emeralds and diamonds in the back, and the semiprecious stones in the front—sun and moonstone, peridot as green as fairy wine, garnets as crimson as red velvet cake. They're cut into ovals and circles and squares, some faceted, and others as smooth as silk, called cabochons.

Someone drapes their arms on the display next to me—and when I look, I'm not surprised that it's Sky. "Are you taking Tenn's advice?"

"What advice?" I snap, trying to slap away the way my heart constricts, hearing his name.

"Make something for Teal. That reminds her of when she liked you."

"How do you know that?" I whisper. "That was in his car this morning. I didn't see you at all."

"Words and stories don't stay hidden for long, Sage."

I close my eyes, jumping when Brian returns, cup of coffee in hand. "Here you go. You let me know if you need anything else."

"Thanks, Brian."

I sip the coffee. This store is too small for me to talk to a ghost no one else sees with their tears, so Sky hops on a display of engagement rings, leaving me to my devices.

The truth is, I have a lot of people I need to remind of when they liked me. I have a lot to apologize for.

First, keeping secrets for so long. Not telling Nadia about her neglect way back when. Not telling anyone about Sky the ghost.

Lashing out at Laurel. Yeah, she was an asshole, but I know she was projecting. I should've hung up the phone and called back later, when she wasn't in the middle of a big shoot, but I let it escalate.

I never properly apologized for outing Teal as a domestic abuse survivor.

And the big thing right now is Tenn. I lied to him, even as I fell for him. The way my heart feels right now—I hadn't realized it until he left in a huff of rage and dust, but I fell *hard*. Too hard. Stupidly hard.

"Everything is broken," I murmur.

"Things have been cracked for so long, Sage," Sky responds. "They *needed* to break. So now the roots and leaves can come out and everything can bloom again."

Her metaphor stops me. If a seed cracks open and the plant can't make its way out, it would either rot or dry out from the inside. Is that how my life has been? Cracked. Dried. Rotting. Yes, it's not pleasant to break. But what if it is needed sometimes, like Sky just said? What if sometimes, we have to break things in order to heal them?

I finish my coffee. "Brian? Could you cut up this moss agate for me?"

He walks over. "Depends on what you're thinking."

This type of agate is so named because it looks like there are green curls of moss captured inside it. It's usually mostly milk white in color, but this one looks like it's been dipped in the blue greens of an Appalachian forest.

It looks like a whole landscape.

It looks like sage, teal, and sky put together in a gem.

"Three rounds," I say. "Five millimeters in diameter apiece, cut right here, at the horizon line." He takes a wax pencil and sketches one of the cuts, directly on the stone. "Yes. That's perfect."

Brian gives me a smile. "Come back at the end of the day. I'll have them ready then."

NEXT STOP, ONE I'VE *BEEN* PUTTING OFF. AMÁ SONYA'S.

I cry all the way there, and so by the time I pull up, my eyes are swollen, my nose is sniffly, and Sky is as visceral and hard-edged as any living human.

She accompanies me toward the front door. "You think that Farmer Whitey's home?" I ask. Sky snorts. This is Teal's nickname for Sonya's current husband.

Sky closes her eyes. "He's not."

I guess that's those words and stories she's sensing now.

The door opens, and there's Amá Sonya. "Hello, Amá," I say pleasantly.

She stares at me like I just suggested we try cannibalism for fun. "What brings you here today?" She pushes the door further, and then she looks *right* at Sky. "Ah." Goose bumps crawl over my back and arms. I had *wondered* if she, too, could see Sky after I'd had a good, hard cry. And lucky for me, I'm not running out of tears anytime soon. Especially today of all days.

"I've got some questions," I say, sniffling. "About ghosts."

"Shhh," Sonya hisses, looking around. "Get inside, fast. Before anyone sees you. *Either* of you."

"What's the problem?" I ask as we follow her in. "Are your neighbors the ghost police?"

"Hilarious." She's wearing a cream blazer and a matching pencil skirt and kitten heels. I couldn't guess if she just got home from some banquet, or she's got an important appointment soon, since I'm pretty sure she dresses like that whether she goes out or not. In fact, if Sonya decided to announce that these were her pajamas, I'd not blink once.

"Can you hear me, too?" Sky asks, her eyes wide. Apparently, she wasn't expecting Amá to see her.

"Of course I can hear you. Even your thoughts. They're loud." Amá gives her a hard look. "You've been spying on your neighbor's grandson."

"You have?" I ask Sky, the second she cries out, "Amá!"

"Whose grandson?" I ask.

Sky is blushing. "Old Man Noemi's. He drove up to stay and take care of him."

I ponder this for a moment. "So you, what? Watch him shower?"

"Jesus, Sage!"

"The both of you, sit. And be quiet." Sonya starts grabbing coffee mugs and tossing pastries on a serving dish.

"I haven't seen anyone at Old Man Noemi's," I whisper.

"That's because you hole up in the attic like a bat."

I snort. "Well, is he hot?"

"Sage Esmerade," Sonya says in a warning tone.

Yes, Sky mouths when Sonya turns away.

After a brutal, silent few minutes, Sonya sets coffee in front of us.

"Sky can't drink that."

"You drink it for her, then."

Sonya sits, sips her coffee as daintily as possible, and then says, "Well. You have questions."

I nod. May as well get to the point. "You said ghosts don't dream, they don't affect the material world, and they don't age." I gesture to Sky. "She dreams, she leaves me cups of raspberry chocolate coffee, and, well. Look at her."

Sonya does just that, her eyebrow raised as she appraises her dead granddaughter as though she were a common antique I'd brought by to sell.

"You *said* if a ghost does those things, then they're not a ghost," I add.

Sonya narrows her eyes at Sky. "You cannot travel worlds, then?"

Sky looks incredulous. "How the hell would I do that?"

"It's natural to ghosts. You can jump from the world of the shadows, to the world of dreams, to the living, to the dead, to . . ." She pauses and then lowers her voice. "To the world of the old ones."

"So," I say. "That's ghost rule number four, then."

Sonya gives me a look of disgust. "There are only three rules. Traveling the worlds *goes without saying*. Just like the fact that a person must die in order to become a ghost to start with." She glares. "Every ghost traverses the worlds. It's why ghosts tend to be so bothersome." She rolls her eyes and shakes her head like she can't believe how dumb I sound.

"Well, I can't do it," Sky says. "I wouldn't even know where to start."

"You've never stepped into a dream?" Sonya asks. "That's the easiest world to slip inside."

"No! I have not." Sky narrows her eyes. "Though it sounds really cool. Can you explain to me how I'd do that?"

"You *can't* do that," I say. "Because you're *not* a ghost. That's the whole reason we're having this conversation to begin with! Right, Sonya?"

Sky and I look at Sonya expectantly. She makes a little humming noise and continues to drink her coffee as though we're not there.

"Well!" I throw my hands up. "What is she, then?"

"How am I supposed to know that?" Sonya says, exasperated. "My gift isn't identifying things that are not ghosts."

"So you *do* have a gift, then."

"I didn't say *that*." Sonya sighs. "Look, we knew something odd had happened when they couldn't find the body. What that was, I couldn't guess."

"Who's 'we'?"

"Me and Nadia and your other tía, Anya."

"Well, why was it odd? The detective said she might've been . . ." I glance at Sky. "Taken. By animals. And that it's a big park."

Sonya scoffs. "I *know* animals scavenge. But to not even leave a hair? A drop of blood? There were nothing but rocks under that gate."

She has a point. I search my brain for other logistics. "Well, it rained—"

Sonya stops my sentence with a piercing look. "It didn't rain until after Teal came back, lightning blazing. That was what, three days later? After the police combed the bottom of the cliff with dogs?"

"So what are you saying, Sonya?" Sky explodes. "What else could possibly have happened?"

Sonya blinks. "I promised I wouldn't say."

"This is *my* body we're talking about. I think I'm allowed to know."

It's a standoff. We stare at each other, guns cocked, waiting to see who will make the first move. Finally, Sonya shrugs and tosses her hair. "*I* am not the one who *knows*, am I?"

Sky and I look at each other. I know we're thinking the same thing. It's not Sonya's gift to *know*. It's Nadia's.

31

THANKFULLY, NADIA'S HOME. TEAL'S NOT, WHICH IS A small mercy. Lord knows we don't need explosive thunder on top of the conversation we're about to have.

Sky's the one who opens the door, stomping inside. I follow.

Nadia's sitting in the kitchen, pouring two shots of espresso, her eyes wide, following the booms of Sky's footfalls.

"Where is it?" Sky demands. "Where am I?"

"She can't hear you, Sky."

"Can she hear this?" Sky slaps a serving spoon inside a cast-iron pot on the stove. Both Nadia and I jump.

"What's this?" Nadia finally asks.

"Where is Sky's body?" I ask.

Nadia shakes her head. "I don't understand . . ."

"Where's Sky's body, Nadia?"

Nadia sips her espresso, staring right out the window, at the glitter of leaves in the wind and the sun. "They looked and looked, for weeks—"

"But you *know* something, Nadia. You *know*."

Nadia stares at me for a moment, then glances at the cast-iron pot, still vibrating from the spoon like a bell. "Come on." She lifts the espresso and pours it into a travel mug, clasping the lid shut. She walks to the front door, sliding her keys from the counter as she goes. "I already know you're not going to stop until I show you. So let's go."

MY HEART'S BEATING A LITTLE TOO FAST. I TAKE A FEW DEEP breaths to slow it down, trying to focus on the landscape around me as Nadia drives. Old red farmhouse, half caved in. Collection of goats lying under a big banyan tree. Piggly Wiggly.

That last one reminds me of Laurel. I wonder if she'll ever divorce Jorge.

And that reminds me of how she'd seen Tenn there, at *that* grocery store, as I was moving back home. How when she said his name all the way back then, my heart dropped. Like I knew he was somehow gonna break it all over again. And I was right. I mean, yeah, it was all my fault. But I was also right.

Nadia breaks my thoughts. "Sage."

"Yeah?"

She glances at me. "Sky here?"

I look back. Sky's more nervous than me, I think, fidgeting her hands, tapping her feet. "Yeah, she is."

Nadia nods. "Sky, you remember. You were my little flan helper."

Sky and I both smile a little. Once, Nadia was going to start her own bakery named 24 Flans. Flans were always Nadia's specialty, and twenty-four was her lucky number. And Sky was going to help her get it all done, when she graduated high school, while she started classes at Cranberry Community College downtown.

"When I lost you—when we lost you—I prayed to the old

gods to keep you. I prayed because I didn't think I, or we as a family, could sustain another loss like that."

I know she's talking about our mama walking out on us. She didn't die, but it still caused us all to grieve like she had.

"And while I was praying, I had the *knowing* come over me." That's how Nadia describes her gift. I haven't heard it put that way for so long, goose bumps scatter along my arms like rain. "And I knew where your body ended up."

"Why didn't you tell anyone?" I ask softly.

"Because I didn't want to find her, mija. I didn't want to find her half-eaten and half-gone. I thought she should be at peace, where the old gods had chosen to take her."

"What do the old gods look like?" Sky asks. I relay the question to Nadia.

"I don't know," Nadia says. "They must be golden, though, from the footprints your mama and I used to find in the park."

"Golden . . ." Sky murmurs.

We pull up to the parking lot of Cranberry Falls State Park. I put my hand on Nadia's arm. "I'm scared." I don't want to find the skeleton of my sister. I don't want to see her teeth last not on her smile but on her bare skull. I don't want any of that.

"I am, too. But it's clear she needs this. Otherwise she wouldn't have come to you."

With that, Sky and I hop out of the car and follow Nadia through the woods.

"Sage," Nadia says, surprising me a little. I'm on edge. I don't want to talk and I didn't think she'd be down for it, either, right now.

"Yeah?"

"You know, among you and your sisters, you look most like your mother."

"I do?" I haven't seen many photos of Mama, but the few I have show her as elegant. Lean. Her hair wavy like Teal's, her smile as mischievous as Sky's.

"You do. When we lost your mom, I lost la hija de mi corazón." Nadia's breath is a little labored. I don't think she hikes much anymore. I offer her my arm but she shakes her head. "I was lost in my own sorrow. A part of me knew that leaving you in charge was wrong. And yet I convinced myself that you would do a better job than me. I was depressed. I could hardly look after myself. I didn't think I could look after you all, too . . . and in order for me to maintain this . . . narrative, I had to convince myself that Teal was a child, and that you were not." Nadia looks right at me. "It was wrong. And I'm sorry." She hesitates and adds one more thing: "I should've made her clean her own room."

I feel like my heart's breaking all over again. I want to say *Thanks*. I want to scream *Why couldn't you have realized this before it could damage me beyond repair?*

I don't say anything, though, because Nadia then walks off path, into the woods.

To the right, in the far distance, is the cliff Sky fell from. The police and park rangers told us she died instantly. People rarely survive falls higher than forty feet, and from the railing to the rocks was a good eighty. Nadia doesn't go toward the rocks, though. She leads us deeper into the trees.

We walk for another twenty minutes, wild blackberry branches getting caught along our legs before I remember that I, too, have a gift and start asking plants to clear ahead for us. Immediately, like an inhale, the path opens before our bodies—as though invisible arms hold branches and brush back. They snap back into place when we pass. Exhale.

I see it from far away long before it's confirmed that Nadia's leading us straight there. And somehow, I know. I know the oak tree right ahead is it. It's wide and low-branched, just like the old oaks in Tenn's mom's woods. One side of it is lined in the yellow gold of sunlight; the other, the cool blue of summer shadows. It's huge, it's ancient, it's deeply wild the way anything with roots as long as towns must be. It's where Sky's body lies.

My heart thumps right along with my feet. I start to get sloppy and trip a little. *I can't do this*, I think, but my legs somehow keep moving. We get closer and closer until we are at its aboveground roots, as big and curved as ocean waves.

Nadia sits on a root. "Give me a minute."

I can't give her a minute. Instead I circle the tree. I want to get it over with, and Sky does, too, I think, because she's way ahead of me.

I touch the bark of the oak and its consciousness vibrates under my palm like the buzz of bees too close. It's old—when I wonder its age, my cells hear the cells in the tree respond. Five hundred and eighty-six years.

A small car could fit inside its trunk, which is hollowed deep in a shadowy cave. Its branches hang low, making a canopy wide as a home. It's cooler under here, in the shade of the tree, and it's not just from the shadows. It's also from its breath.

"Sage?"

I walk toward Sky's voice. She's bent over . . . Oh my God. It's a foot, sticking out of the tree cave.

It's been eight years. Eight years, why is there still flesh on those bones?

There's a big opening next to it, wide like a cave. I crawl in and my heart feels like it stops for so long, I wonder why I don't collapse next to her.

Because *there* is the body of my sister.

There's a wispy spotlight on her and I look up. Light, from a big hole open to the top of the tree.

There are leaves all over her, arranged in a pattern that makes me think it was knitted together. I reach and touch a leaf, and in that moment, they break apart, swirling around in wind. I swallow my gasp.

I can't see that well, so I reach for my phone, turning the flashlight on. All around me there is the glitter of gold, but I don't pay attention to that.

Sky the ghost has crawled up next to me.

"Do you see that?" I whisper.

"See what?" Sky hisses. "See my own body right there, dead?"

"Not dead, Sky. Look. There's *breath*."

We watch as a shadow rises and falls. Rises and falls.

"Mary Magdalene." Nadia's made it in, her eyes as wide as an owl's. "She's alive?"

"How can this be?" I ask. "How can her ghost be here and her body be there?"

Nadia watches the silhouette of Sky's body. Sky's wearing the same clothes from that day. Jeans—though now too short from her growing. An *X-Files* T-shirt she'd stolen from me. *I want to believe.* Next to her are tattered sneakers that definitely wouldn't fit her anymore, either.

"Espanto," Nadia says.

"Terror?" I ask. That's what espanto means.

"It's what we call it when something terrifying happens, yes, and the soul leaves from fear. It's not a ghost. It's her soul." Nadia touches a piece of bark and shows me her finger. It's like she raked it through gold leaf. Her eyes shine with tears. "The old ones have been keeping her here. Safe. Just as I prayed."

"But what do I do?" Sky asks. "How do I get back in there?"

"How does her soul get back?" I ask Nadia after I remember she can't hear Sky.

"Step in. Just step in, mija," Nadia says.

Sky swallows. "I'm scared."

"I'm scared, too, Sky," I say, my voice breaking. "But I'm not leaving you. I'm going to be right here, and no matter what happens I am not leaving you ever again."

Sky bites her lip and closes her eyes, like she's imagining something. Whatever it is, it gives her strength, because she looks at me again and nods. "Okay."

"Okay." I whisper it.

I watch with held breath as the soul of Sky stands, shaky, inside the tree. Wind rushes through and glittery gold goes with it—floating around her like the wispy seeds of dandelion in sunset light. She looks eternal, her edges lit in sunlight fire. She looks like an old god, I think.

And then Sky steps in.

32

IN THE BEGINNING, NADIA USED TO TELL US, HER THREE LITTLE witches, curled up in one twin bed. *In the beginning, there were only gods. Gods and this earth.*

Nadia would go on to explain how all the worlds came to be, how before they split into distinct dimensions, they existed *within* each other. The world of dreams sewn through the world of shadows, inlaid against the world of the living, swirled around the world of the dead.

The moment before Sky *becomes* once more, I feel like for a split second, this is exactly what I witness. A breath in which the worlds merge once more. A breath in which I can see every creature that has lived and died, every shadow made, every god that has roamed this earth, all around us like layers of silk spun by spiders.

And then it—this glimpse of divinity—it passes. As it must.

I exhale as Sky—our only Sky now, curled in the curve of an ancient oak tree—inhales sharply. She pushes herself up, her waist-length hair sliding over her shoulders. I reach and grab her hands. "Are you okay?" I ask. "Are you okay?"

"Yes," she whispers in a way that makes me think that maybe she doesn't know yet.

But she's here.

She's alive.

That's okay enough for me, for now.

AFTER A GOOD DEAL OF CRYING, AND HUGGING, AND KISSING, we make plans.

Nadia says it probably isn't the best idea to tell the police that Sky's been in a tree, her soul following her big sister for the last eight years until we could get them back together again. I agree.

And yet, Sky's long been declared dead. We need *some* explanation.

We argue back and forth, on the way home, me and Nadia. Poring over hypotheticals and logistics until Sky speaks up.

"I woke up in the woods. That's all I want to say."

"But—" I begin, and she shakes her head.

"That's all I want to say. That's all I will say. I woke up in the woods today. I don't know what happened but I am here."

Nadia and I look at each other. If that's what she wants, then okay.

"We have to tell Teal," I say. "She has to find out now, from us, not anyone else." This is a small town. The second the sheriff hears what's happened, it's over.

"You tell her," Nadia says. "Call her right now."

I wince. "She won't pick up for me."

Nadia hands me her phone. With shaking fingers, I pull up Teal's name and hit the call button.

"Hello?" she answers.

"Teal," I say, and then for the zillionth time that day, I begin to cry.

"Sage? What is it? Did something happen to Nadia?"

"No." I can barely talk but I get it out. "It's Sky." I take a deep, deep breath. "Sky is *alive*."

THE SHERIFF COMES, ASKING SKY TO REPEAT HER STORY. *I WOKE up in the forest. I walked to my aunt's house and knocked on the door.* These are the only two full sentences she gives him. He has all kinds of questions, and I know it's because so many things do not add up. She couldn't have survived the woods through Virginia winters, even coastal Virginia winters. He thinks she's had amnesia, because obviously someone took care of her.

I imagine one of Nadia's favorite sayings in that moment. *There are many things older than God.*

And then Teal bursts in, and the sky around us reflects every single one of her emotions. There's a rainbow, thick and bright, amid sunshine and lightning. Thunder rumbles, shaking the house. Then the clouds all clear once she practically jumps on Sky, sobbing, on Nadia's red sofa, and won't let go, not even when the ambulance arrives to take Sky to the hospital.

Of course, we all go with her—me and Teal in the ambulance, Nadia driving behind us. I meant it when I said I wasn't ever going to leave her, and I think Teal and Nadia have the same idea.

Cranberry Medical Center keeps her for two days. They run all kinds of tests and are astounded that she's not dehydrated or famished, nor is there any evidence of broken bones. There isn't even dirt under her nails. It is as though she was placed in a hibernation vault, sealed, and then released after eight whole years.

She's grown two inches and is five-eleven. She's skinny but her hips have grown wider than they were. All this indicates she's been well-fed. She's been getting her vitamins and minerals. But the question of *how* is what propels this scenario from weird-small-town-incident to viral-on-the-internet with loads of strangers trying to solve the mystery themselves.

Headlines begin like *Cranberry Hiker, Thought Dead, Returns Home after Eight Years*, and only four days later, they look like *UFO Expert Claims Resurrected Cranberry Hiker Was Abducted for Reptilian Agenda*. Journalists line Catalina Street. Calls come in on Nadia's landline at any given time, and soon, all our cell numbers are compromised. I turn my phone off for a good, long while after I get an anonymous text saying yr sister isn't human anymore. u know that right?

Of course, all Sky wants to do is lie down in her bed, sleep, and watch movies. We bring her whatever food she craves—a double black bean cheeseburger with extra pickles? On it. Homemade tamales with a side of cheese-stuffed olives? Coming right up. She gets a hankering for a grilled cheese with roasted red pepper? I'm on my way to the store for bell peppers before she can finish her request.

Sometimes I just watch her sleep. I won't even know I'm doing it—I'll come in and reassure myself that she's there, yes, still breathing, heart still beating. I'll sit at the edge of the bed and make sure she's not too warm or too cold and then, thirty minutes later, realize I'm still counting the rise and fall of her breath. Sometimes, at the right angle, she looks like she did when she was a toddler, when she insisted I be her pillow when she didn't feel well or had a nightmare.

At sixteen, Sky was a little gangly and awkward. Her limbs grew too fast for the rest of her, long and bony, and her face still had hints of baby fat at her cheeks. Now, though, she's all woman. She's twenty-four and doesn't look a day younger. Her cheekbones are sharp. Her thighs have thickened up. Before, her shape was like a tree trunk; now she's a figure eight. Her hair is deep honey in color, just like it used to get every summer. Her eyes, still dark, still sparkly. Her lips are fuller, I think, and the dimple on her left cheek is more pronounced when she can manage a smile. She tries to stay cheery for us, but come on. She lost eight whole *years*.

When I'm not checking in on Sky every half hour, on the dot, I'm working in my room. When Sky came home, I pulled open my *SCHOOL/WORK* box and unloaded my supplies. Blue jewelry wax, in several different kinds of hardness. An electric wax carver. Non-electric carving equipment, stainless steel and sharp and surgical.

Make her something that reminds her of who she was when she liked you.

This is my new goal for *everyone* I've hurt.

And even though some memories of my old job hurt, I'm not mad about it anymore. I miss my students, yeah. I miss my studio. I don't know if I'll ever stop missing those parts.

But my creativity right now, flowing like sap from syrup trees in the spring—nothing can stop it. Not Tenn being mad at me, and certainly not what's been stopping me, crappy old memories of Greg. In fact, it's like Greg never even happened. Because all of a sudden, what consumes me is what *matters*. My family. My friends. Everyone I love. And the truth is, Greg never mattered to me. Not like that, anyhow.

Brian's daughter Kate casts my carvings in silver, and then I polish the weird skin that metals get after being cast. Then I set stones. Three moss agate rounds—Brian gave them to me, no cost. *You've had a hell of a week*, he says, to explain. I don't contradict him. When I'm done, I slide the castings onto chains.

Then I carve a lighthouse, setting a tiny pearl the color of aurora borealis at its light source.

The last thing I do is carve a mushroom. Oyster, naturally. *Make him something that reminds him of who he was when he liked you.*

I do more work in three days than I've done in six months. But it's the only thing that keeps me from going out of my mind— between Sky, between thinking about Tenn, between text messages from Laurel I just haven't been able to respond to yet. It's weird. I know I haven't returned from a yearslong comalike state, but it almost feels like I have. It feels like my cells have rearranged and I can't return to where I was, not without a big reckoning. That's why I'm working so fervently. This is *my* becoming. This is my putting the pieces together again.

IT'S ONE WEEK AFTER SKY RETURNED. ONE IMPOSSIBLE WEEK after Sky impossibly returned. It's after dinner—she requested enchiladas—and it's not even seven thirty and she's already passed out in bed.

Everything is ready. Everything is set and polished. My bag is packed. I throw it over my shoulder and make my way to the second floor, stopping in front of Teal's room. I take a deep breath and then knock.

The door opens so fast, it's like she was waiting for me. "What's up?"

I swallow. Then I reach in my pocket and hand her the necklace.

She wordlessly takes it, the sparkling chain, cradling the pendant in her palm. A wide flat expanse of silver frames the piece of agate.

"It's us," I start to explain, but she finishes for me.

272 RAQUEL VASQUEZ GILLILAND

"The whole landscape." When she glances up at me, her eyes shine with tears. "Sage, teal, sky."

We say nothing for a good while. And I realize, maybe things won't ever be amazing between us again. That's something I'm just going to have to accept. So I turn to leave, but she stops me with a single sentence.

"I heard Nadia tell you to clean my room that morning."

I turn to her. She swipes the tears from her cheeks. "I didn't like how shitty my room got back then. I was depressed, I think, you know? But that wasn't your fault. It wasn't your mess to clean up."

"Teal—"

"I knew that you'd clean my room eventually, just like you always cleaned the whole house. Just like you always took care of us. I was selfish. When I heard Nadia tell you that, I should've stepped in and said I'd do it myself. I knew the mess had gotten nasty. But I just didn't want to. And Sky and I, we were just so stupid. Daring each other to balance on the gate. There's like, five feet of flat grass before the cliff even starts. I didn't think we'd get anywhere near the edge, even if we fell." She sniffs. "God, I was so dumb."

I inhale. "But—she's here now, and—"

"She's traumatized to hell, Sage. She's got eight years she's never going to get back. That's *my* fault." The tears keep coming, and she angrily wipes them away. "I couldn't face what I did, so I blamed you. That's why I said it was your fault. I knew it wasn't. I knew it was a dumb accusation. You weren't even there. And the reason you weren't there was because of me."

I bite my lip so hard, it cuts. "I should've been there, though."

"No, Sage. You shouldn't have. You weren't our mother. It wasn't your job to be there for us like you were. And I'm sorry, okay? I'm sorry that when I got mad at Mama, I took it out on you. I'm sorry that when I ruined Sky's life, I took it out on you. I'm sorry that every time I could get my way with Nadia, I did, and I'm sorry that it was usually you I kicked out of the way to do it."

"It's okay," I whisper, because I hate to see her cry like this.

"It's not, but I'm going to make it okay." And then Teal hugs me.

It's a raw, painful hug. I haven't held her since she was maybe ten, and we've been through so much since then. I'm sniffling now, too, and she pulls back, takes a look at my bag, and says, "Where are you going?"

I shrug. "It's an apology tour."

"Okay." Teal turns and pulls on a hoodie. Then she pulls socks from a drawer, bending down to slip them on her feet.

"What are you doing?"

"I'm coming with you. To help."

I hesitate. "Teal . . . I might be committing a felony tonight."

She gives me a look. "What, like that's supposed to scare me?" She steps out the door. "Let's go and do some crime."

There's a creak and I turn to see Sky sticking out of her room, a mischievous smile alight on her face. "Did somebody say 'crime'?"

I close my eyes and lift my face to the ceiling. "You can't go, Sky. Sorry."

"What? That's not fair!"

"Life's not fair. Go back in your room." Teal waves her pointer finger like she's done this mom crap all her life.

Which is not the case at all. I mean, right now I'm looking at Teal with bug eyes, because, what? I have never heard her help with Sky before. Ever. Usually it was them against me, and I always had to be the bad guy. *No, you can't eat chocolate cake for dinner*, and *No, you can't steal an elephant from the circus* (which Sky can legitimately do). Stuff like that.

It kind of feels nice, though, to have backup.

"You can come next time," I say gently.

"Oh." Sky nods. "The next time you two decide to commit a felony. Okay, sure. I'll hold you to that."

"Glad you agree," Teal says, walking toward the staircase.

"I *don't* agree! I was being *sarcastic*."

Teal doesn't respond as she stomps down the stairs.

I take a deep breath. "Sky, you *just* got back. From basically the *dead*." I wave my hand. "We need to keep you out of danger, you know?"

She scoffs. "Okay, but you two are acting like I'm eleven years old. I'm twenty-four now."

"Even so. You need to stay safe."

"Safe, right. In my room. In Nadia's house. Forever. Nice life I've come back to, all the way from *the dead*." She makes spooky-hand motions with the last two words.

I tilt my head. "You're the one who hasn't wanted to do anything but eat falafel gyros and watch movies, though."

She throws up her hands. "Yeah? Well, maybe I'm tired of that now. Besides, you and Teal never invite me anywhere! All you do is stare at me from the door like I'm a freak of nature!"

Before I can respond, she retreats, slamming her bedroom door shut behind her.

Sigh. I hate being the bad guy. Even if there's two of us now.

Teal insists on packing snacks and water to keep our strength. Teal's idea of snacks, though, is soggy-ass homemade kale chips and dry-ass protein bars. I grab the tub of cheese balls to balance things while we "do some crime."

First stop isn't crime, though. It's Laurel's.

She's been texting a lot since everything went down with Sky, but she knew I needed space, so it was a lot of *Take your time* and *Please call/text when you're ready*. I'm excited to see her again. Despite how we left things last, I've been missing her like crazy.

"I think these kale chips are expired," Teal says, lifting the bag up to the passenger window as I drive.

"That's literally how they're supposed to taste, I think. Like they're expired, I mean."

Teal looks at me like I'm nuts. Like *I'm* the one holding a bag of freaking kale chips. "Have you ever even had warm, homemade—"

"Here, have some cheese balls." Sky's voice, head, and cheese-ball-filled hand appear over the console, and Teal and I both give screams that could conceivably wake the dead. My hand slips on the steering wheel and we scrape the median, and before we're even done screaming, cheese balls fly down on us like shrapnel.

"Jesus Christ, Sky," Teal gasps.

I'm just trying to get back in the lane while hyperventilating. It's not an easy thing to do.

Sky, however, is back there laughing her ass off. "You guys. Your faces!"

"What the hell are you doing here?" Teal demands. "We told you to stay home."

Sky shrugs. "I climbed out my bedroom window."

"Oh my God," I say, putting a hand to my head. "You? Snuck out your *second-floor window*? After everything that happened eight years ago?"

"Come on, Sage. I wasn't an idiot about it. I just jumped to the porch roof. Then to the top of the compost bin. And that's right next to the driveway. Y'all were still in the kitchen when I got to the van. Which you didn't even lock, and you want to lecture me about safety."

"We're bolting that window shut tomorrow," I mutter.

"I heard that!"

"So what are we going to do? Take her back?" Teal asks me, taking a cheese ball from her décolletage and popping it in her mouth.

"No. Don't take me back. Please. I want to have fun with you guys. Just like the old days. You know?"

I look at Teal and we both sigh. "Only if you promise to never climb out your window again."

"Well, I can hardly do it again if you're going to bolt it shut."

"Promise me, Sky!"

"Fine. I promise." She puts a hand on her heart.

"You're going to clean all this cheese powder out of my van, too!" I add before turning down Laurel's street.

Laur's on the porch, with a threadbare brown robe on over one of her nightgowns. Her car is the only one in the drive, and so I pull up right next to it.

"Cheating motherfucker isn't home," Teal says.

"I guess not. Thank goodness." I don't think I'd be able to restrain myself, to be honest.

Laurel blinks in the headlights, but when I turn them off and we get out, she rushes to me, barefoot and all. "Sage, holy shit." She throws her arms around me in her classic hug, tight, long, swaying. "Oh my God, how are you?" She pulls back. "How's Sky?" Then she sees Teal walking up and she can't hide her surprise. "Oh, how are you doing, Teal?"

"Sky came, too," I say, and Sky steps up, shyly, rubbing what I'm guessing is cheese ball dust off her hands onto her olive cargo pants. Note to self: we need to take that girl shopping and update her wardrobe from 2007.

"Sky. Holy shit." Laurel hugs her carefully but fiercely and

Sky's face cracks into the biggest smile. This is the first time any old friend outside the family has seen her, and it feels right that it's Laurel, who basically watched her grow up alongside Teal.

Laur turns to me. "What's up? How are things? You want to come inside?"

I ignore all the questions, because before anything else, I have to apologize. "I came to say I'm sorry." I pull the lighthouse necklace from my bag. "And to give you this."

Laurel pulls the chain closer, to get a better look, and then she bursts into sobs. "No, Jesus. Sage. I was the asshole. I was the stupid ass who didn't want to do what I had to do, so I lashed out at you instead. I'm sorry. I'm so sorry." I can barely understand her, but she says, between gasps, "Jorge . . . I kicked him out. I kicked his ass to the curb."

"Yes!" Teal cheers. "Where'd he go?"

"His parents'? His mistress's? I don't care. I kicked him out and you know what that fucker told me?" Laurel's voice is loud but I get the feeling like she's been bottling this up and there's no way it's coming out in a whisper now. "He said I owed him *money*. He said I owed him because he's been the breadwinner for the last four years."

"That *bitch*," Sky gasps.

"He wanted me to empty my photography savings account, and for what? For making his meals every day? For bringing him beers? For enduring sex with a man who wouldn't know if a woman came even if her vagina swallowed him whole in the process?"

"Holy shit," Teal says, and yeah, it's getting graphic. But also amazing. I didn't think I'd see the day, to be honest.

"And so I grabbed his fancy-ass briefcase, I threw his phone, his computer on the fucking porch and told him to get the fuck out of my house." Her eyes are *crazy* beautiful. "And then I bought the fucking lighthouse."

Goose bumps break over my skin. "Holy shit, Laurel. You *bought* it?"

"I went right up to Darren Lavender, its real estate agent, remember? I said I could pay cash if they gave it to me for ten grand less. And they did. I signed the contract this morning."

Now I'm hugging her. "Shit, I'm so proud of you." Before I break away, Teal and Sky join us for a group hug, swaying just a little in the pine tree breeze.

"I know, right?" Laurel says, her eyes shining. "I'm all out of money, and I have no idea what's next, but I own the freaking *lighthouse*."

I smile so big. "I'm best friends with the owner of a lighthouse."

"Damn *right* you are."

Then we squeal and jump up and down, dancing a little. Teal walks back to the van. "Get in, bitches," she calls. "We've got crimes to commit."

"One crime, Teal," I clarify.

"Ándale, then!"

Laurel runs inside to grab boots and lock up, and then she and I hurry to the van.

33

THE SUN'S ALREADY DIPPED INTO THE HORIZON LINE, THE sky fading from aquamarine to lapis lazuli, the beginning of stars to our right. They twinkle and wink so much that I momentarily forget they're actually burning, and some have been burning for longer than the earth has *existed*.

I park in front of our destination and . . . and, *shit*. Tenn's mom's forests are already half bulldozed over. I knew they would be, but it doesn't make this any less devastating.

Teal, Laurel, Sky, and I stand in front of the construction, the deep yellow vehicles created for the purpose of digging, smothering, flattening, killing, all hovering over ripped-open red clay. Trees are piled in heaps and I can only imagine what Tenn would feel were he here, seeing his mama's dream demolished to pieces.

"So, how the hell am I supposed to know what to dig up?" Teal asks. She's got a hand shovel in her grip. Laur's got a big stainless steel trowel. I hold the big shovel. Meanwhile, Sky has the plastic planters and trays. She protested, saying she wanted to dig, too, but both Teal and I told her she had to take the least dangerous tool. I know it's not rational to think Sky would somehow impale herself on a trowel, but that's where Teal and I are at right now, as far as our trauma.

"Earth to Sage. What are we digging here?" Teal asks again.

"Right. You can ask me, or ask the plants." I pause. "Just don't grab poison ivy. Or Virginia creeper. That can give you a reaction, too."

"That's helpful, considering I have no idea what they look like."

"Leaves of three, leave them be," Laurel says.

"That's right. The creeper has sets of five leaves, though." I clap my hands. "New rule: don't touch any vines at all."

This understood, we move to the patch of forest just behind the construction, untouched. As soon as we step in, the sounds of cricket love songs press in on us, and there's fluttering high in the trees. It's a reminder that when we rip apart forests, we don't just lose plants. We lose birds, the eggs they so carefully tend in their nests, the butterflies forming in their cocoons, the mushroom network underfoot connecting it all. It's a set of dominoes, slapping the next down until it eventually reaches us, the humans who refuse to see our own loss as a part of it. My heart breaks even more, but I shake my head, pushing it down. We have a job to do. And we need to do it as fast as possible, before anyone might see.

We spend the next thirty minutes frantically digging, potting, and repeating. I'm not sure what everyone else gets, but I find a blueberry bush seedling the size of my palm, and a curl of black raspberries. The last thing I dig up is a sapling—dogwood. It whispers to me that its flowers will be pale pink once it becomes big enough to bloom.

I feel so raw right now that the voices of plants press in on my skin from everywhere. And the thing is, they know. If you approach a plant with clippers, with the intention to cut it, its stress hormones increase. If you were wondering if something similar happens when you approach a forest with a skid steer, the answer is yes. The answer is yes and I don't know how to make people value wilderness. *This*, all around me—these trees, this ecosystem, this wise, living web brimming with life is *where we come from*. We need *this* to survive. And no one wants to remember that.

It's all enough to drive someone to despair, and right now, I have to focus. I dig and pull, pot, and repeat. And before I wipe my hands on my jeans for the last time, I turn toward the brush, to its cardinals, asleep in its centuries-old trees, to the baby chipmunks curled in their burrows, their bellies full from their mother's milk, to the berry brambles spiraled around and around like a labyrinth and heavy with sweet fruit. And I say a prayer of apology. There is nothing else I can do, so this must be enough.

Once the containers are filled, we rush them to the back of the van. As soon as I shut the door, the smile of victory already curling on my face, I pause. "Wait, where's Sky?"

Before any of us can freak out, we hear her. "I'm here."

She has one of the black trays in her hand, and inside are . . . I narrow my eyes. "Are those rabbits?"

She approaches, and yes. Sky is holding a tray of rabbits. "They were right next to the construction, Sage. In their little burrow. They'll be buried alive first thing tomorrow if we don't do anything."

"They're so cute," Laurel squeals. And okay, they're adorable. There's the mama and her three—no, four—babies, each smaller than the palm of my hand, with fur as soft-looking as clouds.

Before I can remind Sky about Nadia's no-animals-in-the-house rule, though, blue and red lights flash at us. And then there's the chirp of a siren. We all turn slowly, horror-stricken, and yep. There's the deputy's car, a smooth silhouette behind all its lights.

"Shit," Teal breathes. "Shit!"

"I told you it was illegal," I hiss. "You insisted on coming anyway!"

"Shut up, the both of you," Laurel says. "They might hear you freakin' confessing here."

The driver's side of the police car opens, and out steps a woman. She walks up slowly, her features revealed, one by one. An angled bob. Brown lipstick. Short. "Laurel," I whisper. "That's Alexa Ramirez."

"Who's Alexa Ramirez?" Sky asks in a low voice, holding a baby bunny to her cheek with a smile.

"Jesus." Laurel glances around. "Where do I hide?"

"Didn't you date her in high school?" Teal asks.

"*Yes*, that's *why I'm trying to hide*."

"Good evening, ladies." Alexa's voice is cheery and cautious at once. "What are y'all up to tonight?"

"Oh, nothing," I say, with a smile.

"I have bunnies!" Sky announces, and I put my hand over my face. I'm sure there are *hundreds* of laws against taking wildlife if you're not authorized to.

Alexa raises an eyebrow. "O-kay . . ."

"Sky came back from the dead!" Teal bursts out.

"Well," Sky says, placing the bunny back with his mother. "It wasn't *exactly* the dead—"

"Laurel kicked her husband out!" I yell, then clasp my hand over my mouth.

"Sage!" Laurel's voice might as well slap my face.

This information, though, makes Alexa blink and tilt her head. "Laurel? That you?"

Laurel steps forward, into the light. "Uh, yeah. How you doing, Alex?"

Alex, Teal mouths to Sky, who giggles.

Alexa lets her eyes drop down Laurel's nightgown and then back up again. "I'm doing good."

"Sweet-talk her," I hiss through my clenched jaw.

Laurel coughs, then gives Alexa a shy smile. "That's good to hear." Then she glances at me. "Uh. You know, Sage here is doing fieldwork for Nate Bowen, over at Cranberry Rose. We came to help her, to see if we could save plants before they"—she gestures to the construction site—"were chopped to bits."

Alexa's smile falls. "Did Nate Bowen get permission, or permits, or—"

"He didn't, not that I know of." Laurel chews on her lip. "But, the thing is, we went *around* the construction site."

"It's all private property. That'd still be trespassing."

Laurel's silent. I think that's the extent of her sweet-talking powers. "Maybe you should wink at her," Teal says under her breath.

"Or see if she wants to hold a bunny," Sky adds in a whisper.

Laur shoots us all a glare, but then she sticks out her hip and does just what Teal suggested. She *winks* at Alexa Ramirez!

Alexa snorts, then shakes her head. "Okay. Here's what's going to happen. I'm writing up a warning. You make sure your employer hears about it so you're not sent on any more . . . *fieldwork* like this. I'm going to drive around this block here. And when I come back down the street, I don't want to see any of you *or* your vehicle. Got it?"

"Yes," I breathe.

As soon as she hands me the warning, we turn, readying to sprint into the van, when Alexa says, "Oh, and Laurel?"

We freeze. "Yeah?" Laurel calls.

"Maybe you could text me and we can grab a drink. You can tell me all about how good it felt, kicking that husband out."

Laurel widens her eyes and then smiles. "Yeah? Sure. Great idea."

And with that, we're off.

"WOW, THAT'S A BEAUTIFUL CABIN," LAUREL SAYS, SCOOCHING up between me and Teal in the front of the van.

Nighttime is officially here, I'd say. Here in front of Tenn's place—or Abe Arellano's place, if we're going to get technical—the songs of crickets are so loud, we can hear them right in the van, like they're in here, too. The sky is ink indigo, the stars white quartz sand spilled all across it, some parts so thick it looks like clouds made of those stars. The lights are on inside, all amber and gold. I don't see any movement or anything, but that doesn't stop my heart from trying to beat out of my chest. I take a breath to try to calm it.

"Are you ready?" Teal asks me.

I nod. "Yeah. Let's do this."

I grab my bag and we jump out, opening the back of the van, reaching for the pots and trays. I walk up first, placing the plants next to the doorway, then walk back to the van to grab more. Between the four of us, we're done in five minutes, even with Sky checking on the bunnies in the back seat every thirty seconds. We sort of stand there, huddled around the front door, Laur shivering in her nightgown as cool air sweeps around us in a gust of wind.

"What now?" Teal whispers.

"Well, I—" I clutch my bag. I mean, I *planned* this. I know what's supposed to happen next. But I'm starting to freak out a little. A lot. A part of me wants to head back to the van, drive home, and pretend this night, this whole broken-heart-thing never happened.

But then fate, or maybe us being loud as hell, decides the next step for me. Because the door flies open, and there is Tenn.

He's wearing a white T-shirt and faded jeans, holes frayed at the knees. He's barefoot. His arms are crossed over his chest, and the cords of veins in his arms, in his neck, are visible even as he's lit from behind. His jaw is sharp enough to flay a wild animal. His eyes are dark and narrowed.

He looks good.

He also looks pissed.

Finally, he speaks. "What are you doing here, Sage?" His voice comes out really gruff and clipped.

I wince and glance at Teal and Laur and Sky. "We'll be in the van," Laurel says, grabbing Teal's arm, who in turn grabs Sky's arm. As their footsteps fade behind me, I swallow and force myself to look at Tenn's face.

"I—uh—" I inhale. He waits. I start again. "My sister came home. The one who we thought died."

He nods, his gaze softening, his eyes glancing behind me, maybe at Sky's retreating form. "I heard."

I shake my head. "That's not what I came to tell you, though." I gesture for him to step out, and he does. He doesn't look as mad, but those arms are still crossed over his chest, so I tread carefully. "I stopped by your mom's property. Or, what was your mom's property. Or, rather, Teal and Sky and Laurel and I did. I didn't ask them to, but they came anyway, to help."

His eyebrows knit. "To help with what?"

I point to the containers all around him. My hand's shaking. "There's a dogwood tree sapling," I say, bending to touch its leaves. "This will be a blueberry bush someday. Remember it likes its soil a little acidic. And there's . . . oh my God." I stand, lifting one of the pots. "One of them found a *pawpaw* sapling."

"Pawpaw?"

"It's indigenous to right here, to Virginia. It makes fruit the size of your hand, and it tastes a little like banana, but with a custard texture? Anyway. You'll need another for pollination, but, one of them, this one—" I blink, and tears helplessly river my face. "This one came from your mother's land. And so did this black raspberry, and that mountain mint, and that dandelion, and all this dirt, Tenn." I inhale. "And remember when we were talking about literal reincarnation? And how you put your mom's ashes in the woods? And I'm so sorry I said that the land, getting the land wouldn't get her back. I was being stubborn and insensitive and dumb." I'm babbling now, and sobbing a little, but he hasn't hopped back in the house to slam the door in my face, so I keep going. "I know that land meant *everything* to you. And I've been trying to think about, how can I help? How can I make this . . . *destruction* of it better? You know? And it hit me. The night we got Sky back. It popped right into my head: *mushrooms.*"

"Mushrooms." His tone is still sharp, but there's curiosity in his eyes. It gives me the strength to keep talking.

"Yes! Mushrooms. The whole, invisible network of mushrooms, the microscopic little strands that connect every plant, every tree, every flower, that feed the bugs and the criaturas, including us. If I could get the dirt from her woods, and if we don't let it dry out, you'll have those mushrooms, her mushrooms, forever. You could put it all in a big pot, or if Abe lets you put it in his yard for safekeeping, till you get your own patch of woods? And if you need me to, I could touch it, I could make sure it stays healthy with my gift." I inhale sharp and long, and he looks right in my eyes and I feel it, I feel that lightning in his gaze all the way to my toes. "Because when I was in those woods tonight, Tenn, I *felt* you. I felt your mama, I felt *everything* in that dirt. I dug it up with my bare hands because I kept feeling it. I felt how the whole universe held it together with stories, and how every story is held together with love. And I *love* you. And I know you wanted that piece of your life back, that's why you wanted to find Silvergurl—"

I reach into my bag and pull out a folder and hand it to him. He flips it open, and his jaw goes slack. "When we used to IM, I copied and pasted *every single* conversation into a Word doc and printed them out. *Every* Friday night. It took me forever to find it, but thank God Nadia never throws away anything that resembles a book." I keep forgetting to breathe. I inhale again, in a gasp. "And I know I can't take it back, what I did. The lie. The lies. But I'm giving you this. Because this is from the time you remember being happy, right? Maybe this could have just a taste of that happiness for you."

I don't let him respond. Instead, I reach in my pocket and grab the last piece of silver I carved. The oyster mushroom. And I reach over, and open his big, warm hand, and place it right in the center. "It's a button I made," I say. "I saw your Santo Domingo leather bracelet. And the button was broken. So here's a new one." I don't add, *I hope it makes you remember when you liked me*, because that seems a little too big to hope for right now.

His eyes aren't exactly warm, and I feel like it's because he thinks I'm trying to manipulate him. Which, fine. I'm human. I'm trying to earn forgiveness, which I'm not even sure I deserve.

"Anything else?" he asks with a cough.

I start to shake my head, but then I say, my voice cracking, "You make the best soup *ever*." And then I run back to the van, before he can break my heart any more. I'm not even sure it can be broken any more, but I don't want to give him, or me, or anyone else the chance.

34

"WHERE TO NOW?" LAUREL ASKS.

"Home," I say, and at the same time Teal insists, "The Lounge."

"Ooh! I've never been to the Lounge," Sky says.

I groan. "I don't feel like going anywhere."

"Come on. It'll be fun."

Laurel frowns thoughtfully. "I could use a drink."

I sigh, deep and long. "Fine."

"I'll buy this time," Teal says.

I give her a cautious smile and she smiles back, grabs my hand, and squeezes.

Luckily the Lounge isn't too far, and I take the highway, getting us there in under ten minutes. Inside, it's as dark as ever, the skull fairy lights and candles and skeleton lanterns casting their honey citrine glow on us.

Laurel begins, "You sure the bunnies will be okay in the . . ." before trailing off.

Because despite the dim lighting, all conversations in the bar come to a crashing halt when the four of us come into view. "What the—" Laurel says, and I'm confused for a second, too. Until I see wide eyes and a few discreet pointer fingers all angled at Sky.

"That's her," someone mutters. "The one who *claims* she—"

"Sage," Sky says with a shaky voice.

Before I can react, though, Teal steps forward. "What the *fuck* are you assholes looking at? Huh?"

Teal's pretty scary. Just about everyone jerks their gaze away, and awkward, stilted conversation starts to fill the room. She lets out a breath and glances at Sky. "You good?"

Sky nods. "I'm good."

We each order something different—Teal gets her whiskey, Laurel orders a martini, Sky requests a blueberry beer, and I ask for a mint julep. We take our drinks to a dark booth, the flames in the candles dancing wildly as we sit.

"How'd it go with Tenn?" Laurel asks.

I shake my head. "Not ready to talk about it." I shrug. "Maybe once I drain this drink, or four more like it."

"That bad?" Teal asks.

I shrug. "Who can say, really." I shake my head again. "Someone, distract me from my miserable love life." I glance at Sky. "What about Old Man Noemi's grandson?"

She shrugs. "Old Man's all healed up. Adam—that's the grandson—went back to New York."

"Wait, you were seeing someone?" Laurel asks Sky. "How'd I miss this?"

"Well, maybe because he wasn't seeing me. As in, he couldn't. Because I was dead, remember?" Sky makes absurd ghost sounds until we're all cracking up.

Teal takes a long swig of whiskey. "I dumped Nate."

"*What?*" Consider me sufficiently distracted. "Why?"

Teal shrugs. "He was a rebound. I mean, sure there was some mutual attraction, but it was mostly sex, and after that excitement wore away . . . there was, like, nothing to talk about."

"That's fair." Maybe in another universe, I'd be spitting mad now, because I thought *I* could've loved Nate. But in that universe, I'd have to not fall in love with Tennessee Reyes again. Impossible. "Is Nate okay?"

"He was a little bummed, but I think he'll get over it."

I look behind her. "Speaking of bummed. My two o'clock. There's Carter. Pretty sure you stomped on his heart that day when you left here with Nate."

Teal groans, burying her face in her hands. "He's not supposed to work tonight. I swear to God, it's like he has a radar . . ." She turns and we're both watching Carter ordering drinks at the counter.

"Is he allowed to drink at work?" Laurel asks.

"I doubt that," I supply. "Plus he's not in uniform. I don't think he's working."

And then, a tall, gorgeous blond woman walks up to him and slips her hand behind his back pocket as she kisses Carter on the mouth. And it's, like, a legit kiss. Short, but definitely with tongue.

"Yeah, that boy's not on the clock," Laurel says with a snort.

I have a quip on getting tips for kisses, but stop short when I see how pale Teal looks. "Hey. You okay?"

"I'm fine." She shrugs, schooling her features back to neutral. "Dunno what he's doing with that *bitch* over there, though." Out the windows, lightning flashes across the sky, causing the low lights of the Lounge to flicker. The following thunder rumbles so loud, I can feel it in my chest.

"Are you seriously that drunk already?" I ask.

"No. I'm not." She squares her jaw. "I just . . . dunno. He could do so much better than her."

"Do you know her?" Laurel asks.

"No. And I don't want to, either."

A smile curls on my face. "Wait a minute. Wait a *minute*."

She knows what I'm going to say. "Shut the hell up, Sage."

"You like Carter."

"Shhhh! Don't fucking scream it!"

I say it again, lower, but in a singsong voice. "You like Carrrr-terrr."

"Is it true?" Laurel asks.

Teal hesitates to respond, which tells me all I need to know.

"Yes, it's true!" I say with glee.

"Come on. He's dorky. He talks too much. He likes to text *good morning* and *good night* like a total nerd."

"And . . ." Laurel says to her.

Teal sighs. "And he was the best kiss I've ever had." She glances down at her nails. "I haven't been able to stop thinking about it. That's the real reason I broke up with Nate."

"I knew it!" I say, pointing. I calm down, though, when I see how gloomy she is. "Now you need to tell *him* that."

"Hell, no. He's on a date."

"I don't mean right now. But sometime. Soon."

We all four glance back at the same time, to where the blonde is practically sitting in his lap at the bar.

Laurel nods. "Sooner rather than later, for sure."

We each turn back to our drinks, and then Teal stands. "I'm done. I'll be in the van."

"Right behind you," I call to her as she saunters away. She doesn't spare Carter or his date a glance. But he double-takes when he spots her. In fact, he doesn't take his eyes off Teal until she's well out the door.

WE DROP LAUREL OFF AND THEN HEAD TO NADIA'S. WE ALL trudge up the stairs, sore and dirt stained. When we get to the second floor, I remind Sky about her promise about sneaking out of windows. She rolls her eyes. "O-kay, Sage." Then she grins. "Thank you for letting me help commit crimes." And she gives us the biggest hugs before disappearing into her room, but not before I catch what I'm pretty sure is a baby bunny down her shirt.

"The bunnies were supposed to stay in the garden, Sky. Nadia's going to kill you!" I call through her door. From inside, Sky cackles in response.

Before I pass Teal to get to the attic, she says, "Sage?"

"Uh-huh?"

She leans on her hip. "Thanks for threatening Johnny's ass for me."

I furrow my brow. "How do you—"

"I left my candle-making supplies at his place—"

"Hold on." I lift my hand. "You make *candles*?"

"Just as a hobby. It's not a big deal."

I just blink for a second, then shake my head. "Okay. Go on."

"Anyway. I stopped by to get them, right? He saw me on his porch and I swear he almost pissed his pants. He *ran* inside and locked me out. I had to bang on the door, and when he heard what I wanted, he threw my supplies in a box and tossed it on the porch. He said to not tell you a single word. That he didn't want to be murdered by plants." Teal raises an eyebrow.

I nod. "That sounds about right."

She chuckles. "Anyway. Just. Thanks." She holds my hand, just for a moment, before disappearing into her room.

When I get up to the attic, there's one more thing I need to do before the whole bedtime routine. I pull up my phone.

Tabby's husband and I messaged each other back and forth, and he sent me a link to a charity the family had started for her. She had *loved* her job as a pre-K teacher and was doing all she could—including spending her own money—to make sure the littles had books, snacks, and other supplies. Now folks could donate to the school in her name to make sure every child had what they needed to thrive.

I click on the link and hit donate, depositing my whole last paycheck. Just like that.

Afterward, I pull up Tabby's Facebook page, perusing through her profile photos until I stop where she looks the happiest—dancing and laughing on her wedding day. "I'm sorry I dragged you into this," I whisper to her. "I hope that helps, even just a little."

SOMETHING SHIFTS IN MY BED. I KEEP MY EYES CLOSED. "I'M tired."

"It's late. It's almost afternoon, even."

At Sky's voice, I sit up. Seeing her there, perched on my bed, the light around her just a little bright and blurry . . . it brings back some bad memories. I grab her arm, tightening my grip on her until I'm certain she's solid.

"Ow."

"Sorry. I just—" I'm breathing fast, like I had a mini panic attack or something. I let go, drop my arm on the bed.

She knows exactly what happened. "You were scared I was still a ghost?"

I nod. "It's dumb. But it's the first thing that popped into my head."

She grabs my hand. "It's not. I feel that all the time, too." There's intense grief in her voice. "A dozen times a day, I question my flesh."

God, I wish I could take away all her pain. All her loss. "That sounds like some epic Bible verse."

She bites back a smile. "Nadia's making me go to therapy for it."

"That's probably a good idea."

She sighs. "I still have dreams about it, you know? Being there. In that little golden cocoon." She bites her lip. "I can travel, in the dream, just like when I was a ghost. I can still spy on people." Her face pinkens. "I probably shouldn't tell that to a therapist, huh?"

I laugh. "Depends on the therapist, I guess." I shrug. "I dunno. It sounds like you got some *extra* magic from your time in the 'in-between.' You know? Ancient cultures thought the 'in-between' was super sacred."

Sky nods. "I can see that."

"You're basically a priestess now. So you can say things like *A dozen times a day, I question my flesh*. And everyone will say *Oh, don't mind her. She's a temple priestess*."

We both laugh, and then Sky gets sober. "People are saying a lot meaner stuff than that about me, aren't they?"

I shrug. "Well, you know—"

"It's okay. I know they are."

"Well, you know all you have to do is let me and Teal know

who's talking shit and we will deal with it." I sit up more, leaning back on the headboard. She looks so sad. I decide to change the subject. "So what are you planning on doing now? With your new lease on life and all that?"

"You mean besides sneaking along for your nighttime adventures?" She nods. "I have a whole list I've been working on."

"Wow. What's on it?"

She blushes. "I don't want to say *everything*. But . . ." She sighs. "Get my GED. Start a business. Take a trip." She shrugs. "It's all hypothetical."

"I'll help you. With any of it. All of it. Just let me know."

She smiles. "Thanks, Sage." She gazes down at my neck. "Teal said you made one for me, too."

"Oh!" I grab the moss agate necklace under my collarbone. "Yeah. I totally forgot to give it to you last night."

"Understandable, considering I wasn't supposed to be there last night." Sky grins.

I stand and reach for my bag, which I dropped off in front of the bed. "Here." I hand it to her, and she puts it on immediately.

"Is that why you came up here?" I ask.

"Well. Sorta. I wanted to go on the balcony for a bit."

"Oh, hell no." I step up until I'm in front of the French doors, putting my hands on my hips. "You're not allowed near any ledges for the rest of your very long, very healthy, very ledge-free life."

Sky rolls her eyes. "Come on, Sage."

"I think *not*."

She crosses her arms, slouching. Even doing all that, she towers over me. I can't believe she's almost six feet tall now. My baby sister.

I take a breath. "Look, you might be ready, but I'm not. Not yet. You don't understand how much it about killed me, hearing that you scaled your freaking window last night. Maybe in six months I'll be okay with you free climbing and diving out of airplanes to your heart's content, but right now *my* poor heart can't take the idea of you anywhere near a spot more than four inches off the ground."

She worries her bottom lip. "What would it take for you to be okay with me visiting the balcony?"

I pause. "If me and Teal were there, in front of you, holding your hands."

She shrugs. "Fine. But I'm holding you to your word. In six months, I'll be skydiving."

"That was a joke, you little asshole."

We laugh and then I walk up to the bathroom, running water to wash my face. Sky stands behind me, leaning on the open doorway. "You might want to dress pretty."

"Why?"

"There's someone downstairs. Waiting for you."

I freeze and turn. "You mean Tenn? Is Tenn down there?"

She grins at me, skipping toward the door. "Guess you'll have to see for yourself!"

That's gotta be a yes, right? She wouldn't mess with me that bad, would she?

I finish freshening up fast, adding some lip gloss and mascara. Of course I don't want to look like I got a hot tip and therefore am trying too hard . . . so I change out of my old, yucky pajamas into a cute pink lace set that I never wear because the lace cuts into my skin when I lie down in it. Pajamas aren't "too hard," are they? Even if they're kind of sexy? Whatever. I'm too nervous to change again now.

I walk downstairs, my heart beating along with each thump of my feet, and then round the corner, and . . .

Tenn.

He's sitting in the kitchen, chatting with Nadia about coffee, I guess because she's made him a cup. They both turn to me as I creep in, obviously not as stealthy as I thought. "Hi?" I say, and then want to hit myself for sounding so uncool.

Tenn gives me a shy smile as he sips his coffee. "Morning, Sage." He glances at the stove clock. "Afternoon, rather."

I nod. "Good afternoon."

We stare at each other for a few seconds before Nadia clears her throat. "Well, I've got to grab more pepperjack from the store. Sky won't stop eating grilled cheese this week." She winks at me and it warms my heart. Yeah, it's a little late, but she's sharing the caretaking now, too. "Text me if you need anything. Nice meeting you, Tenn!" And then she's off.

I clear my throat and then reach for a mug—my lilac-against-a-lightning-storm mug, the one a student made for me way back when I still taught. She gifted it to me earlier this year, even, but that feels like one hundred lifetimes ago. I fill it with coffee, pouring slow. I'm not really hankering for coffee right now—my stomach is doing too many wild flip-flops—but this gives me *something* to do.

"You're probably wondering why I'm here." His voice is deep, calm. Resonant in this tiny sunflower-yellow kitchen.

I shrug. "It's crossed my mind."

He gives a laugh that I feel deep in my belly. It sounds so much like before—before I'd ruined everything—that hope sparks in my chest. "I came by to bring this." He reaches down and lifts a big ceramic pot onto the table. I recognize it immediately. It's the rose—the blue rose. And it looks *awful*.

"Oh my God." I put my mug on the counter and bend over the plant. Almost every leaf is brown and dried. There are only three with any green left in them at all. "What happened?"

He frowns. "I—well. I mean, that's obvious, right? I didn't listen to you."

I take a breath and sit down.

"I gave it fertilizer. I gave it the most expensive dirt I could find. I sprayed it with this nasty follicular liquid I found at the store . . ."

I snort. "And how did that smell?"

"Like literal fish ass."

I swallow a giggle.

He smiles, and it's a little sad. "I got too much in my head. You ever do that? You ever get an idea that couldn't ever possibly happen, and you fool yourself into thinking if you do things the exact right way, you could defy all logic?"

I smile and look down. I mean . . . he's just explained me, trying to pull off lying to him while loving him. "Yeah. Of course."

He nods. "That's what happened to me when I saw that blue rose. My thought process became a runaway train. I thought I could get my mom's land back. I thought I'd been blessed with a miracle. But I was humbled instead." He looks at me. "And then you brought some of Mom's land to me."

I nod, my eyes filling with tears. "It was the least I could do."

"It was everything you could do, Sage. Thank you." He takes a big breath. "Today, I looked up YouTube videos on how to sew a button."

"How'd that go?" He lifts his hand toward me. The leather strap is on there, held together with one little silver oyster mushroom. "Looks good," I say with a nod. And then he lays his hand on top of mine. I inhale sharply. He looks at my fingers and then back up at my eyes. "I'm sorry I said your gift—and its wisdom— was bullshit."

"Oh." I whisper it. "That's okay."

"It's not. And I'm sorry." He rolls the tips of his fingers over the back of my hand, making goose bumps move up my wrist, up my arm, on the curve of my neck and down my spine. Until I can feel him touching me all the way in my toes. "That's not the only thing I came here to say."

"It's not?" I can barely breathe. His touch is actual lightning against my skin, frazzling my brain. I'm surprised I managed two words just now.

"I've loved you since I was sixteen, Sage. I've loved you since before I knew your name. You know that, right?"

Well, my breath's back now, double-time, even. "Yeah?"

"Yeah. I know I fucked up back then. I was so nervous to meet you."

I wipe away the tears from my cheeks. "I was really nervous, too."

"I'm so upset I missed your cute blue dress." He lowers his gaze down my lace pajamas. "And your cookie dough perfume." I burst out laughing as he continues. "I was wondering if we could . . ." He squeezes my hand. "Start over."

I bite my lip. "Like, hi, I'm Sage . . ."

"Like, hi, I'm Tennessee. I think we used to IM back in the day."

I smile. It's slow but it gets big, bigger than I've smiled in a week. "Oh. Well. I'm Sage. I think we did, too. My screen name was Silvergurl? With a *u*?"

We laugh and he says, "Yeah, that was you, all right." He slides his hand up my arm, nudging me forward, until I'm sitting in his lap. He's so warm. He smells like leather and Earl Grey tea. He feels so good, I want to cry. "You never told me why you were Silvergurl with a *u*."

"Silver was because I liked making jewelry. Sky called me Silver Girl all the time. The *u* seemed cool."

"It *was* cool."

"Oh my God. Was *not*."

"It was. And I think, considering how *obnoxiously* cool I am, that I can declare a thing like that cool. And it would be true, just like that."

"Just like that, huh?"

He grins, his eyes on my mouth. "Just . . . like . . ."

I kiss him before he can finish. The kiss starts soft, but I open my mouth, urging our tongues to meet, and next thing I know, my hands are under his shirt and his are gripping my ass. It's rough and amazing. Sweet and mind-blowing. "Tenn?" I say, pulling back.

"Yeah?" His mouth is almost red, his pupils inked out, making his beautiful dark eyes even more dark. Even more beautiful.

"I know you said 'let's start over,' but do you think we can skip right to sex this time around?"

He smiles so big, it's the sunset and the sunrise and the moon and the whole galaxy, not just the one above us with its infinite stars, but the one below us, the mushroom tendrils connecting *everything*, just everything. "I like that idea." And then I stand and lead him up the stairs, to my attic, and our clothes basically evaporate. And then I realize I don't have any condoms, but we're so frantic we put our hands, our mouths, our tongues all over each other until we're moaning and shivering, and then soon thereafter, we're ready again, so I have to sneak into Teal's room wearing a sheet to steal a condom from her nightstand.

He cups my face when he's inside me. "Tenn," I whisper, my thighs shaking. "I love you, too."

"I know you do, baby." And then we make each other come again, the clouds rushing past out the window, in front of all the basil, in front of the ancient, wide, glittering-in-the-sun trees peeking in just beyond Nadia's yard on Catalina Street.

Afterward, we're finally exhausted enough to just breathe, to talk, to hold each other. "You never told Nate about the blue rose?" I ask him, my head resting on his shoulder.

He shakes his head. "I told him that we found something real special. And then I thought better of it. And then your sister came back, so I told him it'd be a few days."

"So he's still waiting for something special?"

"Uh-huh."

I stand, grabbing the sheet around me again. "Remember when we first went plant hunting? And that awful ranger was there?"

He chuckles. "I remember."

I reach on the basil shelf and grab two pots. "Look." I hold them out to him. They're the irises from that day—blue flag. But pink. I'd been working on them, here and there. That one little rhizome piece is now two fully formed plants. And both are blooming, the pale pink of them almost white in the sunlight pouring through the windows.

Tenn smiles. "That'll do it."

"I think it will, too." I place the pots back.

"Do you think you can save the blue rose?" He's frowning a little, leaning back on one arm, the quilt twisted up over his chest and hips, leaving his thick legs exposed.

"Uh—" I blush. Easily distractable, that's me in the presence of a naked Tenn Reyes. "I'll try. You wanna help?"

"I do."

So that's what we do. We find the best spot in Nadia's yard and plant the rose with plenty of compost. I hold my hands over it and yes, thank God, I can feel its consciousness. Its heartbeat. And it's all faint. I don't know if it will make it—if it even *wants* to make it. But sometimes when you're working with plants, the best and only thing you can do is wait and see.

And then we order pizza, and Teal comes home from work and has dinner with us—me, Nadia, Sky, and Tenn. Throughout dinner, I keep thinking about how wild fifteen-year-old me would think this is. Tennessee Reyes, here. Nadia. My sisters. The way everything had to break in order to root, to sprout. To heal.

And the second we're finished drying dishes, I drag Tenn upstairs, raid Teal's nightstand again, and we do it another two times, promptly falling asleep, tangled up with sheets and each other.

Sometime around midnight, there's something sharp poking at my back. "What the hell," I grunt.

"Come on, Sage. Let's do this so we can go back to bed, huh?"

I open my eyes and see Teal there, next to Sky. "Come on," Teal continues, whispering. "I'm tired."

"And I'm naked!"

"We know. Your man just turned over and we almost saw his junk."

I swallow back a snort. "Lower your voice," I hiss. "You're going to wake Tenn. Pass me that nightgown." I get it over my head and march them toward the door. "What are you two doing?"

"You said I could go on the balcony if you and Teal were there holding my hands." Sky lifts her head and folds her arms. "And I want to look on the balcony."

"Sky, it's the middle of the night."

"The moon's just coming out. I want to see her, up close, just like when we were little."

I look at Teal, who shakes her head. "Like I said, let's just do this. The sooner it's done, the sooner we're back in our warm, cozy beds."

I glance at Tenn, who's still passed out. "Fine."

The balcony doors open with witchlike creaks. I grab Sky's left hand, and Teal grabs her right.

"Ready?" They nod.

We take exactly one step onto the balcony, and I say, "That's enough."

"Sage, we're barely on here."

"I don't care. I told you, I'm not ready for this."

Sky sighs but eventually, we turn and stare at the moon. It's a quarter full, and it looks blue. The blue of Montana sapphire, of aquamarine, of blue lace agate, lit from within like an impossibly blue lantern. Like an impossibly blue rose.

The sea is somewhere in the distance, but it's too dark to make out right now. The wind rushes through us, and I shiver.

Sky giggles. "We're the Three Musketeers, back together again."

Teal snorts. "More like the Three Stooges."

"You're both wrong," I declare. "We're witches. We're Nadia's three little brujas."

And we all watch everything around us, just a tiny bit longer, before going to bed. The clouds, framing the moon like whipped cream over pie. The sea, distant but still here with its salt air. The trees, their silhouettes blacker than night, shimmering against moonlight. The landscape in here—Sage, Teal, and Sky—looking at the landscape out there—sage, teal, and sky.

That's us. The Flores witches, together again.

Thank all the old gods.

ACKNOWLEDGMENTS

All witches—and storytellers, and poets—know a Rule of Three, whether in reference to rhythm, plot points, or spellcasting. I find it fitting, then, that *Witch of Wild Things* owes its origin to a set of three.

When I first began *Witch of Wild Things*, I was recovering from a painful writer's block. It was particularly devastating because up until then, I wasn't even certain if I believed in such a thing.

I had written two manuscripts, both of which needed major revisions. I chose one—the adult romance—to focus on in revising. I spent over one year deleting and rewriting and moving chapters around, and for all my effort, at the end of the day I still had a hot mess of a book. Moreover, I'd completely run out of ideas on how to fix it.

My wonderful and patient agent, Elizabeth Bewley, suggested cutting some fat. She sent me some notes with suggestions on where to start.

I dedicated an entire weekend to cutting thirty thousand words. By the end of it, my thought process went, "Do I love that? No? Okay, delete!" At some point, I realized I loved very little about the book. In fact, I scrolled back up to the beginning and, upon reviewing it for maybe the one hundred thousandth time, I realized I loved almost none of it.

I sat down and asked myself, "Well, what *do* I love about this book?"

There were only *three* elements total that I loved: The idea of wild magic. The flawed female elder. And a tattooed love interest.

I wrote these three seeds down, and after a whole season of not writing, I picked them up again and realized they had germinated and taken root. From them bloomed the romance of Sage and Tenn, a story of which I loved every single word.

I owe much gratitude to so many people who helped me craft this beloved love story.

First, my family. Thank you, Ansel, my greatest love, for your sweetness. Thank you, Jordan, for always reading the first drafts, no matter how messy they are. To Mom and Dad, Jessica, Matt, Oliver, Logan, Joey, Aries, Sophia, Daniella, Aria, and the little one on the way. Thank you to Junior, and to Nana especially for always talking and singing to plants, and to Polo, rest in peace, Welito. Thank you to Tina, Tod, Carroll, Ivan, Faith, and Robert for always being there for us.

Thank you to my agent, Elizabeth Bewley, for being the most amazing and understanding partner an author could ever ask for. I'm so glad we're a team. Thank you to Kristine Swartz, for your enthusiasm for this book from the start, and for your brilliant input to make Tenn and Sage's story as gorgeous and fulfilling as possible. Thank you to Miranda Hill, who believed in my book at first read (at first tweet, even!), and who helped shape *Witch of Wild Things* to become the best version it could be.

So much gratitude to Amy J. Schneider, Lindsey Tulloch, and Christine Legon for all your thoughtful and necessary notes, suggestions, and calculations. Thank you to Mary Baker for your knowledge and patience with all my questions! An emotional thank-you to both art director Sarah Oberrender and artist Carrie May for creating a cover more beautiful than I ever imagined. I am especially touched by the gorgeous renderings of the Indigenous plants of Virginia, all of whom have been guides in one form or another throughout this story, its writing, and within this cosmic and earthly creative life.

To literally everyone at Berkley, would it be too embarrassing to admit that I cried when I found out you would be the home of *Witch of Wild Things*? I can hardly believe the company this book keeps. I am so honored to be a part of this publishing family.

Thank you so much to India Holton and Brittany Kelley for reading this novel, back before I had sifted through it to find three seeds, when it was still a crappy first draft. I'm so grateful for your time and feedback and I'm proud and honored to call you both my friends. Also, thank you to everyone at the Las Musas Collective who helped me figure out the best and most magical way to translate "the plant whisperer." I'm so grateful and honored to be a part of this sacred community with you.

Thank you so much to Christy Shivell, and to your beautiful, sacred farm, which inspired Cranberry Rose Company (including the enormous herb spiral made of cinder blocks!). For anyone in Appalachia who is interested in visiting a beautiful, peaceful nursery dedicated to native plants as well as healing herbs and unusual heirlooms, please consider Shy Valley Farm in Fall Branch, Tennessee.

Thank you to Jessica Brody for writing *Save the Cat! Writes a Novel: The Last Book on Novel Writing You'll Ever Need*, and to Beth Revis for writing both *Paper Hearts, Volume 1: Some Writing Advice* and its corresponding workbook. These books were the publishing equivalent of guardian angels as I broke through writer's block and developed and outlined *Witch of Wild Things* with only three little seeds to start with.

Thank you to Mary Reynolds, Kate Clearlight, and Robin Wall Kimmerer for reminding me about the heart of the work I do in being a land steward. Thank you to *Deep-Rooted Wisdom: Skills and Stories from Generations of Gardeners* by Augustus Jenkins Farmer for inspiring Tenn's and Sage's job positions as plant-hunters. Thank you to *The Reason for Flowers: Their History, Culture, Biology, and How They Change Our Lives* by Stephen L. Buchmann for teaching me everything there is to know about blue roses. And big, big thanks to Kathy McFarland from Baker Creek Heirloom Seed Company for answering all my questions about how seed-hunting works.

Thank you to my spirits and guardians and ancestors, both in the world of plants and the land and elsewhere and beyond. Everything I love on this miraculous earth, and around this miraculous earth, and woven in the secret, magic places of this miraculous earth is because of you.

I hope it's not weird to thank myself. This author journey hasn't been easy, and I am so grateful I never gave up, not even when I had every reason in the world to.

Thank you to the librarians, booksellers, and teachers who love and support my work. If you can imagine the Ace of Cups, with the cup just overflowing like a great, misty waterfall, that's the image of my gratitude for you.

And last, but never, ever least: thank you to my readers. I can't tell you how many times I have read your kind messages and reviews to help me when I was having a bad day. I wish you all nothing but the best things—a garden full of herbs and fruit, a home full of warmth (and perhaps a ghost or two), and a TBR pile full of life-restoring books.

Witch
of
Wild
Things

Raquel
Vasquez Gilliland

DISCUSSION QUESTIONS

1. Sage and Tenn first met through AOL Instant Messenger when they were teenagers. How do you think Sage's internet anonymity helped shape their relationship back then? Did it bring them closer together or keep them further apart? Have you ever had an anonymous online friendship?

2. When Nadia sees Sage's basil plant, she tells Sage, "I thought you'd given it up." In return, Sage wants to ask, *How can you give up something that you're made of?* Do you think Sage, or any of the Flores women, could ever truly give up their gifts? Would their lives be easier or harder without their gifts?

3. For most of the story, Teal is very resistant to patching up her relationship with Sage. Why do you think this is? Is Teal right to blame Sage for what happened to Sky? What could Teal and Sage have done differently to fix their relationship sooner?

4. Do you think Sage was right or wrong to make a deal in bad faith with Tenn?

5. Nadia says the gifts the Flores women have are a punishment. Do you agree with her? Why or why not? If you could pick from Sage's, Teal's, or Sky's gifts, which would you choose?

6. When Sage first learns that Sky the ghost breaks all three rules of ghosthood according to her grandmother Sonya, did you suspect that maybe Sky wasn't a ghost after all? What were you anticipating when Sage finally discovers Sky in Cranberry Falls?

7. Plant hunting is a centuries-old profession. Had you heard of it before reading *Witch of Wild Things*? How do you think the job suits Sage and Tenn?

8. When was the moment you think Sage fell for Tenn (again)? When do you think Tenn fell for Sage? What do you see in their future after the book ends?

RAQUEL VASQUEZ GILLILAND is a Pura Belpré Award–winning Mexican American poet, novelist, and painter. She received her BA in cultural anthropology from the University of West Florida and her MFA in poetry from the University of Alaska Anchorage. Raquel is most inspired by folklore and seeds and the lineages of all things. When not writing, Raquel tells stories to her plants, and they tell her stories back. *Witch of Wild Things* is her third novel.

CONNECT ONLINE

RaquelVasquezGilliland_Poet